THE MASTER'S WIFE

Cornwall, 1882. Now owner of her late father's shipyard, Caseley has drifted apart from her husband, Captain Jago Barata. Following the loss and heartbreak they have recently suffered, their marriage is at risk of collapse. When Jago is commissioned to undertake an important voyage to turbulent Egypt, Caseley, convinced she is about to lose him, risks everything by deciding to go with him. Will their marriage survive the dangers they are sailing into – and will they ever make it back to England?

THE MASTER'S WIFE

THE MASTER'S WIFE

by

Jane Jackson

Magna Large Print Books
Long Preston, North Yorkshire,
BD23 4ND, England.

British Library Cataloguing in Publication Data.

A catalogue record of this book is
available from the British Library

ISBN   978-0-7505-4426-9

First published in Great Britain 2016 by Accent Press Ltd.

Published in Large Print 2017 by arrangement with
Accent Press

Magna Large Print is an imprint of Library Magna Books Ltd.

Printed and bound in Great Britain by
T.J. (International) Ltd., Cornwall, PL28 8RW

Chapter One

Cornwall, 1882

Caseley Barata kept her gaze lowered as she walked along the pavement towards Market Strand. She had come only because Rosina insisted, and she lacked the energy to argue.

She was perfectly capable of walking unaided. But when Rosina had taken her arm she welcomed the support. Now all she wanted was to get back home again without being stopped and asked how she was.

Horse-drawn delivery wagons rumbled along the street. Ragged urchins dodged between them, shouting to each other. Women bustled in and out of shops. Barrow-pushing tradesmen whistled, and nesting seagulls screamed from the rooftops. The air was warm and a gentle breeze blew puffs of white cloud across a cornflower sky.

''Twas only right and proper you stayed in your black over the winter,' Rosina said. 'But 'tis May now. Soon be a twelve month since–'

As Caseley tensed, the housekeeper left the sentence unfinished. 'Time you was thinking of going into grey or mauve. No one would think any the worse–'

'Do you think I care for anyone else's opinion?'

'I should hope you don't. I'm just saying now the weather is getting warmer you could start thinking

9

about it. It'll be a year by the time you've had dresses made up. That's long enough, my bird. You was never one for drawing attention to yourself. Not like your Aunt Margaret. Remember how she carried on after your dear father died? I never seen the like. Drooping around the place in head-to-toe black for a full year. Dear life, it was ridic'lous. She was his sister-in-law, not his widow.'

'That wasn't grief, Rosina. It was guilt. If Uncle Thomas hadn't nearly bankrupted the company, Father might not have died–'

'Yes, he would. He was sick long before that. 'Twas you that kept him going. Some proud of you he was.' Rosina patted Caseley's hand. 'But that's water under the bridge now. What I'm saying–'

'I hear you. Maybe you're right. It's just–'

'You won't never forget, my sweetheart.' Rosina's voice was gentle. 'But 'tis time you stopped punishing yourself.'

'And new dresses will help?'

Rosina met Caseley's stormy gaze placidly. 'I've looked after you since you was born. Dear to me as my own child you are and I'd cut my arm off sooner than hurt you.'

'I know that–'

'Then hark to what I'm saying. Leave them go, my 'andsome. You can't change the past. Time you was looking to the future. Now don't we go and see what Mr Gedney have had come in? Liza-Jane showed me a notice in last week's paper about him taking a new delivery of watered silks, taffetas and satins.' She steered Caseley towards the double doors of Gedney's Drapery Emporium.

'You and Liza-Jane–'

'Think the world of you as you well know. So–' Rosina suddenly changed direction. 'I tell you what, let's go and have a cup of tea first.'

'No, this was your idea. Besides, we're here now. So why–'

'I'm sorry, bird,' Rosina murmured, looking towards the shop door.

Caseley followed her gaze. Shock jolted through her as a dark-suited male attendant held it open for a departing customer and Caseley came face to face with her husband's former mistress.

A small wicker basket swung from one gloved hand as Louise Downing emerged, wearing a close-fitting emerald jacket that emphasised a full bosom and rounded hips. Across the front of a narrow skirt adorned with tiers of ruffles, a swathe of purple taffeta was drawn into a puffed and fluted bustle. Her small hat, decorated with emerald and purple rosettes, perched on frizzy hair the colour of marmalade.

All this Caseley absorbed as she turned in response to Rosina directing her attention to something in the display. Looking at Louise and herself reflected in the shop window, Caseley saw a thin, sad crow and a plump, self-satisfied peacock.

''Afternoon, Mrs Barata.'

As her housekeeper's grip tightened on her arm, Caseley glanced around, pride keeping her spine straight as she inclined her head in a brief nod. 'Good day, Mrs Downing.'

Louise paused long enough for Caseley to read the triumph in her smirk then sauntered out onto the street, head high, basket swinging.

Realisation was followed by a jagged knife-

11

thrust of pain. He wouldn't – he *couldn't*. Yet there was no denying what she had seen. Louise Downing had been gloating. She turned to the woman who was her surrogate mother.

'Did you know? Don't lie to me, Rosina.'

'I don't believe it.' Caseley noticed Rosina didn't answer her question. 'You know what this town is like for gossip'

'People are talking about Jago and Louise Downing?'

Rosina made a dismissive gesture. 'There's always rumours and nothing loses in the telling. It don't mean nothing, bird. A man as 'andsome as Mister Barata will always attract talk. But whatever went on there was years ago and over before you wed. So don't you go upsetting yourself over the likes of her, you hear me? Come on, now.'

Gossip and rumour meant people would be whispering, claiming there was no smoke without fire. Caseley let Rosina draw her into the shop. Mr Gedney himself came forward to serve them, pulling down bolts of watered silk in delicate shades of pearl grey, oyster, lavender and violet. He and Rosina discussed colours, design and occasion. Caseley feigned interest but her thoughts were with her husband.

She had missed sailing with him. But with two boisterous young boys who needed her it hadn't been possible. She had continued doing translation work for her Uncle Richard, who managed the shipping office, but this rarely took more than a couple of hours each week.

A woman's role in life was to be a wife and mother. So she had poured her energy and devotion into caring for her family, finding her happiness in their welfare. Until both her sons had succumbed to putrid throat.

Fighting the fever with every remedy she knew, she had watched helplessly as the infection reached their lungs. Philip and James had died within hours of each other, aged just five and three, their short lives ending before they had properly begun.

Ten months on, raw-edged grief had numbed to a deep, endless ache.

Jago had been at sea when the epidemic broke out. For three weeks she and Rosina scarcely slept. While she nursed them, watching them grow weaker, she prayed he was on his way home, that he would arrive that day, or the next. But he hadn't. Her grief and his guilt at not being with her had driven a wedge between them. Within weeks he had returned to sea. She was glad to see him go, but missed him terribly and hated him for abandoning her.

Her life as a mother was over. After James's birth Dr Vigurs had told her it was unlikely she would be able to bear another child. So what now? What was the point of her life?

'What do you think?' Rosina nudged her gently. 'I like that pearl grey, and the lavender.'

Aware they were watching her, Caseley made an effort. 'They are both very nice.'

'Mrs Roskilly will be pleased to make the gowns up for you,' Mr Gedney said. 'I believe she has your measurements.' His hesitation was brief and he continued smoothly. 'Should alterations be required they will easily be accommodated at the fitting.'

'No bustle or train,' Caseley said, glancing at Rosina whose mouth opened to argue. 'No,' she repeated softly. Rosina's mouth closed.

'As you wish, Mrs Barata,' Mr Gedney bowed. 'May I suggest a plain bodice split at the back to allow a cascade of frills and a matching frill on the hem?'

'That would be acceptable, thank you.'

They walked up the High Street towards Greenbank and home.

'You never was one to follow every fashion,' Rosina said. 'Truth is, I never did see the sense in having all that there material dragging along behind. Only thing that's good for is to save Liza-Jane sweeping the floor.'

Letting her rattle on, Caseley kept seeing Louise Downing's sneering, triumphant smile. Was it not enough that she had lost her beloved sons? Had she lost her husband as well?

Jago Barata walked up wide granite steps and through the open door. William Broad & Sons, cargo brokers, occupied offices a short distance from Bonython's, proximity that had proved beneficial to both companies.

'Good afternoon, Captain Barata,' a black-suited clerk said, moving from his desk to the counter as Jago walked in.

'I received a letter from Mr Broad asking me to call?'

'If you will come this way, sir, Mr Broad is expecting you.'

They crossed the passage. The clerk knocked,

announced him, then withdrew, closing the door quietly. William Broad's dove grey tailcoat and dark trousers were expertly tailored to flatter his stocky figure. Over an upright collar a maroon cravat was fastened with a pearl pin and tucked into his waistcoat.

Aware of his sun-faded navy reefer jacket and blue trousers tucked into salt-stained leather boots, Jago shook the proffered hand. 'Forgive my appearance, but your letter said the matter was urgent.'

'So it is, Captain Barata. So it is. I take it kindly that you have come by so quickly. Please,' indicating the visitor's chair, Broad resumed his seat behind a plain kneehole desk of burr walnut. 'See, what it is, this here trouble in Egypt is growing worse by the week. You don't need me to tell you how much trade we do there, not just buying cotton, but all the goods coming through the Suez Canal. Mr Gladstone don't have no choice but to do whatever's necessary to protect Britain's interests as the major shareholder in the Canal. I b'lieve in the past you done secret work for the government. Am I right?'

Jago gave a brief nod.

'In that there safe,' Broad pointed, 'I got £20,000 in gold. Came this morning it did, from the Treasury. I'm to ask you to take it to Egypt.'

'Why me?'

'You got a reputation for making fast passages. This business is urgent. And, like I said, you've done this kind of work before.'

'Who is this gold for?'

'Far as I can make out, it's a gift to the Bedouins

15

so they'll take our side against this here Egyptian who's causing so much trouble.'

'In other words, it's a bribe.'

Tapping the tips of his fingers together, William Broad shrugged. 'You catch more flies with jam than vinegar.'

'What guarantee do we have that the Bedouins will honour the agreement?'

'None. But the gold is here, so the government must think it's worth the risk. Word is that these Bedouins do govern theirselves. They don't owe loyalty to no one, not Egypt nor the Ottomans. Once word reaches this Colonel Arabi that the Bedouins are on our side, he will see his nationalist ambitions haven't a hope of success. That's the plan, anyway. Last thing Mr Gladstone wants is a costly war. I wish I could say go home and think about it. But there isn't time, not if–'

'I'll go.' As the words left his lips. Jago visualised Caseley's face, the shock and disappointment she would try hard to hide. But if she didn't want him to go, why didn't she offer him more reason to stay? As shame suffused him he shoved it away.

Relief spread across Broad's face. 'That's 'andsome. I wasn't sure you'd want to take it on; what with... How is your good lady? Been some terrible time–'

'As well as can be expected,' Jago interrupted. *Everyone's concern was for her. Of course it was. How could he begrudge a moment's sympathy to a mother who had lost both her children?' He didn't. He wouldn't. But it was his loss too...*

'Hammer and Jimbo Caddy will be here at 7.30 in the morning to collect the gold. I assume it's

16

in a strongbox?'

Broad frowned. 'Yes, but I don't–'

'Which will require two strong men to carry it.'

'Yes, but–'

'Mr Broad, if I am to catch the morning tide I have a great deal to do. Over the past ten years my crew and I have faced death on more occasions than I care to remember. They have my total trust. Either accept my word on that or find someone else.'

'No! Please, I didn't mean no offence.'

Jago fought anger that prowled inside him, seeking an opportunity to escape. 'Then I take none.' Standing, he offered his hand. 'Good day, Mr Broad.'

'Good day to 'e, Captain. I'm very much obliged.'

Jago strode through the open double gates beneath the large curved sign that read 'Bonython's'. Though he and Caseley held equal shares, neither had wanted to change the name that for three generations had been synonymous with expert boat building and repair.

He had hoped one day his own sons... He slammed a door on that thought, mind and gut churning with guilt, anger and misery.

Bypassing her younger brother, Ralph, Jago's father-in-law, Teuder Bonython, had left the yard to Caseley. Selling his foreign interests to invest in it, he was expanding the business, proving his worth and his earning power.

He wished he might have spent more time with the boys. But both home and family were a

17

woman's domain. His role was to provide for them.

Society judged him a successful man. Yet with his sons' deaths he had lost his stake in the future. If Caseley had reached out to him ... but she hadn't. So he could not turn to her. Could not betray his need for comfort. Not when he was the rock everyone depended on.

As long as he honoured his obligations he could do what he wished. Sleeping with Louise offered brief escape from demands, grief, guilt. But it wasn't enough, could never be enough.

The tide was out and the lower half of the stone slipway was green and slimy. Seaweed hung in brown bunches from the granite blocks of the quay. *Cygnet* was moored fore-and-aft to iron bollards. But wooden props had been jammed under her keel to hold her level.

He saw Hammer and Jimbo brushing boiling pitch over a patch of fresh caulking in the schooner's hull. The throat-catching odour lay heavy over the familiar stink of mud as he called down to them. 'We sail on the morning tide.'

'Right,' Hammer said.

'Where we going?' Jimbo asked.

'Egypt. I need a strongbox picked up from Broad's at 7.30 tomorrow morning.'

The men glanced at each other. 'Barrow and a tarp to cover'n with?' Jimbo said.

Jago nodded and turned away. They never questioned, never asked him to explain. Their trust saved time and effort and now he took it for granted.

Across the busy yard he heard the clang of

18

hammer on anvil. A cloud of steam billowed from the blacksmith's shed along with the acrid reek of burning coke and red-hot metal. The dry coconut smell of fresh rope wafted from the riggers' store. Fresh sawdust lay in golden drifts between the sawpit and a stack of seasoning timber.

Reaching the yard office he ducked his head to avoid the low lintel made from a huge square balk of timber and stepped inside.

Toby Penfold, the yard foreman, rose from a wooden chair behind a battered desk that was strewn with scraps of paper, a couple of rolled plans, several oak blocks, a spliced end of rope, a sailmaker's fid and palm and a rumpled cloth holding the end crust of a pasty. One shelf above a cupboard was crammed with ledgers and in the grate a small fire had burned down to glowing embers.

Short and square, Toby had a weathered face deeply creased around eyes that were sharp and missed little. The ancient seaman's peaked cap he usually wore lay on the desk. His pale scalp was fringed with fine grey fuzz.

Beneath an open waistcoat he wore a woollen shirt with the cuffs rolled halfway up scarred and sinewy forearms. A broad leather belt buckled under his belly held up filthy serge trousers.

'Is it true what I heard?' Toby swiped crumbs from his mouth with the back of his hand.

'What did you hear?'

'That you beat the crap out of Mickey Croggan.'

Jago glanced at the split skin and purple bruising on his knuckles. 'Yes, so?'

'Word is he'd be dead now if you hadn't been

19

pulled off. What was that lightskirt to you any-way?'

'Nothing.'

'Then what was you thinking of?'

'She turned him down so he hit her. He's twice her size, he's a vicious drunk and he needed a lesson.'

'You need to watch your temper. You killing someone will bring your missus even more grief. She don't deserve that.'

Anger roared through Jago. But before he could speak another man entered.

'Afternoon, Cap'n.'

Turning, Jago saw Will Spargo, Bonython's senior captain on coastal trade. He shook the outstretched hand.

'Will.'

'I was sorry to hear about your boys. Me and Mary lost our middle son to the scarlet fever when he was just a little tacker.'

'I never knew that.'

''Twas a good few year ago. No point going on about it, is there? It's not like we was the only ones.'

'Even so, you have my sympathy.'

'Much obliged to 'e, Cap'n.'

Jago wanted to ask how long it took Will's Mary to get over her loss. But he was afraid of the answer.

'I'll leave you to get on. See you tomorrow afternoon, Toby.'

'She'll be ready.'

Touching his cap in salute, Will Spargo left.

Jago turned back to the foreman. 'I need *Cygnet*

20

ready for tomorrow morning.'

After a moment's silence, Toby nodded. 'Where to?'

'Egypt.'

'That's some trip. Take 'e–'

'At least three weeks.'

Toby sucked air through his teeth. 'Right. Hammer and Jimbo'll be finished within the hour. I'll send Mart down to Curgenven's. He know what to get to revictual her. Afore you go I'd take it very kindly if you was to give the riggers a bit extra in their wages. Same for your crew. Nathan done some 'andsome job with they spars. Worked like the devil they have, every man jack of 'em.'

Jago nodded. 'See to it.'

'A word of thanks wouldn't go amiss neither.'

Jago stiffened. 'Be careful, Toby.'

'No, 'tis time you was told. You got the best crew in Falmouth. They deserve better than you're giving 'em.'

'For God's sake, they're grown men! I'm not their father.' He could have bitten off his tongue.

'You're their captain. 'Tis next best thing,' Toby yelled back, not giving an inch. 'They'd follow you to hell and back. But you're driving them too hard.'

'No harder than I'm driving myself.'

'D'you think I don't know that? But you're going to kill yourself and them along with you.' Toby stabbed a forefinger at him. 'Broken spars, snapped ropes, ripped canvas, half the port rail gone and the hull leaking like a sieve. That's not weather damage, not every voyage. *Cygnet* can't take that kind of punishment and neither can you.'

21

Jago glared at the foreman who glared right back. Then, like curtains parting, he saw past Toby's anger to the concern that inspired it. Shame swept through him, dissolving his fury. He rubbed his face.

'I beg your pardon.'

''T isn't me you should be saying it to. You don't need to say it at all. Just ease up. Now, if there's nothing else, I better get on.'

Jago left, briefly gripping Toby's shoulder as he passed.

Chapter Two

Caseley wished she hadn't gone into town, although having Rosina with her meant she could simply nod and smile in response to greetings *and keep walking*. She didn't have to stop to respond to people's enquiries.

Most meant well. But their lives hadn't been devastated, and their polite expressions of sympathy made her want to hit them. These sudden urges to violence were unnerving and she felt like a stranger to herself.

She was so angry: with Jago for not being here when she desperately needed him; with herself for failing at the most basic task of being a mother, to protect her children; and with God for taking her two innocent and much loved sons. *Why?*

Before Jago left on his most recent voyage she had sensed a change in him and hated her suspicions. But she hadn't *known*, not for certain. Not until today. Had she given in to Rosina's urging, she wouldn't know now. Would it have been better to remain in ignorance? *While the town gossiped?* Now she knew she couldn't pretend she didn't. So what was she to do?

Rosina took Caseley's cape. 'Just say you're right about Mrs Downing–'

'We both know I am.'

'It don't mean nothing. Mister's a man, and men... She's no more to him than scratching an itch, and that's the truth.'

The front door slammed.

'I'll fetch a tray of tea. Listen, bird, p'rhaps it isn't my place to say–'

Caseley smiled wearily. 'When has that ever stopped you?'

'You aren't the only one hurting. He took it very bad that he wasn't here for you.' She hurried out.

Caseley moved to the window and looked down onto the busy river. She heard him speak to Rosina, his deep voice so beloved and familiar. She wrapped her arms across her body, pressing them against the constant gnawing ache in her stomach and fought for composure.

She would never forget the look on his face when he burst into the room a week after she had watched two small coffins lowered into the ground, one on top of the other. She had insisted the boys remain together.

But in the torrent of questions that poured from Jago's lips she had not heard comfort or sympathy or understanding, only accusation. Unable to bear any more pain she had withdrawn deep into herself.

The door opened. She turned and saw him, tall, strong, his dark curly hair untidy. With him came the vivid memory of Louise Downing's triumphant smirk.

Crossing the room he brushed her cheek lightly with his lips then stood at her shoulder looking out of the window. Longing for more while wanting to hammer him with her fists, she realised his close-bearded face was leaner than she remembered. Creases surrounded his eyes and scored a groove between his dark brows. What changes did he see in her?

'How was your day?'

She braced herself to give him the news. 'My cousin Charlotte is expecting her first child.'

His frown deepened. 'How did you learn of this? If Margaret Bonython came here and upset you–'

'No, she sent a letter. I do not begrudge her plea-sure, and I wish Charlotte well. But Aunt Margaret could not resist comparing Charlotte, wed only six months, to poor Emily Lashbrook who has been married seven years and whose failure to produce is causing both families great anxiety. Her gloating was unpleasant. Though I always found Emily spoiled and selfish, I feel for her. The pressure must be very hard to bear, especially for someone to whom everything came easily.'

He nodded, but she could see his attention was elsewhere. Hopelessness welled up like a tide.

'I have to go to Egypt.'

Startled, Caseley looked up at him. 'Egypt? When?'

'As soon as possible.' His gaze held hers.

24

'But–' She stopped. They both knew he had been home only a week. 'Why?'

'See for yourself.' Handing her an opened envelope he crossed to the fireplace and tugged the bell-pull. 'This was waiting for me at the office. I went straight to Broad's then back to the yard.'

Caseley read the letter twice. She cleared her throat, determined to hold her voice steady. 'How long will you be away?'

He shrugged. 'It's hard to say. Even with favourable winds, the voyage to Alexandria will take at least three weeks. Then I have to reach the people I'm supposed to see. I think it unlikely I'll be back before August.'

There was a brief tap on the door. Though Caseley expected the housemaid, she was not surprised to see Rosina behind her. Jago turned.

'Rosina, tell Ben to repack my trunk. I have to leave early tomorrow morning.'

'Dear life, you only just got home,' she muttered and stomped out.

Caseley gazed at the letter but saw Louise Downing's mocking triumph as clearly as if the woman were standing in front of her. She heard faint echoes of her children's laughter. Her eyes stung and burned but remained dry. She had wept until she had no tears left.

When Jago left she would spend three more months alone, reliving a past she could not change but could not escape. The rumours would grow and spread. Every time she ventured out she would be studied. Sympathy for her bereavement would be weighted with sympathy over her husband's betrayal. She could not face that.

25

'I want to go with you.' She hadn't known she was going to say it. The shock on his face mirrored her own. But now she had spoken she realised those words held her only chance, their only hope.

He hesitated as something flashed in his eyes. Then he shook his head. 'No.'

'Why not?'

'Caseley, you read the newspapers. Egypt is in ferment. Mr Gladstone is preparing for intervention. The English Channel fleet is already on its way to Malta. It will be dangerous.'

She stared at him for a moment. Then shocked them both by laughing. But it was a harsh sound and filled with pain. 'Dangerous? Tell me, Jago, what exactly do I have to fear? The worst has already happened. What can hurt me now?'

His gaze met hers. Anguish tightened his features and she glimpsed utter desolation.

'Please, Jago.' *Why? Why did you not turn to me? Why did you go to Louise Downing?* Could he not see this was pointless? Her desire to go was stronger than any argument he could raise against it.

'I will not risk your safety.'

'You are willing to risk your own.'

'I have no choice.'

'And I have no purpose here.'

'Caseley–'

Emotion would not sway him – he had cut himself off from it, and her. But logic might. 'You are bound for Egypt, but you do not speak Arabic.'

'Nor do you.'

'That's true. But in Alexandria French is the common language. I speak French. You do not. I

26

am also familiar with consular work.' It was through her assumption of her father's consular duties during his final illness that she had met Jago Barata.

'I need no reminder.'

She tipped her head in acknowledgment as a pulse throbbed in her throat. 'Then surely you see I can be useful.' As the silence stretched her restraint crumbled. 'You must let me – I cannot stand – everywhere I turn I see them. I hear their voices.'

He grasped her hand, held it to his chest. It was the first spontaneous move he had made in nearly a year. She fought the urge to lean on him and weep.

'We can move. I'll sell the house–'

'No! No. I love this house. But I need to leave it for a while.' She needed far more than that. She wanted the man she had fallen in love with, the man who had chosen her, with her damaged foot and untameable chestnut hair, above all the others he might have had. But after eight years, two children and tragedy, they were no longer the same people. There was no going back, so the only way was forward. Even at the risk of more pain she could not continue living as she was.

'I love this place. But being here all day – and you have said so little.'

'You thought I didn't care?' His expression was appalled.

'No, I never made that mistake. I know you feel deeply. But you hold your emotions under iron control. Your stoicism – I felt abandoned, Jago.'

As he looked away she saw the muscles bunch

27

in his jaw. He was the only man she had ever loved. She had pledged him her heart and soul. But no longer would she accept being pushed to the fringes of his life.

Outside the door the housekeeper coughed loudly.

Jago released her hand. Caseley remembered a time when he would not have done so, a time when he never missed an opportunity to touch. Even outside the privacy of their bedroom they had found comfort and promise in the brush of fingers, linked arms, his gloved hand covering hers, confidences whispered and private smiles that made words unnecessary. It seemed so very long ago.

'Come in, Rosina.' Caseley crossed to sit on a sofa and waited while Rosina placed a tray of tea on a low table in front of her. Ask Ben to fetch my trunk down from the attic, will you?'

The housekeeper's eyebrows shot up. Then she frowned and opened her mouth. Caseley didn't give her the chance.

'Now, please? I'll be with you shortly. There's a lot to do.'

Closing it again, Rosina bobbed a stiff curtsey, and with lips pursed in anxious disapproval, she sailed out.

Jago shook his dark head. 'I cannot like it.'

Caseley's hand trembled as she poured a little milk into each of the bone china cups. Setting the jug down, she reached for the teapot. Then she spoke. 'I do not ask you to. But for this at least you need me.' The silence that followed hummed with tension and too much left unsaid. He broke it.

'Forgive me if I do not join you. I must return to the yard.' He paused at the door. 'Caseley, are you sure–'

She didn't let him finish. 'Both trunks will be packed and ready to be carried to the ship first thing in the morning. Will you hire a cab?'

He shook his head. 'It'll be quicker for Hammer and Jimbo to collect them by boat from the slipway across the road. Have your dinner. Don't wait for me.' He left.

The front door closed. She poured tea then set the pot down carefully.

Was she sure? No, she wasn't. But if she didn't get away she would go mad

Jago strode through the town. He should have refused, but how could he argue with her need to escape the constant reminder of her loss? Though slender as a reed, she had always been strong. Now her pale fragility, emphasised by her black mourning gowns, increased his guilt.

She could not blame him more than he blamed himself. Had he been at home – it would have made no difference. Dr Vigurs had assured him that Mrs Barata, Rosina and Liza-Jane had done everything possible. Indeed, he had been forced to speak very sharply to Mrs Barata to get her to rest at all.

What tore at Jago was that for those final terrible days, and afterwards, he had not been here to comfort and support her. At sea, he had not even known his sons were ill. By the time he arrived back in Falmouth, they were buried. When his family had needed him most he had failed them.

How did he live with that? A man was supposed to protect those he loved.

His sons, two fine boys, were gone. His beloved wife, the light of his life, was suffering and he couldn't put it right. His helplessness made him ashamed and deepened his guilt. He had not protected. But he could provide.

In the past ten months he had sailed to the Azores for fruit and twice to Halifax in Canada for timber. The Atlantic in winter was wild and lashed by storms. At least Egypt promised warmth.

'You can't!' Rosina wrung her hands. 'You aren't thinking straight. Look at you. Lost pounds, you have. A strong breeze would blow you over.'

'I'm going, Rosina, and that's final. What I want you to do is help me sort out which clothes to take.'

'Listen, you got more sense than to take any notice of gossip–'

'What are they saying?' Caseley pressed the heel of her hand to her breastbone to ease the sharp pain beneath. 'Poor Caseley Barata lost her sons and cannot keep her husband happy?'

Grabbing her shoulders, Rosina shook her. 'You stop that right now! None of this is your fault. You're still grieving. You need looking after. Last thing you should be doing is gadding off to some heathen country on the other side of the world.'

Caseley pulled open a drawer and took out several neatly folded shifts of fine linen. 'It will be hot there, so–'

'Beg y' pardon, ma'am,' Liza-Jane said, poking her head around the door. 'Your brother have just

30

come. I've put 'n in the morning room.'

Laying the shifts on the bed cover, Caseley smoothed the front of her black silk dress. She never enjoyed her brother's visits. Thankfully, they were rare. What misfortune had befallen him this time?

'You wanted me out of my mourning clothes, Rosina. You have your wish.'

'Listen, bird–'

'I cannot wear black there.' Caseley turned at the door. 'Questions would be asked. I would have to explain. I could not bear–'

Hurrying across, Rosina hugged her. 'All right, my sweetheart. I don't like it, not at all I don't. But if you're set on going–' She sucked in a breath. 'Right, you'll want your lightest dresses. I got a length of holly green ribbon. Won't take me long to add a bit of trim to your white spotted muslin. There'll be enough to trim your second-best straw bonnet. The lilac is all right as it is and so's your floral cotton. For the boat you can wear that navy jacket and skirt. I'll pack the gold and green dress in case you got to go anywhere formal. You'll want bed linen, towels, and I'll put all your underwear in a spare pillowcase.' She sighed. 'You best get on down and see what your brother want. He'll be whingeing about something. Or on the scrounge. 'Tis the only time he ever come near the place.'

Entering the morning room, Caseley saw her brother sprawled in a chair. His clothes were unkempt, his hair greasy and overlong. His eyes were bloodshot, his pallor unhealthy, but at least he was sober.

'Good afternoon, Ralph. How are you?'

31

'As if you care.' He gazed round the room with a dissatisfied frown.

Smothering a sigh, Caseley perched on the edge of a chair and folded her hands. 'Of course I care, you're my brother and I–'

'Then let me come and live here. You can't say now that you don't have room.'

Air hissed between Caseley's teeth at his casual cruelty. He didn't even notice.

'It's not fair. I'm no good at looking after myself. George Trembath is refusing to pay for his portrait. All right, it was a few weeks late. But a painting takes as long as it takes. Do you know what he called it? A travesty. Perhaps that's what I'll call him: Travesty Trembath. The man has no taste. He wouldn't recognise talent if it jumped up and bit him on the a–'

'Ralph, was there a reason for this visit? Only I'm rather busy.'

'Doing what?' he sneered. 'You really ought to stop wearing black. You look positively Gothic.'

Caseley stood up. 'I'm going to Egypt.'

Ralph sat up. 'Can I come?'

'No. I'm sailing with Jago. He has business there.'

He brightened. 'Can I stay here while you're away? Rosina and Liza-Jane could look after me–'

She shook her head. 'No, Ralph, you can't. I'm sorry–'

'No, you aren't. You don't give a damn about me. You're just like the rest of them. It's not my fault if–'

'It never is,' Caseley said quietly.

He lurched to his feet. 'If that's your attitude I

32

may as well go.' But he didn't move towards the door. Caseley knew he was waiting for her to back down or offer a compromise. He expected it, believed he was entitled. But she had nothing left to give.

'I think that would be best.'

He pushed past her, leaving a stale sour reek in the air. A moment later the front door slammed.

Caseley pitied her brother. He was a talented painter. But he was lazy, nursed grudges, and when things went wrong he blamed everyone but himself. His visits, thankfully rare, always unsettled her, provoking worry that she ought to do more for him, even though her help in the past had made no difference whatsoever. He took everything offered, wanted more, but refused to help himself. He hadn't changed. It appeared unlikely he ever would.

Though she wished he hadn't come, seeing him gave her strength to fight the doubts crowding in to undermine her. The house was full of devastating memories, yet the prospect of leaving its security and the reassuring presence of Rosina, Liza-Jane and Ben terrified her. But if she wanted things to change, she had to change them. No one else could do it for her.

Chapter Three

Cygnet's mate, Nathan Ferris, welcomed Caseley aboard; his callused hand enfolding hers was reassuring as he helped her onto the deck. Beneath the long cloak of navy serge that had kept her warm and doubled as an extra blanket during past voyages, she wore a hip-length fitted jacket over a white camisole and a petticoat with flounces at the back to support the plain navy skirt that fell straight to her instep in front. It was two years old but the gathered fullness at the back gave a nod to fashion.

Because of her damaged foot she always wore ankle boots that were flat or had a low chunky heel. Easier for walking, they were also far safer on the brass stairs or a sloping deck. Her simple straw bonnet had a broad brim and two navy ribbons that tied under her chin. She had studied her reflection in the long glass before leaving.

Etiquette demanded full mourning for a year. She was still two months shy of that. Guilt pricked like sharp thorns. She fought it. This voyage was not about her, and black would provoke questions, elicit sympathy. She didn't want that, for her sake and Jago's. He had a job to do.

For the first time in years he needed her help. Could this be the first step on their journey back to each other? A vivid memory of Louise Downing's triumphant smile made her recoil. She closed her eyes, breathed. She had lived through the worst a woman could suffer. She would survive this.

'Good to see 'e again, missus.'

'Thank you, Nathan. I hope your family is well?'

'Going on fine they are.'

'I'm glad to hear it.'

'All right, missus?' Hammer and Jimbo each touched a knuckle to their foreheads in a salute as they hurried to unlash the two huge fore-and-aft sails and haul them up the masts.

Seeing Martin, now a stocky muscular twenty-year-old, stowing sacks and crates of provisions in the galley shack, Caseley remembered the skinny twelve-year-old he had been on her voyage with Jago to Spain. Glancing up, he gave her the same salute. Caseley made herself smile. 'Are you still the cook, Martin?'

'He isn't fit for nothing else,' Jimbo panted, heaving on a rope.

'We keep 'n in the shack so he don't get under our feet,' Hammer agreed.

'If it was left to you pair we'd starve,' Martin shouted back. 'Burn water, you would.'

'Truth is,' Nathan told her, 'Mart do a good job. He got a gift for it.'

'I hope you'll find these useful, Martin.' Caseley handed the young man a cloth bag. 'Two fruit cakes, two fresh loaves, a crock of butter and two jars of homemade raspberry jam.' Rosina had been busy baking until late last evening while Liza-Jane ironed then carefully rolled Caseley's dresses so they wouldn't crease.

Martin flushed, grinning with pleasure. 'Proper

job, missus. Much obliged. Go down a treat, they will. We never go short of porridge and treacle, meat and veg. But cake,' he held up the bag. 'Good as Christmas this is.'

As Caseley descended the brass stairs she saw the door to Jago's day cabin wedged open. His trunk was pushed against the ship's side below the sliding door of the sea berth.

He was sitting writing the log and rose as she entered, sliding out of the narrow space between the triangular table and the padded leather bench.

'Thanks, Nathan. I'll be up directly.'

As the mate returned topside, Jago's gaze lingered on her cloak. Was he remembering Spain? 'If you've changed your mind it's not too late.'

'We've already had this conversation,' she broke in quietly. 'My trunk?'

Gesturing towards an alcove screened from the cabin by the folds of a thick dark curtain, he moved to the open doorway 'You know your way around. I want to get underway.'

'Yes, of course.'

They were husband and wife and as wary as strangers. He disappeared and she heard his boots clang on the chased brass treads of the companionway. Alone now, she pressed a gloved hand to her dry throat as her heart thudded. *Not too late...* With all her heart she hoped so.

Everything was as she remembered: the table designed to fit the narrowing stern and edged with a wooden lip to prevent things sliding off, the shelf above filled with books and sea junk secured by a beautifully turned fiddle rail, the shallow brass lamp suspended beneath the open skylight.

Her gaze moved from the clock and barometer to the squat stove standing on its protective metal plate in front of the forward bulkhead and bracketed by a full coal-bucket and basket of logs.

Through the open skylight came the sounds of a ship making ready for sea: the rattle of blocks, snapping canvas and the crew's banter. Six years had passed since her last trip and it was exactly as she remembered.

She crossed to the sleeping alcove. Pushing back the curtain she saw the nightstand. Beneath a hinged lid was an enamel basin. A cupboard underneath held a chamber pot. Light fell across the berth and her breath caught in her throat.

Immediately after proposing to her, Jago had instructed Hammer to widen the narrow berth so it would comfortably accommodate them both. She had made a mattress to fit and bought new blankets.

In that small private space they had discovered each other, shared their pasts and talked of their plans for the future. Their elder son had been conceived there. She had slept in Jago's arms, safe, loved, until her advancing pregnancy had made it uncomfortable and unwise.

The berth had been reduced to its original size. Rejection stung like a slap. She lifted the blankets and saw the mattress had been made smaller to fit. Their time together, her presence here, her part in his seafaring life, he had erased it all. She had believed herself numb to further pain. She wasn't.

But, having insisted on coming, she could not complain. Nor could she stay down here. If she did not show herself topside he would come to find out why. Pulling herself together, she left the door wedged open and returned to the deck.

Jago was at the helm steering a course through anchored ships of every size and rig. The crew ignored her, busy hoisting additional sails and coiling ropes over wooden pegs. Martin was in the galley shack lighting the stove.

Caseley leaned on the weather rail with warm sun and cold breeze on her face, and felt relieved. She didn't have to talk and no one wanted anything from her.

She glanced back as the distance between *Cygnet* and the Cornish coast widened. Whatever this voyage held could not be worse than the past she was leaving behind.

At sea the main meal of meat, vegetables and a pudding was always eaten at midday. Martin put a plate in front of her containing two thick slices of boiled ham, three boiled potatoes and a spoonful of sliced carrots. In the centre of the table stood a small pot of mustard and a jar of apple and onion chutney.

'That enough for you, missus? I wasn't sure–'

'It's just right, Martin.' She smiled up at him.

The others were served, Martin slid in beside her and the meal began. She wasn't hungry but, with Jago watching, she knew she had to eat. She used her knife to take some chutney then cut into a potato. After swallowing the first mouthful it was easier to take the next. The men ate quickly, focused on their food.

Caseley finished and put her knife and fork together. 'That was delicious, Martin.'

'Look at 'n, blushing like a sunset,' Jimbo teased.

'Don't say no more, missus,' Hammer warned. 'He'll never get his swelled head in the galley shack.'

Aware of Jago's gaze, she slid out from behind the table. 'Will you excuse me?'

'Don't you want no afters?' Martin started to get up. ''Tis treacle pudding.'

'I couldn't manage another mouthful,' Caseley smiled at him. 'Perhaps tomorrow.'

'I'd like to say we could use 'em for cannon balls,' Jimbo said. 'But truth is, Mart do make 'andsome suet pudding, and jam roly-poly. Make someone a lovely wife he will.'

'Giss on!' Martin's blush deepened.

'I'll look forward to trying some. Please don't get up,' she said quickly, as all three started to rise. Leaving them she went up on deck.

Nathan was at the wheel and, apart from a brief nod, he tactfully ignored her as she walked round the side of the wheel shelter and opened the door to the latrine.

Beneath a wooden seat fixed on two stout battens screwed to the plank wall was a bucket. Another bucket contained ashes and a small scoop. Small squares of newspaper pierced in one corner hung from a string suspended from a nail in the wall.

Each evening the latrine bucket was emptied and rinsed with seawater containing diluted pitch. Each morning when the stoves were cleaned out the ash bucket was refilled. It was basic but efficient and Caseley was glad of it.

After tea, while Jago took the helm and she had the cabin to herself, Martin brought down a ewer

39

of hot water. The routine followed a pattern established when she sailed with Jago during their first year of marriage. But it wasn't the same. Then she had prepared for bed in shy yet eager anticipation. Now – now she burned with anger and ached with loneliness.

After a strip wash she put on her nightgown, then brushed her hair and plaited it into a loose braid. Curled up in the berth listening to the creak of the timbers and the hiss of water against the hull she lay awake.

She heard the door open and quietly close, heard him moving about, then the creak of the padded bench. If she moved the curtain she would see him at the table writing the log and marking the chart. Only a few feet apart, they might as well have been on opposite sides of an ocean.

By the second afternoon the Cornish coast was no longer visible. With a strong steady breeze filling every sail, *Cygnet* headed southwest towards Spain and Portugal.

At tea time Caseley managed a slice of bread and butter but it felt like a wad of cotton in her mouth. Forcing it down with a few sips of tea, she begged them to excuse her.

Jago followed her down. 'Are you unwell?'

'I'm fine,' she lied as chills raced over her skin and her head pounded. 'Just tired. It's a long time since – the constant motion of the ship–'

'You're not seasick.'

Had she not felt so awful, the mingled accusation and disbelief in his tone would have made her smile. But her amusement was fleeting. He would be debating whether to return to Falmouth.

'No, I'm not. Nor have I ever been, as you should know.'

They reached his day cabin and she fumbled with the door handle. If she didn't lie down soon she would fall down. 'It's nothing. I will be better tomorrow.'

He hesitated in the doorway. She remembered a time when he would have closed the door on the rest of the ship, undressed her himself, then held her, lain with her, comforted her and she would have drawn strength from him.

But that was before. Before the bottom fell out of her world. Before he turned for comfort not to her, but to Louise Downing.

Feeling ill and utterly wretched Caseley dragged off her clothes, leaving them where they dropped. Wearing only her shift, she pulled the pins from her hair and, as it tumbled over her shoulders, slid beneath the blankets. She closed her eyes and felt herself falling...

Awareness returned. She was warm, comfortable and deeply relaxed. But where–? Then the motion and the nearby sound of rushing water brought it all back. She was aboard *Cygnet*. She drew in a deep breath and stretched. Her hand thumped against the bulkhead.

She heard booted feet. The curtain was pulled back and Jago stood in the doorway.

'So, you're back.'

She sat up. 'Back? I don't understand.'

He sat on the edge of the berth, elbows on his knees. 'Five days, Caseley. You barely stirred for five days.'

As she tried to take in what he was saying and what it meant, she saw strain and exhaustion etched on his face. 'Oh, Jago–'

'We should reach Gibraltar tomorrow–'

'*What?* How–?'

'Gales.' The terse reply told her everything she needed to know.

'Was there much damage?'

'A broken yard and a ripped topsail. We got off lightly.'

'You have a first-rate crew.'

'I'm putting you ashore. I'll arrange with the governor for your passage on the first ship returning to Falmouth. In the meantime–'

'I'm not leaving *Cygnet*, Jago. Not until we reach Alexandria.'

'I should never have agreed to this.'

'But you did.' She paused, then added softly, 'I'm sorry if I caused you worry.'

'You're sorry?' He shoved an unsteady hand through his hair. 'It's – you have no idea–'

'I was tired, that's all.'

'Five days, Caseley. That's not tiredness.'

'But I'm perfectly well now. Truly. What's the time?'

'Why?'

'If Martin's not busy with dinner, could he heat some water? I would dearly love a wash.'

He gazed at her a moment longer, his lips pressed together as if to physically prevent words escaping, and strode out. As he clanged up the stairs, Caseley swung her legs out of the berth. As she stood up, the cabin floor seemed to rock. She sat down again, taking slow deep breaths, until

42

her head stopped swimming. She would feel stronger after a meal.

The skylight above the table was open and she heard him shout for hot water, heard Martin's yelled reply, 'Aye, Skip.'

Jago took the wheel from Nathan. He was furious with Caseley for frightening him. He had a job to do and didn't have time for this. He kept seeing her lying there unresponsive and relived his mouth-drying terror at the thought of losing her.

Realisation had shocked him like an icy wave as he realised it must have been the same for her as she nursed the boys, watching them get worse and helpless to prevent it.

He shouldn't have let her come. But her determination to do so had allowed him to hope there might be a way back for them. He should have realised she wasn't well, that exhaustion and grief had taken far more out of her than either of them realised. But she hadn't complained, not to him. If she had, would he have heard? Self-loathing burned inside him.

Refreshed after a top-to-toe wash, Caseley put on a clean shift, stockings and her shoes. She brushed her hair and twisted it into a coil on the nape of her neck. After fastening the hooks of her corset she stepped into a petticoat with flounces at the back, then her skirt. Both corset and skirt sat more loosely on her waist. Buttoning a clean camisole she put on her jacket.

The small mirror Jago had fastened to the bulkhead reflected a pale, oval face, green eyes with purple shadows like bruises beneath them and high, sharp cheekbones. The rounded softness she had acquired during motherhood had vanished. *She was no longer a mother.* So what – who – was she now?

She turned away, clutching the back of the padded bench for support. *She couldn't do this.* Yes, she could. She must, if she was to change her life. Being on *Cygnet* was not simply a voyage to a foreign country, it was a journey to find a new self.

Jago needed her assistance. There was no going back to what had been. Could working together again help them find a new way forward? She straightened her spine, drew a deep breath and left the cabin.

The crew's welcome brought a lump to her throat. After each one had asked how she was feeling, Jago snarled at them to look to their tasks.

Startled, Caseley met his gaze. The bright sunlight revealed dark smudges of exhaustion under his eyes and a furrow of tension between his brows. About to speak, he shook his head and turned away. 'Hammer, clear a space on the cargo hatch so my wife has somewhere to sit.'

Chapter Four

Cygnet sailed across the Bay of Algeciras. Ahead Caseley saw the tall limestone promontory of Gibraltar jutting out into the Strait from the end of an area of low, flat land.

It was just after two when they entered the harbour and moored alongside one of the quays. Leaving Hammer on watch, Nathan went down to have his dinner and a customs officer came aboard.

After introducing Caseley, who remained topside to give them privacy, Jago took the officer down to the day cabin.

That morning she had left off her navy cloak in favour of a skirt and matching long-sleeved fitted jacket of cream cotton printed with tiny green flowers. When she had finished dressing she looked down at herself. It was wrong, too soon…

Her fingers had gone to the buttons. Then she had lowered her hands. The navy cloak needed washing and was too warm now they were in the Mediterranean. Wearing cotton was a simple necessity, not a lack of respect. After nearly a year in unrelieved black she needed time to get used to wearing ordinary clothes again – *and time to overcome guilt at her relief.* The straw bonnet Rosina had re-trimmed with holly green ribbon shielded her eyes from the bright sunshine.

Jimbo and Martin came towards her. 'We're going up the town to buy provisions, missus,' Martin said, raising a forefinger to his forehead in salute. 'Anything you want, is there?'

'Will you post this for me?' She handed him the letter she had written to Rosina with reassurance that all was well. Telling her the truth would only make her worry, which wouldn't be kind. 'Perhaps some fruit? You'll need money–'

'Cap'n took care of that, missus.'

As the pair left, the bowser cart arrived and

45

Hammer started refilling the freshwater barrels.

The customs officer reappeared from the companionway hatch and nodded politely. Jago followed, pausing beside Caseley.

'I have to go ashore for a short time.'

'May I come?'

He shook his head. 'I'm only going as far as the Custom House. We are to have a passenger. A reporter employed by Reuter's Agency needs to reach Alexandria as soon as possible. I'm going to meet him and pick up a case of photographic equipment. Apparently it's addressed to Miss Collingwood at the Consulate.'

'That's fortunate. As you need the Consul's help, being the person to deliver the case will surely weigh in your favour.'

'We must hope so.'

When she entered the saloon for breakfast that morning she had seen his gaze linger on her dress but he had not commented. Of course he hadn't. Nor would he in front of the crew. Since then they had not been alone. Should she explain?

'The only spare berth is in Nathan's cabin,' he said. 'I have already spoken to him.' He lowered his voice. 'Go below, Caseley. You aren't yet used to the heat.' He started to follow the officer then turned back to add, 'I'm glad you changed your dress.' Then he left.

She went to the day cabin, removed her bonnet and jacket and dropped them on her bed. Once more she looked in the small mirror. Was he concerned in case she fell ill again, which might put his mission at risk? Or was it because he cared? But if he cared, if she mattered to him, how could

46

he have resumed his affair with Louise Downing?

She poured cold water into the nightstand basin from the jug Martin had left and scooped it over her hot face, then pressed her wet hands to the back of her neck and throat. Straightening up, refreshed, she blotted away water with the towel, surprised by how much better she felt. She dried her hands, tidied her hair and replaced her jacket, then sat down at the table and opened her journal.

She had started keeping one after the boys were born, a record of when their first teeth appeared, their first words were spoken and first steps taken without a supporting hand, so she could share them with Jago when he returned from a voyage.

The entries stopped when they fell ill. While she was nursing them she had had no time. Then after – after she could not bear the reminder. She wasn't sure what had prompted her to put the leather-bound book in her trunk.

She couldn't read it, not yet. Instead, leaving several blank pages to separate *before* and *after,* she had begun writing a few sentences each day describing daily life aboard the ship.

She was on a journey. One day she might look back to compare *then* with *now* and recall events along the way.

Hearing footsteps on the stairs, and voices, she closed the journal as Jago walked in, automatically ducking his head to avoid the lintel. Caseley rose as another man followed him.

'Caseley, this is Mr Pawlyn, a reporter with considerable experience of Egypt. Pawlyn, may I present my wife,' Jago said.

Caseley saw a slim fair-haired man wearing a

47

slightly crumpled lightweight suit and narrow bow tie. He carried a hat with a round crown and narrow brim. His face was tanned and his smile deepened, creases radiating from the outer corners of his blue eyes.

'How do you do, Mr Pawlyn.' Caseley offered her hand.

'It's a pleasure to meet you, ma'am. I am most deeply obliged to your husband for his kind offer of a berth. I have spent several days waiting for a ship bound for Alexandria. Indeed, I was beginning to fear the Custom House might start charging me rent.'

As the tension that had gripped her dissolved – *he didn't know*, so she would not have to respond to his commiserations – Caseley warmed to the reporter. 'Before we left Cornwall I read in the newspaper that people are leaving the city.'

'Not just the city, ma'am, they are fleeing the country. Having made their fortunes in Egypt, bankers and merchants are scuttling away like rats from a sinking ship.'

'Yet you are going back.'

'I am indeed. Officially, I am replacing a colleague who is ill. The truth is that my predecessor fears war and wants to escape before it starts.'

Seeing Jago's expression harden, for this was *his* fear, and the reason he hadn't wanted her to come, Caseley kept her tone light. 'Clearly his decision to go is wise. Leaving at such a momentous time in Egypt's history proves he is not cut out to be a reporter.'

Pawlyn's grin held admiration. 'An astute observation, Mrs Barata.'

48

'I'll show you your berth,' Jago said, shepherding Pawlyn out as Jimbo came in carrying a large wooden box.

'Cap'n said to put this under the sleeping berth if that's all right, missus.'

'Go ahead.'

'We got oranges and peaches,' he said, emerging a moment later. 'Mart would have brought back a barrowful if I hadn't dragged 'n away. Peaches won't keep long in this heat so you'll be having them every meal.' Caseley smiled at him. 'I can't imagine anything nicer.'

After tea the crew went topside, leaving Caseley, Jago and Pawlyn at the mess table.

'It was the murder of Lord Frederick Cavendish, new Chief Secretary for Ireland, and Mr Burke the Permanent Under-secretary, in Phoenix Park on May 6th that changed Mr Gladstone's mind.' Pawlyn's mouth curled in contempt. 'Now, instead of supporting Egypt's aspirations to self-government, he is backing armed intervention to prevent it.'

'The Suez Canal must be protected,' Jago reasoned. Caseley recognised at once that he was baiting Pawlyn in order to discover the reporter's true opinion.

'That is simply a convenient excuse. Nor is it legitimate. Colonel Arabi has stated publicly on several occasions that trade with England *must* continue in order for Egypt to pay off its debt. At the moment neither the French nor the Canal Company believes the Canal to be threatened. But invasion might well change the situation. I

49

beg your pardon. ma'am. I have no wish to cause alarm.'

'Nor have you, Mr Pawlyn. So no apology is necessary. Have you been to Alexandria before?'

He nodded. 'I have worked there and in Cairo for four years until family business required me to return to England for a few weeks. I'm glad to be going back.'

'Even under current circumstances?' Jago asked.

'Especially now,' Pawlyn said. '*The Times* and the *Pall Mall Gazette* are being fed information by correspondents bribed through money or favours to write whatever best suits the ambitions of the Consul-General or the English Financial Controller. After the newspapers are printed in London, copies are telegraphed back to Egypt and translated into French and Arabic. I dread to think what Egyptians must make of the bias and half-truths being published as fact.'

'With so much at stake, feelings are bound to run high,' Jago pointed out.

'That I can accept. What I find offensive is deliberate distortion and scare-mongering.'

'You think that's what's happening?'

Pawlyn nodded. 'I know it is.'

'Do you speak French, Mr Pawlyn?' Caseley asked.

He nodded. 'And Arabic. Both are vital if you want to know what the Egyptians really think.'

'I would welcome the opportunity to practise my French,' Caseley said. 'Also to learn a few words of Arabic, if you would be so kind.' She glanced at Jago and realised with a shock that he had been studying her. She willed him to under-

50

stand. At his barely perceptible nod she returned her gaze to Pawlyn.

'Arabic is not an easy language,' he warned.

'And we have only the time it will take to reach Alexandria. But even if my accent is poor, being able to greet Egyptian people and say please or thank you must surely be considered a courtesy.'

'It will indeed. Few English ever bother. They don't even learn French though it is the city's official language.'

'My wife also speaks Spanish,' Jago said, and the undertone of pride in his voice thrilled Caseley, even as it made her want to weep.

After Jago left to go topside, Caseley and Pawlyn remained in the saloon for her first lesson.

An hour later, exhausted, her throat aching from the effort of achieving sounds that, to her untrained ear, sounded like harsh throat-clearing, she raised her hands in surrender.

'No more,' her smile was wry. 'When you said it was difficult, you were not exaggerating.'

'Don't be disheartened, Mrs Barata. You are a quick student, and you have an ear for the subtleties. Truly, you have exceeded my expectations.'

'*Shukran,* Mr Pawlyn. You are very kind.' As she slid out from behind the table he got awkwardly to his feet. 'Tomorrow?'

'At your service, ma'am. *Salaamu aleikum.*'

'*Wa-aleikum as-salaam.*' With a polite nod she left the saloon and walked up the companionway stairs.

Her sails taut in the wind, *Cygnet* sped through the darkening water, her foaming bow wave turning to liquid gold by the setting sun.

51

She stayed on deck for a while, enjoying the evening air. Jago was at the wheel.

'How did your lesson go?'

'It was hard work. There are sounds we don't have in English. They made me cough.' She gave a self-deprecating shrug. 'Apparently Bedouin is the plural of Bedawi and means "those of the desert". But English people use Bedouin as a singular noun and add an s to make it plural.' She shrugged again. 'Mr Pawlyn was generous and said I had done better than he expected.'

'If he knew you he would not be surprised.'

Before she could respond, Martin shouted from the galley shack, 'Want your water now, missus?'

'Yes, please,' she called over her shoulder then looked at Jago, wanting – she wasn't sure what she wanted. There was too much to say and she didn't know where to start.

'Goodnight, Caseley.' His voice was gentle.

Relief battled disappointment as she turned away. 'Goodnight.'

In the cabin she topped up the fire with a small shovel of coal. Damped down it would last all night, keeping the cabin comfortable and their clothes aired and free from the mould that was always a risk on a long voyage.

Cool and refreshed she put on her nightgown, brushed and braided her hair, and was sitting at the table, a soft shawl around her shoulders, writing her journal when Jago came in, yawning.

'I thought to find you asleep.' He closed the door and wearily took off his jacket.

'I wasn't tired.'

'What are you writing? Surely Pawlyn didn't

give you written work to do?'

'No, thank goodness. The book is just a journal. I write a little about each day's events. I must say I never expected to write that I'm learning Arabic.'

'It was a good idea to refresh your French.'

Martin knocked, calling through the wood. 'Hot water, Skip.'

Jago took the ewer and bucket. 'You needn't wait; I'll bring them when I relieve Nathan.' The door closed. 'As you're still up, would you mind me using the nightstand basin?'

'No, of course not.' She had left the curtain pulled back to allow air to circulate in the small space.

Re-corking the squat inkbottle, she heard the bucket clank as he put it down then water poured into the basin.

'When you've finished writing, leave the pen and ink out, will you? I need to update the log.'

She glanced round and saw him strip off his shirt, revealing a broad back and muscular shoulders. Longing pierced her and a flush burned her cheeks. He was her husband, the only man she had ever kissed, touched, held, loved. *He was her husband and he had lain naked with Louise Downing; made love with Louise Downing...*

She choked down a painful stiffness in her throat and carefully wiped the pen nib on a cotton square before laying it on the grooved wooden tray.

Water splashed, she smelled the fragrance of the soap she had used too, heard the soft rasp of the towel as he rubbed himself dry, then the rustle of clothing as he dressed again.

He emptied and replaced the basin then carried

53

the bucket and ewer to the door.

'Goodnight.' Caseley limped into the sleeping cabin, pulling off her shawl and dropping it over the foot of the berth. She reached for the curtain but didn't touch it. With it drawn across, the small space that had once been a cosy, private haven now felt lonely and claustrophobic. She lay down and pulled the blankets over her. Had she no pride? What kind of fool longed for a man who preferred someone else? A tear soaked into the pillow.

When Jago returned to the cabin he sat down and opened the log. Elbows propped on the table, he raked both hands through his hair. Tension made his scalp ache.

He was ashamed of his pleasure at seeing Caseley out of the black that constantly reminded him of his failure. Recognising her uncertainty about wearing a summery dress, he had hoped to reassure her. She was still hurting, her loss still a raw wound. She hadn't uttered a word of complaint. That made it worse. He didn't know what to do and hated his helplessness.

After meeting the reporter in the Custom House, he and Pawlyn had walked along the quay to *Cygnet*. Making conversation, Pawlyn had asked if he had family. He'd said no, and left it at that. Explanations would invite commiserations that were pointless and painful. They reminded him too vividly of Caseley's drawn, grief-ravaged face as he arrived home too late.

How could he ever make it up to her? Did she even want him to? That her rage seemed to have dissolved only increased his guilt. Their conversations were pleasant and their unspoken under-standing of each other's thinking on all other matters was still intact. If only she would meet his gaze, she would surely see everything he could not find words for: how much he missed her, needed her.

Several times, about to blurt it out, he had bitten his tongue to stop himself. Such a confession would make it about *him,* and that was self-indulgent while she was coming to terms with such devastating loss. He would live with the permanent ache at the base of his skull and a gut tied in knots. He would wait for as long as it took. He had adored his sons. But Caseley was the love of his life. So he would wait until she was ready, until she turned to him.

Chapter Five

During the next two weeks Caseley continued her language lessons. After dinner or tea, when Jago was with them and not at the helm, she listened while Robert Pawlyn described the political rival-ries that were turning Egypt into a battleground.

'Egypt is a member state of the Ottoman Empire headed by Sultan Abdul-Hamid. He is thirty-nine years old, shrewd, tyrannical and determined to defend his position. His mother, the Valide Sultan Sherketzya Kadin, deposed the former sultan, Abdulaziz, in favour of her son, Murad. After being ousted, Abdulaziz apparently committed suicide by slashing his wrists.'

'Apparently?' Jago asked before Caseley could.

Pawlyn nodded. 'Late last autumn, following an investigation that took nearly six years, several men were charged with his murder. But that's by the by. After only three months Murad was removed.'

'Why?' Caseley and Jago asked simultaneously.

'Because he was mad: truly insane. So Murad's brother, Abdul-Hamid, took the throne, and has no intention of allowing foreign powers, especially Christians, to tell him how to rule what's left of his empire. Meanwhile, Egypt's head of state, Khedive Tewfiq, is demanding the Sultan's support against the English.'

'What kind of man is the Khedive?' Jago asked.

Pawlyn sighed. 'He's twenty-eight years old and, by all accounts, is a devoted family man. He has a baby son and only one wife, though the Quran allows four. Unfortunately, those are the only points in his favour. As a ruler he is vengeful, jealous, manipulative and weak. The previous two khedives, Said and Ismail, were educated in France. Both wanted to make Egypt more like Europe, but to pay for their ambitions they taxed the people into abject poverty. When that still didn't raise enough money to pay for his grand schemes, Ismail borrowed money from Europe with exorbitant interest rates. His inability to make the repayments brought Egypt to the brink of bankruptcy. That left him no choice but to agree to the French and English taking over financial control. This was what finally turned the people against him and sowed the seeds of rebellion. He was forced to abdicate in August 1879 in favour of his son, Prince Tewfiq, the present Khedive.'

'Why are the French involved?' Caseley asked.

'They built the Suez Canal and have a financial interest in it. But the English government bought a large number of cut-price shares in the Canal Company with money provided by banker Lionel de Rothschild. So, when Egypt faced bankruptcy, England was the main creditor. As a Muslim, Colonel Arabi is loyal to the Sultan because Egypt is part of the Ottoman Empire. But the colonel's demand that Egypt should be run by Egyptians has set him against the Khedive.'

'Why?' Caseley asked.

'Khedive Tewfiq wants to keep government in the hands of the Turco-Circassian ruling class. This is one of the reasons why ordinary Egyptians hate him.'

'What has made Colonel Arabi so popular?' Jago asked.

'He truly is a man of the people. His mother was Egyptian. His father is reputedly descended from the youngest grandson of the Prophet Muhammad. Arabi himself came up through the ranks to become leader of the Nationalist party. He is honest and sincere. All of that is in his favour. Unfortunately...'

Pawlyn hesitated. 'Yes?' Jago prompted.

'Unlike the Khedive and his father, Colonel Arabi has no experience of Europe or its people. He doesn't understand our way of thinking. Nor is he strong on military strategy. But his greatest weakness, and it pains me to say this, is that he lacks the necessary skill to deal successfully with

Sir Auckland Colvin, the English financial controller.'

'Why?' Caseley asked. 'What is so particular about him?'

'Apart from his being a consummate politician?' Pawlyn enquired bitterly. 'He is arrogant, aggressive and fiercely ambitious. Before coming to Egypt he spent a number of years in India. Arabi has no chance against a man like that. He's simply not devious enough.'

A few evenings later Jago entered his day cabin, yawning after coming off watch. His heart lifted to see Caseley still up. With a shawl over her nightgown, she was seated at the chart table writing her journal. In the lamplight her hair, in its single loosely plaited braid, gleamed like a ripe chestnut.

White cotton, with a frill at the high neck and long sleeves, covered her from chin to ankle. No garment could have been more modest yet intimate. He visualised her slender body, slimmer now than before the birth of their sons – he forced the thought away as hunger warred with guilt.

Swallowing the dryness in his throat he shrugged off his jacket. 'How did your lessons go today?'

'Very well, thank you.' She sat up. 'When we first started I was mentally translating into English whatever Mr Pawlyn said in French, then working out my reply and translating it back into French before I answered.'

'That sounds exhausting.'

'It was,' she admitted. 'But thanks to Mr Pawlyn's generosity with his time I'm actually thinking in French now, so it's much easier. I'm still

58

not as fluent as I'd like to be, though.'

Jago fought jealousy. Through the open skylight he had listened to the murmur of their voices. His grip on the wheel had tightened as she grew impatient with her mistakes and Pawlyn made light of them. This afternoon she had laughed.

He loved her laugh. Rich and throaty, it was a long time since he had heard it. Now she laughed for another man. *For pity's sake, pull yourself together.*

'I don't like having to depend on you to translate for me. Not because I doubt your ability,' he added quickly. 'Far from it.'

'You are concerned about accuracy. I do understand how important it is.'

So did he, but that wasn't what worried him.

'Which is why I asked Mr Pawlyn for extra practice.'

Jago nodded. He had known that. Yet hearing her say so gave him a reassurance he felt ashamed of needing. 'He has spoken highly of your progress. But I'm concerned about the strain this is putting on you.'

'I offered,' she reminded him. 'You need me for this, and I want to be useful.'

'You will be. Because of your quiet manner, strangers sometimes overlook and underestimate you.' Irony briefly lifted the corners of his mouth. 'A misjudgement I was guilty of when we first met, though I very soon recognised my error. However, on this occasion it will work in our favour. Your observations will be invaluable.'

For him it had been a simple statement of fact. But seeing her eyes widen and her cheeks flush soft pink brought home to him how rarely he paid her a compliment. She had never sought them. *That's your excuse?* His shame was increased by the tremor in her fingers as she turned the pen round and round.

'Jago, taking into account everything Mr Pawlyn has told us, I can't help wondering about the legitimacy of what you have been asked to do.'

'I've been having similar thoughts myself.' He raked a hand through his windblown hair. She had always been a valuable sounding board, asking questions and raising points that clarified his thinking. He had missed that, missed her. But how could he have admitted to jealousy of his own sons? Wary of pressing for more than she was ready to give, he was desperate to bridge the distance between them.

'When William Broad asked me to undertake this mission he did so as an agent for the government. I accepted and we shook hands on it.'

'Then you have no choice. You are honour-bound to fulfil your obligation. Does Mr Pawlyn know why you have come to Egypt?'

Jago shook his head. 'Not yet.'

'Will you tell him?'

'What would you do in my place?' As her gaze rose to his he saw doubt. 'I'm not patronising you, Caseley. I never have, and never will.' Panic stirred in him as her eyes glistened. 'Forgive me. You must be tired. I should not–'

'I'm glad you asked, truly.' She set the pen down and drew her shawl closer. 'Listening to him has widened my understanding. It hadn't occurred to me to wonder what the Egyptians might want. Or why they were so angry. Of course their debt to England must be paid. But Colonel Arabi is not disputing that. So why was it necessary to send a naval fleet?'

'A deliberate intent to provoke in order to justify retaliation?'

Caseley gasped. 'I cannot believe our government would be party to such a cynical scheme.'

'I would hope not. But consider what's at stake: money and national pride. Politicians always think several moves ahead. Colonel Arabi's lack of deviousness may indeed be his downfall.'

Caseley shivered. 'Mr Pawlyn has worked in Egypt for several years. He knows the country and its politics. And he speaks Arabic. I think you should tell him.'

'I agree. I'll do it tomorrow.'

'I doubt he'll be surprised.'

'What makes you say so?'

She lifted one shoulder in a rueful shrug. 'I could see he was curious about my anxiety not to make mistakes. Shall you invite him to accompany us?'

'I will. Of course, he may not be free to–'

'Really, Jago,' she interrupted with a smile that stopped his heart. 'A journalist pass up such an opportunity? He is more likely to kiss your hand in gratitude.'

As their eyes met, he wanted to reach out and touch her. *It was too soon.* He forced himself to break the contact and, as he did so, heard her slide along the bench seat. He drew the log towards him. 'Sleep well.'

'You too.'

He watched as she disappeared into the sleeping cabin, heard the berth creak as she lay down, and buried his head in his hands.

'What can you tell us about the Bedouin?' Jago asked the following evening from his usual place at the head of the table. Caseley and Pawlyn sat opposite each other. The rest of the crew were on deck.

'They are a lean, hardy people with fine features and dark skin. They love poetry, and skill in recitation is highly prized in both men and women. So is musical ability. Traditionally, it is only royal tribes who herd camels, and only men look after them. Women look after the goats and sheep reared by all tribes for meat, milk and wool.

'They value good manners and all older people are treated with great respect, though it's unlikely you will have any contact with the women.'

'Have you had personal dealings with the Bedouin?'

'No, but I have studied their customs, just in case an opportunity ever arose. I cannot thank you enough–'

'It is I who is in your debt,' Jago interrupted. 'So, what should I know?'

'When greeting tribal elders, don't offer your hand. Wait for them to make the first move. Always stand when speaking to someone older. They appreciate a compliment about their hospitality, or the food that's been served. Although it is perfectly acceptable to say "I hope all your family are well", never ask about wives or daughters. They are not spoken of in public or with strangers.

'If the coffee or teapot is within reach,' Pawlyn continued. 'it is polite to refill the cup of the nearest older person.'

'What must I avoid?' Jago asked as Caseley listened, fascinated.

'That's easy.' Pawlyn smiled. 'Impatience. Negotiations are rarely direct and may take days. Never offer to shake hands with a Muslim woman. And – this is really important – never reveal the soles of your feet or touch someone with your shoe. Either is considered a great insult.'

Caseley edged along the bench and stood up. 'Will you both excuse me? I'm going to write this down while it's fresh in my mind.' Gratitude flashed in Jago's eyes, warming her.

Three days later, they saw the combined English and French fleets at anchor outside Alexandria harbour, ensigns fluttering from mizzen gaffs. The British ironclads had twin smoke funnels, as well as three masts and square yards to allow them to conserve coal on the voyage by using their sails whenever the wind was strong enough.

Caseley had gone below to wash and change into her lilac gown: a fitted, long-sleeved bodice buttoned down the front from a plain round neck trimmed with violet ribbon. The narrow skirt had a matching ruffle at the hem and tiers of ruffles down the back. She had drawn her hair back into a coil on the nape of her neck. A simple straw bonnet trimmed with lilac and violet ribbon shielded her eyes.

Jago was at the wheel. His glance swept over her as she emerged from the companionway. He waited until she was close before speaking. 'You look–'

'Unremarkable?' she suggested.

'Is that your intention?'

She nodded. She wanted to help him, but not to attract attention. Attention meant questions. Questions required answers and the truth – the truth was a private matter.

'Only someone who doesn't know you could think so.'

Touched and unsettled by the compliment, she crossed to join Robert Pawlyn at the weather rail while Jago guided *Cygnet* past the anchored ships and through the harbour entrance made narrower by a long, curved breakwater. On the left was a tall lighthouse surrounded by a rampart and gun batteries.

'That's asking for trouble,' Pawlyn murmured.

Caseley looked at him. 'What is?'

'Egyptian soldiers are reinforcing the batteries. You see those earth ramparts? They're new.'

'As a squadron of foreign ships has anchored within gunfire range,' Jago said, 'you can hardly expect the Egyptians to do nothing.'

'Nor do I. The Egyptians have every right to strengthen their defences against a foreign aggressor. But I doubt the admiral commanding the English fleet will see it that way.'

Intercepting the fierce glare Jago directed at Pawlyn, Caseley remained silent. Jago cared enough not to want her upset by talk of gunfire. He cared enough to pay her compliments. Why, then, could he not have cared enough to–? She pushed the thought aside. The past could not be changed, only accepted and learned from. But what lesson was she supposed to draw from her husband's unfaithfulness?

Her vision blurred and she blinked until it cleared. Between the lighthouse and the city was a complex of buildings set in gardens shaded by trees.

'That's the Khedive's palace, Ras-el-Tin,' Pawlyn said. 'It translates as "garden of figs".'

Ahead of them the city curved in a semicircular panorama of flat-roofed terraces, domed mosques and slender minarets gleaming in the afternoon sunshine. Jetties and quays stuck out like fingers into the turquoise water.

Despite the sea breeze, the air was very warm. It would be hotter still on shore. Caseley breathed in the smells of salt water and baked earth. Threaded through them, faint and subtle, she caught the fragrance of flowers, spices and coffee.

The formalities were quickly dealt with, through a combination of Pawlyn's rapid Arabic and the smooth transfer of folding money from Jago's palm to that of the uniformed customs officer.

'I asked him to order two calèches,' Pawlyn said. 'They are very comfortable but seat only two people. I am not obliged to notify the Consulate of my return, but it's a courtesy and will enable me to learn what has happened while we've been at sea. I don't know Sir Charles Cookson, who is British Consul here in Alexandria. But I've met his deputy, Sir Douglas Collingwood, on several occasions. Our acquaintance might smooth the path for you.'

'You're a very useful man to know, Pawlyn.'

'It's the least I can do. Were it not for you I might still be kicking my heels in Gibraltar.'

At Jago's request, Caseley followed him down to the day cabin. 'Pack a change of linen for us both,' he said. 'Though we made excellent time, you have been without proper facilities for nearly four weeks. You will welcome a bath and a soft bed with clean sheets.'

'I haven't complained, Jago.'

'You never do. That's why I want to give you comfort.'

His words were ambiguous, her head full of images she both feared and craved. So she focused on the job in hand, putting underwear and night-clothes for them both into the battered leather portmanteau.

Jago stripped off his salt- and sun-faded ship-board clothes and washed. While he dressed again, putting on a clean shirt, maroon cravat, dark trou-sers and polished black shoes, she wrapped soap, flannels and toothbrushes in clean towels and stowed them in the bag, then added her journal. He raked a comb through his thick hair, passed it to her and put on a dove grey single-breasted coat.

He turned, devastatingly handsome. Even as she yearned for him, anger flared, leaving her shaken. 'Ready?'

Struggling for composure she nodded and put on her hat. 'What are you going to do about the gold?'

'It will remain on board for now.' He picked up the bag.

Leaving Nathan to supervise minor repairs while Martin went ashore to buy food and arrange for fresh water, Hammer carried the box of photographic equipment to the first of the two carriages each drawn by a single horse.

Settling onto the buttoned leather seat, Caseley looked around as they followed Robert Pawlyn's calèche through streets crowded with people. She saw anxious-looking men in European suits, bearded Jews with black hats and side locks, uniformed Egyptian soldiers and Arabs in long robes and head cloths. Women hurried by in pairs, swathed in blue or black. Some drew their scarves across their faces as the calèche passed. Others were already veiled so that only their eyes were visible.

She heard French, Italian, Arabic and other languages she didn't recognise, and saw donkeys almost hidden beneath their burdens. A group of sailors wearing straw hats laughed and nudged each other, pointing at unfamiliar sights.

They turned onto a wide street with flagstone pavements and tall elegant buildings on either side of a central area, with a double avenue of trees down each side providing shade. At one end was a large circular fountain. Further along, two open pergolas with onion-shaped roofs reminded Caseley of bandstands.

The driver pulled up outside a three-storey white villa with deep windows and a pillared portico. Jago helped Caseley out of the carriage, then picked up the portmanteau as Pawlyn took the box and his own bag.

'This is Midan Muhammad Ali. He was the first hereditary viceroy of Egypt. That's his statue,' Pawlyn indicated with a nod. 'Before the

67

square was given his name it was known as Place Des Consuls because of all the diplomats living and working here.'

As they approached the entrance, an armed doorman bowed. Pawlyn spoke to him in Arabic. The man replied, bowed once more, and stood back to allow them in.

'Hamid says Sir Edward Malet, the Consul-General, is in Cairo,' Pawlyn explained. 'And Sir Charles Cookson is in hospital. Apparently Sir Douglas Collingwood is in charge during Sir Charles's absence.'

Caseley saw Jago frown. 'Mr Broad promised to send a telegram the day we left Falmouth. I must hope it arrived and we are expected.'

They stepped into a cool, airy lobby with white walls, a black and white tiled floor, and green palms in polished brass and copper pots. On the left, a wide staircase curved round to a broad landing edged with a balustrade. On the right was an open door. Caseley heard male voices and a middle-aged clerk appeared. His expression of polite enquiry changed to a smile of surprised recognition.

'Good afternoon, Mr Pawlyn. We thought you'd left us.'

'Only briefly, Mr Everleigh, and I'm glad to be back. Is Sir Douglas available? Captain Barata and his wife have just arrived. They sailed from Falmouth and are expected.'

'I'll just–'

He didn't get a chance to finish as a plump man of about thirty hurried into the hall, radiating self-importance. He had long side-whiskers and thinning brown hair. A bone-coloured suit emphasised his high colour. 'Thank you, Mr Everleigh,' he flicked a dismissive hand. 'You may return to your desk.'

As the clerk retreated, Jago caught Caseley's eye. Sharing his amusement she bit the inside of her lip.

'My name is Blaine. I am Sir Douglas's aide. Good day, Mr Pawlyn.' He nodded coolly then turned to Jago, offering his hand. 'Captain Barata, welcome to Alexandria. I hope you had an uneventful journey?'

'Yes, thank you. Allow me to present my wife.'

'Mrs Barata.'

'Mr Blaine.' His handshake was brief and weak. Caseley guessed it would also be damp and was glad of her gloves.

'Mr Pawlyn, I don't think—'

'I'll wait here.' With a cheerful smile Caseley guessed was designed to rile the pompous Mr Blaine, Pawlyn carried the box towards the downstairs office.

After an instant's hesitation Blaine turned towards the wide staircase. 'Please follow me. Unfortunately, Sir Charles is unavailable. He was taken to hospital last week. This is a very difficult time—'

'So I understand.' Hearing the thread of impatience in Jago's voice, Caseley hoped the aide had the sense to recognise it. 'Please convey our good wishes for his speedy recovery. I understand Sir Douglas Collingwood is acting for him?'

Surprise and chagrin chased across Blaine's face. 'That is correct.' He paused outside a door and knocked. As the occupant called 'Enter,' he opened the door and led them in.

'Sir Douglas, Captain Barata has arrived. With his wife.'

Caseley heard the note of disapproval and sighed. In Falmouth widows took over management of their husband's businesses and young unmarried women worked in offices. Mr Blaine's manner betrayed him as a bigot who believed the only proper place for a woman was at home. *Where she would be now if only–*

She forced herself to focus on the plump man whose red face, shiny with sweat above a white collar and dark cravat, was seated in a high-backed chair behind a large desk covered with papers.

He looked up with a harassed expression. 'Yes? So?'

'You received telegraphs, sir,' his aide reminded, 'from Falmouth and London concerning a potential meeting with the Bedouin?'

Realisation spread across the fleshy face. 'Ah. Yes. Of course.' Pushing back his chair he rose to his feet and extended his hand as Blaine ushered them in. 'Captain Barata. Mrs Barata, I beg your pardon. The situation – you cannot imagine – we barely have time to breathe. Come to dinner tonight. My private apartments are upstairs. We will talk then. Eight o'clock.'

'How kind. If your aide could direct us to a good hotel we will not detain you.'

'He will take you himself.'

'I have a box of photographic items for Miss Collingwood.'

'My daughter is presently at the hotel. She will

70

be delighted to receive it. Blaine, see that it's put...' he gestured impatiently, 'somewhere out of the way.' He turned back to Jago, his smile fleeting. 'Now I must beg you to excuse me.'

Chapter Six

Blaine ordered a servant to take the box to the apartment upstairs. The doorman flagged down two calèches. It seemed to Caseley they had only just settled onto the seat than the carriage was drawing up outside a hotel at the far end of the square.

'We could have walked,' she said as Jago offered his hand to help her down.

'Oh no, Mrs Barata.' Blaine hurried towards them, shocked and disapproving. Robert Pawlyn followed. 'That would not do at all. One must maintain appearances.'

Catching Jago's bland glance, Caseley had to look away, her smile swiftly followed by piercing awareness of how far apart they had grown and how much she had missed their closeness, their ability to communicate without a word being spoken.

Jago drew her hand through his arm. Though his solicitude was salt in the still-raw wound of his betrayal, she was helpless against her response to his touch.

Another porticoed entrance opened into an even grander foyer with a tiled floor and two wide, shallow steps leading up to a reception counter of gleaming dark wood. Against the wall at one end a large arrangement of cream and orange lilies perfumed the air.

A gilded easel supporting an elegantly penned notice caught Caseley's attention. It announced an exhibition of photographs by Miss Antonia Collingwood in the Rose Room.

She tugged gently on Jago's arm, drawing his attention to the notice. 'I wonder why Sir Douglas didn't mention it. You'd think he'd be proud.'

Jago looked down at her and raised one dark brow. 'Did he strike you as the kind of man who would welcome his daughter drawing attention to herself?'

'I take your point.'

'George, Captain and Mrs Barata require a room,' Blaine said loudly to the manager, immaculate in a dark blue coat and cravat over a snowy starched collar. 'With facilities.'

'Of course, sir.' The manager bowed.

'I'd like one, too,' Pawlyn said. The undercurrent of amusement in his mild tone increased Caseley's respect for him.

The manager snapped his fingers to summon servants and directed them to carry the bags upstairs.

While Jago was signing the register, Caseley saw a statuesque woman approaching along the wide passage. A green silk gown styled in the latest fashion emphasised her voluptuous figure and a small hat decorated with green silk bows and a curled ostrich plume perched on her dark hair.

Mentally catapulted back to Falmouth and

engulfed by a wave of dizziness, Caseley bent her head, chiding herself for such foolishness. The hair was different and this woman was ten years younger. But for an instant–

She willed the pain away.

'Are you all right?' Jago murmured.

'Yes, of course. I'm still finding my land legs, that's all.'

'Miss Collingwood! Antonia!' Blaine called, starting towards her.

Caseley saw her hesitate then continue forward.

'Yes, Spencer, what is it now?' Her smile was polite rather than warm and her tone betrayed impatience.

Before Blaine could speak, Pawlyn moved from behind Jago.

'Hello, Antonia.'

'Robert!' Her smile grew warmer. 'This is a surprise.'

'A pleasant one, I hope?'

'How could you doubt it? When did you get back?'

'An hour ago. Allow me to introduce Captain Barata of the schooner *Cygnet* and his wife. But for him I would still be stranded in Gibraltar.'

'Captain, Mrs Barata.' Antonia Collingwood shook their hands. As Caseley sensed herself assessed and dismissed, Jago's arm pressed hers gently.

'Captain Barata brought a box for you,' Blaine announced, taking control of the conversation. 'It's back at the Consulate.'

'Is it my photographic plates?' Her smile was eager as she turned to Jago. 'Please say it is. I have

73

been waiting months.'

Jago nodded. 'I believe so.'

Antonia turned to Caseley. 'Do come and see my photographs. This is my first exhibition, so I'm excited and very nervous. It officially opens this evening. My father was to have hosted it, but the demands of duty take precedence.' Her tone and manner were light, but Caseley recognised underlying hurt.

'Really, Antonia,' Blaine chided. 'You cannot expect everyone to feel about your little hobby the way you do. Captain Barata has far more important–'

'Might we be permitted to attend the reception, Miss Collingwood?' Jago asked. 'That would allow us time to view the photographs with the attention they deserve.'

Antonia's eyes sparkled. 'Indeed you must come, Captain. It would give me great pleasure to see you there – all of you.'

'Now that's settled,' Blaine made no attempt to hide his impatience, 'I really must get back to the office. This is an exceptionally difficult time and Sir Douglas needs me.'

'If you can wait a few more minutes, Mr Blaine,' Jago said, 'I will escort my wife to our room, then Mr Pawlyn and I will return to the Consulate with you.'

'Sir Douglas is very busy. May I suggest you wait until this evening to–?'

'No, Mr Blaine. You may not. My business with the assistant consul is not dinner party conversation. The sooner I have spoken to Sir Douglas, the sooner we can be on our way and out of yours.'

Blaine's high colour deepened to crimson. 'I beg your pardon. I didn't mean–'

Jago turned away, his hand beneath Caseley's elbow as they followed a uniformed porter up the wide staircase. After tipping the man, Jago closed the door on him as Caseley looked round the spacious room.

'Will you be all right?'

'I'll be fine. You had better not keep Mr Blaine waiting. Who knows what disaster might occur during his absence from the Consulate.'

'You see him as the power behind the throne?'

'He sees himself that way. He must be clever in some ways or he would not have reached his present position. But he's very stupid in others.' She moved about the room, pausing to look out of the window, aware of Jago watching her.

'How so?'

'His open disapproval of Miss Collingwood's little *hobby* is unlikely to gain her affection.'

'You think that's his ambition?'

Caseley nodded. 'Marriage to Sir Douglas's daughter would certainly consolidate his position. He was definitely not pleased to see Robert Pawlyn back again.'

Jago laughed, shaking his head. 'You're amazing. You saw all that in just a few minutes.' He turned to the door. 'If there's anything you need just ring. I hope not to be long.' He hesitated.

She waited. The space between them was small in physical distance, but too great to cross. Was she disappointed? Relieved? Caseley didn't know what she felt.

'Turn the key,' he reminded her and left,

75

closing the door quietly.

Sir Douglas leaned back in his chair and linked his fingers over his paunch. 'I find the notion of Englishmen bribing savages to take our side utterly abhorrent for many reasons. One must hope Mr Gladstone knows what he is doing.'

'In different circumstances such an alliance would not be contemplated–' Spencer Blaine began.

Catching Pawlyn's eye, Jago read a reflection of his own impatience. Blaine had a gift for stating the obvious.

'This upstart Arabi needs putting in his place,' Sir Douglas continued as if his aide hadn't spoken. 'Should he be entertaining ideas of defaulting on Egypt's debt–'

'He isn't,' Pawlyn said.

'I beg your pardon?' Sir Douglas looked down his nose at the journalist.

'That was an untrue story put about by Sir Auckland Colvin. Colonel Arabi made a statement refuting it, along with the ridiculous claim that he would burn down the Stock Exchange.'

'You seem to know a lot about it,' Sir Douglas glared at him.

'It's my job, sir.'

'Sir Douglas,' Jago said. 'I appreciate your concerns about my mission–'

'Do you indeed? Then tell me this, what is to stop the Bedouin accepting British gold and still taking the Egyptian side?'

Jago turned to the journalist. 'Is that likely?'

'Honour is a pillar of Bedouin culture,' Pawlyn

76

said. 'If they give their word they will not break it.'

'*If*,' Sir Douglas repeated with heavy emphasis, placing his hands flat on the desk to signal the discussion was at an end. 'Are we to rely on hope that they give it? At least we may be confident that Britain's stand has increased Mr Gladstone's popularity and power.'

'At the cost of the Egyptian people's freedom to choose their own government,' Pawlyn replied. 'I cannot see that as upholding the liberal principles that got Mr Gladstone elected.'

'You are a journalist, not a politician,' Sir Douglas snapped. 'You will not have understood all the–'

'I understand this, sir,' Pawlyn rose from his chair and Jago followed. 'The Consul-General is playing a very risky game.'

Jago watched the battle between contempt, curiosity and fear play across Sir Douglas's face. 'How so?'

'His belief that the arrival of the fleets in a show of force will intimidate Egypt into capitulation is at best naïve, at worst dangerous. What if the threat doesn't work? What next? An invasion and occupation of the country by the British army?'

'Sir Edward Malet is a most experienced diplomat,' Sir Douglas blustered. 'He knows what he's doing.'

Pawlyn opened his mouth, closed it again, and gave an abrupt nod. 'Good afternoon to you, sir.'

Caseley stayed in the bath until her fingertips wrinkled. Cool and refreshed, her skin faintly perfumed with rose soap, she put on her shift then sat

77

on the bed, her head turned to one side as she brushed her hair from underneath to let the air through and help it dry.

Jago stormed in, his face tight with anger, shrugging out of his coat and practically ripping off his cravat. Knowing better than to ask – he would talk when he was ready – Caseley continued brushing her hair.

While he was in the bath she picked up his clothes, shook out the creases and laid them on the bed, then reluctantly fastened the hooks of her corset before putting on stockings and stepping once more into her lilac gown.

He came out of the bathroom, one towel wrapped around his hips, rubbing his head with another.

'Sir Douglas may be a capable assistant consul as long as his superior is present. But right now he's on his own and out of his depth. Damn it–' he broke off. 'Forgive me, but the man's a pompous fool.'

Caseley lifted the mass of gleaming bronze waves over her shoulders and fastened the buttons on the front of her bodice. 'An example Mr Blaine appears to be following.'

Jago tossed the towel over the brass rail at the foot of the bed and picked up a comb from small table. 'I'm aware a consul isn't a trained diplomat.' As his gaze met hers shared memory arced between them.

'No,' she agreed.

'Your father was blunt but never crass.' He raked the comb through his hair, dropped it back on the table without looking in the mirror and ran both hands down his beard. 'Collingwood's attitude towards the Egyptians... It's their country, for heaven's sake. But to hear him talk– He's the worst type of arrogant Englishman.' He blew out a gusty breath. 'I apologise.'

Crossing to the small table she sat down, combed her hair back and coiled it into a bun on her nape that she anchored with pins. Fine tendrils curled on her forehead, temples, and in front of her ears. Behind her she could hear him dressing.

She set the comb down. 'Now you have vented your anger it will be easier for you to be polite during dinner.'

He looked up from buttoning his shirt. 'How do you know these things?'

'Experience,' she said lightly, but kept her face averted so he would not see her mouth tremble.

Two large chandeliers lit the long room in which Antonia's photographs had been hung. Walls painted a soft pink that gave the room its name provided a contrasting backdrop for the mounted black and white photographs.

Antonia greeted them warmly. Immediately, a waiter appeared with a silver tray that held flutes of champagne.

Caseley would have preferred a soft drink, but Antonia pressed. 'You must have one glass, for a toast. I never thought this day would come. Now it has. Unfortunately most of the people I invited have left Alexandria, so I am denied the pleasure of watching them eat their words.'

Jago caught Caseley's eye. She read the warning and realised this was not Antonia's first glass of

79

the evening. As he turned away to talk to Robert Pawlyn, Caseley moved towards the photographs. Antonia followed.

'The loss is theirs,' Caseley said. 'Perhaps a photograph of the exhibition in a newspaper will show them what they missed.'

A slow smile spread across Antonia's face. 'That is an excellent idea. Robert can take one for me. Little hobby indeed.' Raising the glass she swallowed a mouthful. Spencer Blaine is a pompous idiot and I wouldn't marry him if he was the last man on earth. He might suit Maud, but he certainly would not suit me. I have plans and they don't include Spencer stuffed-shirt Blaine.' She glanced at Caseley, then shrugged. 'I'm sorry. It's just–' She shook her head.

'I understand.'

'People say that, but they don't. Not really.'

'I do. You will have noticed that I walk with a limp.'

'Yes, I did. What happened?'

'A childhood accident,' Caseley waved it aside. 'But it means I cannot dance. Nor will my hair ever be considered anything but a disadvantage.'

Antonia's gaze slid away. She looked into her glass. 'That is not what I meant.'

'I hadn't finished. Before my father died, I worked in the company office doing translation work for our foreign customers.'

She had done a lot more besides. Though she had been successful, it had been necessary to keep what she was doing a secret to protect her father and the business. But Jago had guessed, goading her until in desperation, and for the first

80

time in her life, she had let down her guard and spoken with total honesty to Jago. The memory reminded her she had more strength than she gave herself credit for.

'My aunt called me a disgrace to the family and to womanhood.'

Antonia's expression brightened. 'Really?'

Caseley nodded. 'So you see, I do understand. And I suggest that such people are best ignored.'

'I wish it were so easy. The trouble is it's not just my father and Spencer who disapprove. Before most of them scuttled away to Malta after the unpleasantness in Cairo, the English and European wives left me in no doubt that I was letting the side down. They measure their worth by their husband's position. The pinnacle of their ambition is to be decorative, amusing, and good hostesses. But I want more than that. I want adventure and colour and *life*.'

Caseley looked around. 'How many photographs are in the exhibition?'

'Fifty. I selected them from two hundred. It took weeks and I'm still not entirely sure I chose the best.'

'That's the artist in you.'

Antonia studied Caseley. 'How would you know?'

'My brother is a painter. He's very talented but constantly doubts himself.' And was squandering his talent, drowning it in alcohol.

In the centre of the room, two rows of chairs in groups of four were placed back to back, allowing viewers an opportunity to sit and look at the images.

They continued down the room, their progress slow because Caseley kept stopping. One photograph caught her attention and she moved closer. It was a life-sized head and shoulders study of a dark-eyed Arab man of about thirty with an aquiline nose and sculpted mouth. His face was in three-quarter profile as if he had been looking away from the camera then glanced towards it. A white cloth covered his head, the falling end crossing at his throat then thrown over his shoulder.

'That is a striking image,' Caseley said, aware of Jago coming to her side. 'Who is he?'

'Sheikh Imad Abu Quasim al Hussein.' A blush coloured Antonia's face. 'He's a member of the ruling family of the Tarabin tribe,' she announced with a proprietary pride.

Caseley glanced at Jago in time to see him exchange a brief nod with Pawlyn. Then she realised. The Sheikh was the man they needed to see.

'I sent his invitation with Sheikha Sabra's. They are distantly related. It would make such a difference if–' Her gaze shifted to the doorway. 'They've come!' Delight and excitement lit her face.

Caseley turned. Behind an olive-skinned woman wearing a long-sleeved robe of emerald and purple shot-silk, her head covered by a loosely draped purple silk scarf, was the man from the photograph. Beneath a full-length blue sleeveless garment edged with gold braid he wore a long, white robe. His white headcloth was held in place by a thick black woven cord.

Antonia hurried towards them, greeting them in Arabic. The Sheikha took her hands and kissed her on both cheeks. The man merely bowed.

'Do men not shake hands?' Jago asked Pawlyn, his voice low.

'Not with women. For a Bedouin to touch a woman to whom he is not related by blood or marriage would dishonour her.'

Pawlyn's expression as he looked at Antonia told Caseley he envied Sheikh Imad the warmth of her greeting.

Gesturing towards Jago, Pawlyn and Caseley, Antonia led the newcomers forward and switched to French. 'Allow me to present Captain Barata and his wife.'

As Jago bowed, Caseley made a brief curtsey then said in French that she and her husband were honoured to make their acquaintance. Unfortunately, her husband did not speak French. Then, with a polite smile to Sheikh Imad she murmured, *'Salaamu aleikum.'* His brown eyes met hers as he bowed and responded, *'Wa aleikum, as-salaam.'*

Antonia frowned at her. 'You never said you could speak Arabic.'

'A few words, that's all. On our voyage from Gibraltar Mr Pawlyn was kind enough to teach me a greeting and how to say thank you. That was hard enough.' It wasn't strictly true. But she sensed Antonia liked having the advantage and she had no desire to compete.

'You have a good ear, Madame Barata,' Sabra said in French. Then she turned to Robert Pawlyn. 'Good evening, Mr Pawlyn. Welcome back. Your articles have been much missed by those who prefer a balanced presentation of the facts to biased rhetoric.'

As Pawlyn bowed Caseley was touched to see

83

the tips of his ears were bright red. 'You are too kind, ma'am.'

'I'm nothing of the sort, Mr Pawlyn.' She turned to Jago. 'I assume it is business rather than pleasure that brings you to Alexandria at this difficult time, Captain?'

Jago waited while Caseley translated. 'That is so, ma'am.'

'And you, Madame Barata, what do you know of the situation in Egypt?'

'Before I left Cornwall I knew only what the English newspapers reported. But after Mr Pawlyn joined us I learned the situation is not as we had been led to believe.'

Sabra studied her. 'What an unusual person you are.'

'Because I think, ma'am?'

Sabra laughed. 'We will be friends, you and I.'

'You flatter me, ma'am.'

'You will learn that is something I never do.'

Sheikh Imad was speaking to Antonia, complimenting her on the exhibition. She beckoned him across to see his portrait. He followed, keeping a distance between them, his bearing dignified.

Antonia said something in Arabic. He responded in French. After a brief pout she shrugged then smiled at him, clearly delighted to be in his company. Caseley heard Pawlyn's indrawn breath and felt sympathy.

Sabra went to Antonia and drew her away by asking about one of the photos. Pawlyn went with them.

Sheikh Imad returned, asking Jago if his presence in Alexandria was related to the arrival of

84

the combined French and English fleets.

Jago held the Bedouin's gaze as Caseley quickly translated.

'Not directly, sir. I am here on behalf of Her Majesty's government in hope of speaking to the leaders of the Tarabin Bedouin tribe.'

As Caseley gave Jago's reply Sheikh Imad's brows rose.

Jago continued. 'Her Majesty's government recognises the influence the Tarabin might have over the outcome should the present situation deteriorate.'

'The present situation,' Sheikh Imad spoke without inflection, 'is that Egyptians wish to rule themselves. Colonel Arabi has given his promise to repay the massive debts incurred by the present khedive's father. Yet the English government wants the Bedouin to fight against these people?'

As she finished translating, Caseley wondered if the Sheikh would decline on his tribe's behalf without even putting it to them.

She could see Jago was thinking the same. As he glanced at her, his reply showed he was facing the risk head-on.

'Is it your opinion that the Bedouin might decline this opportunity to discuss their potential influence over a matter of great importance to all concerned?'

As Caseley struggled to translate accurately, perspiration dampened her skin so her undergarments clung.

'Bedouin owe allegiance to no government or country. They are free to choose whom to support.'

'Her Majesty's government is aware that commitment to the English cause may involve disruption and expense. That being so, they wish to make an offer of financial compensation in order to demonstrate good faith.'

Sheikh Imad listened politely but Caseley sensed his scepticism. 'Is this compensation a promise to be fulfilled at some point in the future?'

Jago shook his head. 'No, sir. Such promises are too easily given and too easily forgotten. On receipt of a firm commitment from the Tarabin made to myself as agent for Her Majesty's government, a token of gratitude in the form of gold will be handed over to seal an agreement bound by honour on both sides.'

'I see.'

Concentrating fiercely, Caseley still had time to recognise that the Sheikh had offered neither opinion nor commitment. But at least he was listening.

'I would consider it an honour and a privilege,' Jago continued, 'to be granted an opportunity to meet the tribal elders so I could put forward my government's case for their consideration. Naturally they would need to be assured that I am who I say I am, and that I have the authority to act in this matter.'

The Sheikh gestured dismissively. 'I know who you are, Captain. Alexandria is a city of many layers. With access to reliable sources – which I possess – information is easily gained.'

Caseley moistened her lips. Her throat was dry and she longed for a cool drink. She waited for Jago to reply. When he didn't, she glanced at him.

His expression matched the Bedouin's for impassivity. He simply waited.

From the corner of her eye Caseley saw Antonia and Sabra returning.

Eventually, the Bedouin spoke again. 'Tomorrow I go to Cairo. Two days after that I leave for the Eastern Desert to attend the wedding of one of my many cousins.'

Then Caseley remembered Robert Pawlyn explaining that Bedouins rarely approached important matters directly.

'Such an important event will bring together many of your tribe and extended family,' Jago's response told Caseley he had not forgotten Pawlyn's warning.

The Bedouin nodded. 'Such gatherings are rare and a welcome occasion at which to exchange news and discuss current events.'

'Did you say a wedding?' Antonia whirled round. 'Are you going, Sabra?' The Sheikha nodded. 'Please may I come? I would so love to photograph the women – if they do not mind. Surely they won't? A photograph would be a wonderful keepsake.'

Caseley recalled her wedding to Jago. It had been a very quiet, simple affair. With her father having recently died after she had managed to avert a scandal that could have destroyed the business, neither of them had wanted any fuss. Though still in mourning for him it had been the happiest day of her life, until the birth of her sons. Her mind shied away.

Sheikh Imad shook his head. 'I do not think photographs will be possible.'

'Why not? I know they are not seen much in public. But I am a woman myself–'

Sabra gripped Antonia's arm and shook it lightly. Still holding it she turned to Jago, asking in French, 'You wish to keep your discussions with the Tarabin a private matter?'

Caseley saw Jago tense. *How did she know?* He nodded.

'Then if Madame Barata and I were to accompany you, Captain–'

'I should like Mr Pawlyn included. He speaks Arabic and French and so could act as my interpreter in place of my wife.' Jago glanced at Caseley. He was sending her a message, but she was fighting a powerful combination of rejection and relief and could not read it.

'Very well.'

'And me,' Antonia beseeched. 'If Mrs Barata is going you must let me come too, Sabra. Please. You can't–'

'Sshh,' Sabra said, then turned back to Sheikh Imad, still speaking French. 'Women in the party would allay suspicion. A family group bound for a wedding? What could be more innocent?' She held Sheikh Imad's gaze. Caseley translated quietly for Jago. The silence stretched.

Sheikh Imad gave a single nod. Antonia squeaked with delight and clasped Sabra's hands, thanking her. Caseley released the breath she had been holding.

'I must go,' Sabra said, and turned to Caseley. 'We will leave for Cairo on Friday. Come to my villa tomorrow afternoon. Miss Collingwood will bring you.'

Though it was more command than invitation, Caseley didn't hesitate. 'Thank you, ma'am. I should enjoy that.'

'If she wishes, Miss Collingwood may take photographs.'

'Oh, that would be wonderful.' Antonia's delight told Caseley how much the invitation meant. 'Thank you, Sabra. Thank you so much.'

Chapter Seven

Caseley stood to one side watching Robert Pawlyn take his leave.

'It is a superb exhibition, Antonia.'

'Thank you, Robert.'

'I'll see you on Friday, then.'

Though Antonia's eyes shone in her flushed face and her smile was wide and warm, Caseley knew it was not for Robert Pawlyn, but for the man who had just left.

'Will you excuse us for a moment?' Jago drew Pawlyn away.

It was nearly seven. Caseley wanted to go upstairs for a few minutes' quiet before they had to leave for the Consulate and dinner with Sir Douglas.

'Miss Collingwood–'

'Please, you must call me Antonia. I feel we are already dear friends. I can hardly believe it!' She pressed her clasped hands to her full bosom. 'To be invited to the wedding of Sheikh Imad's

89

cousin is such an honour! You must be so glad you are here.'

Caseley could have pointed out that it was Jago's presence and the promise of gold that had secured the invitation, but she had no wish to burst Antonia's bubble of happiness.

'I do wish more people had come tonight,' Antonia sighed.

'Your father told us that many Europeans have already left the city.'

'Others have stayed.' Antonia made no effort to hide her impatience. 'I have gone to a lot of trouble over this exhibition. Some support would have been nice. I know what it is. They didn't come because they disapprove. I have worked hard to develop my talent and they are jealous.'

Egypt may be on the brink of war. Surely that is a more likely reason for their absence? Surprised by the depth of Antonia's self-absorption, Caseley changed the subject. 'I must apologise for not being able to change for dinner tonight. I don't have another gown with me.'

'Don't worry about it. You don't have time, anyway. You and the Captain will be the only guests, apart from Spencer, and Maud of course. There will be no ceremony. No one will even notice.'

Abandoning her resentment Antonia released a contented sigh. 'I wish there might have been more visitors. But at least Sheikh Imad and Sheikha Sabra came. And I have something wonderful to look forward to. What an adventure it will be! I know Sheikh Imad said I might not be able to photograph the women. But I shall take my camera anyway. I must go. Maud will be driving

90

the servants to distraction.'

She started towards the door then turned back. 'She has my father in her sights as husband number three. Fortunately, he has been too busy to notice. Now she's losing patience. I wish she had left with the others.'

She pirouetted in a circle with outstretched arms. 'But nothing is going to upset me tonight. I'm going to a Bedouin wedding with Sheikh Imad. Isn't that romantic?'

Maud Williamson's handshake was brief, her smile practiced, her blue gaze condescending.

'How do you do, Mrs Barata. I hope you are comfortable at the hotel?'

No ceremony, Antonia had said. Clearly no one had informed Mrs Williamson. Her fair hair was drawn back in a complicated coiffeur decorated with silk flowers and a jewelled aigrette. Her magenta silk gown was of the very latest fashion. Edged with lace, the low neckline revealed soft white flesh. Around her throat she wore a cameo pinned to a black velvet ribbon. Elbow-length sleeves ended in deep frills and ribbon bows, and over her flat ruffled skirt horizontal folds of pale pink silk were gathered to form a bow on top of an enormous bustle.

'Very comfortable, thank you,' Caseley replied politely, aware her simple hairstyle and lilac day gown had been assessed and found wanting. Maud turned to Jago.

'Captain Barata. I'm delighted to meet you. Though I fear you will find our society sadly lacking as so many have departed.'

'Then it's as well I have no time for social life, ma'am,' Jago said.

She laid a slim, pale hand over his, her manner both arch and playful. 'All work and no play–'

'Gets the job done.' Jago's smile matched hers for insincerity. 'As I'm sure Sir Douglas will agree.'

'Quite so, Captain.' She turned back to Caseley. 'My dear Mrs Barata, I see you are limping.' Her expression was all sympathy. 'Have you suffered an accident?'

Caseley realised she was paying for Jago's rebuff. 'Not recently.'

'My wife was a child at the time, Mrs Williamson. We rarely notice unless it is remarked on.'

His hand at her waist was comforting. He was protecting her and she was grateful. But no one else could hurt her as he had, because no one else mattered as he did.

A servant approached with a silver tray holding wine glasses of sherry and Madeira. Jago took sherry. As Caseley smiled and shook her head, the servant bowed and returned a moment later with a small tray on which stood a crystal tumbler half-full of cloudy liquid.

'Citron pressé, Madame?' he said softly.

Caseley took it gratefully. *'Merci beaucoup.'*

Watching Jago exchange pleasantries with Sir Douglas and Spencer Blaine, while Maud Williamson spoke quietly through a fixed smile to Antonia who made no effort to disguise her irritation, Caseley was suddenly overcome by doubt. What was she doing here?

A dark-skinned Egyptian wearing a spotless white robe with a scarlet sash, a scarlet brimless cap and white gloves announced dinner. He stood by the dining room door as they filed in and took their places at a long table set with a snowy cloth, crystal glasses and silver cutlery. Down the centre shallow bowls of lilies perfumed the air, flanked by silver cruets and multi-branched candelabra with beeswax candles that cast a gentle flattering light.

Her chair was held and she sat. Another servant carried a silver tureen to the sideboard. Why had she demanded to come? She was in mourning, not only for her children but for life as she had known it.

A small eggshell-thin bowl decorated with hand-painted flowers was set in front of her. She was relieved to see that it contained not the thick brown soup she dreaded, but a clear consommé. She picked tip her spoon. Not too hot; the soup was delicious. The first mouthful loosened the knots in her stomach, making the second easier to swallow.

Would it not be more sensible for Jago and Robert Pawlyn to go without her? But with Sabra and Antonia in the party, how could she back out?

He caught her eye. Seeing his concern she pulled herself together and smiled to signal all was well.

'Naturally,' Sir Douglas said, leaning back to allow a servant to remove his empty bowl, we have discussed with the French how best to protect the Suez Canal.'

'Forgive me,' Jago pretended puzzlement. 'As I understand it, both the French and the Canal Company are of the opinion that the only danger to the Canal lies in intervention.'

'Exactly. And the likelihood of intervention increases with every day that Colonel Arabi continues his reinforcement of the gun batteries in the forts.'

Spencer Blaine nodded. 'The British government appealed to the Sultan to order the work stopped.'

'Just a few weeks ago, Arabi announced in the press that he would guarantee public order.' Anger reddened Sir Douglas's fleshy face. 'And what happened?'

'A riot,' said Spencer Blaine.

'Yes, thank you, Blaine,' Sir Douglas snapped. 'I think I can manage.' He turned to Jago. 'An argument between a Maltese and a donkey boy attracted a crowd and things got out of hand. But instead of taking control, the police were nowhere to be seen. So what started as a mere scuffle exploded into a full-scale riot. Proof, if it were needed, that Arabi makes promises he cannot keep.'

'Perhaps I have it wrong, but is it not the case that the police could only be called out on the orders of Alexandria's civil governor?'

Sir Douglas looked at his aide, clearly expecting him to deny Jago's claim. But Blaine, helping himself from the proffered dish of lamb cutlets and green peas, appeared not to have heard.

Jago continued. 'As I understand it, the governor's background is Turco-Circassian. So he has no sympathy whatsoever for the nationalist cause. He is very much the Khedive's man and, I am reliably informed, hopes to take Colonel Arabi's place as minister of war. In those circumstances, one might be forgiven for thinking he had every reason to let the riot continue.'

Frowning, Sir Douglas opened his mouth to respond, but Antonia spoke first.

'For heaven's sake, Papa. Enough of politics. Surely we can enjoy one meal without talk of riots and guns and threats?'

'Antonia is right,' Maud said at once.

Ignoring her, Antonia continued. 'I have some wonderful news. Sheikha Sabra came to my exhibition late this afternoon.'

'Good of her, I'm sure,' Sir Douglas dabbed his mouth with his napkin then raised his wine glass. 'If I weren't so busy–'

'Yes, I'm sure you would have.' Antonia's tone contradicted her words. 'But never mind that, Papa. Sheikh Imad was with her. He has invited us to attend the wedding of one of his cousins out in the desert.'

'Us?' her father said.

'Yes. Captain and Mrs Barata, Mr Pawlyn and I.' She beamed with pride and excitement.

'Why would he invite you?' Sir Douglas demanded. 'Not that it matters, as you cannot accept.'

'It would not be at all wise,' Spencer Blaine added, having waited to see his patron's reaction.

'Really, Antonia,' Maud began. 'You cannot–'

'Sir Douglas,' Jago leaned forward, his eyes gleaming like a cat's in the candlelight. 'In normal circumstances I would agree with you. But circumstances are far from normal. Unfortunately, intervention does look increasingly likely. Should this come about, having the Bedouin tribes on the English side will ensure that resistance by Arabi's forces is swiftly quashed. Sheikh Imad's invitation offers the perfect opportunity for me to meet tribal elders.'

'Such a meeting is no place for women,' Maud argued.

'Indeed it is not. Nor will they be involved. But the invitation offers an opportunity we cannot afford to ignore. Travelling as a party of guests bound for a wedding perfectly disguises our true purpose.'

Sir Douglas put his knife and fork together. His plate was immediately removed. A fresh dish and cutlery were laid in its place as another course of strawberry jelly, pastries, almond pudding and a soufflé of rice was offered.

Caseley took a feather-light honey and almond pastry.

'I take your point,' Sir Douglas conceded. 'Very well, it seems I must withdraw my objection. Though I cannot like it.'

'We should congratulate Captain Barata,' Spencer Blaine's sour smile would have curdled milk. 'For someone so recently arrived he has a remarkable grasp of local events.'

'Too kind.' Jago's grave bow had Caseley biting the inside of her cheek.

Blaine flushed and turned to Antonia. 'Sir Edward's absence in Cairo means your father cannot leave the Consulate. So if you insist on pursuing this harebrained scheme, I must escort you.'

Caseley held her breath, anticipating an outburst. But Antonia surprised her.

'That is so good of you, Spencer,' she cooed, smiling at him. 'But though I appreciate your offer, you must know I cannot accept. You are my father's right hand. How could you even contemplate leaving the Consulate, or my father, with matters in so parlous a state?'

Watching him torn between the jealousy that demanded he keep an eye on Antonia and his equally strong desire to prove himself indispensable to her father, Caseley was surprised he had not yet mastered the art of hiding his thoughts. Jago was no diplomat but he had that skill.

Even as the thought occurred, he caught her eye. Seeing the flash of amusement, she knew he recognised and appreciated Antonia's adroitness. She looked down at her plate. If she could read him now, why had she felt so cut off from him for all those months?

The meal finally ended. Thanking Sir Douglas and bidding the others goodnight, Jago draped Caseley's cloak around her shoulders and they left to return to the hotel.

The padded seat and back of the calèche were comfortable, the night air cool after the day's heat. Caseley could smell coffee, roasting meat and the sea. With the driver high on his seat in front of them, the brisk clop of the horse's hooves and creak of the carriage masked Jago's voice.

'What are your impressions of our host?'

Caseley glanced at him. 'Honestly? I think Sir Douglas is out of his depth. Mr Blaine considers himself indispensable to Sir Douglas which allows him the illusion of having power.'

'Illusion?'

Caseley nodded. 'He is simply Sir Douglas's echo. I doubt he has formed a thought of his own in years. He prefers others to bear the responsibility.'

Jago gave a mock wince. 'Harsh.'

'You did ask.'

'What about Miss Collingwood?'

'She reminds me a little of my brother.'

'How so?'

'She has the same self-absorption. I don't understand–' she broke off, shaking her head.

'What don't you understand?' he prompted gently.

'It's rather sad. Mr Pawlyn clearly thinks a lot of Antonia. But while she's friendly with him, she makes no secret of her attraction to the Sheikh. Though I see no chance of a relationship between them.'

'Why? Because she's English and he's a Bedouin?'

'No, because she tries to excite his interest in public. That is not modest behaviour, and Mr Pawlyn told me that modesty in women is of great importance to the Bedouin.'

'So what don't you understand?'

'What it is that Sheikh Imad and Sheikha Sabra have in common with Miss Collingwood. I can understand her wanting a connection with them. Their rank gives them considerable status, which obviously enhances hers. But how does acquaintance with her benefit them?' She felt his arm, strong and powerful, against hers.

'Perhaps they find Miss Collingwood's opinions of interest?' Jago lowered his voice still further. 'I would expect her to have been warned against repeating anything she hears in the Consulate.

98

Perhaps she was. But either she has forgotten, or chooses to take no notice.'

Caseley looked quickly at him. 'They are using her?'

'I am reserving judgement. But I'm glad of your opinion. Your comments are astute.'

The calèche drew up outside the hotel. After he had paid the driver, Jago drew her arm through his as they walked up to the entrance.

Caseley's heartbeat quickened as her nervousness returned. This would be the first time they had shared a room – a bed – since...

On board *Cygnet* she had lain alone in the tiny sleeping cabin and he had used a sea berth hidden behind a sliding panel in the day room.

She had insisted on accompanying him. It would be reasonable for him to think she wanted to resume their married life. Was that what she wanted? Yes. No. She missed being physically close to him, missed his knowing familiar touch, the taste and caress of his mouth, his passion and gentleness.

She ached with loss and loneliness. But her mind filled with images of him touching Louise Downing the way he had touched her, awoken her to the joys of physical love. She wasn't stupid. She had known she wasn't the first woman he had made love to. But in her naivety she had believed that when they married she would be the last.

Louise's triumphant face filled her vision and her yearning turned in on itself, desperately trying to hide.

'Caseley? Are you unwell?'

His tone held concern. But was it for her or for himself and the mission? She hated him, loved him. She wanted to batter him with her fists for hurting her when she had already been hurt beyond bearing. She swallowed the sob threatening to choke her.

'Just tired.' She avoided his gaze. 'It has been a long day.'

As they entered the reception area Robert Pawlyn was at the counter. He turned and saw them.

'Pawlyn,' Jago greeted before the other man could speak. 'Would you care for a nightcap?'

'I–'

'Allow me to escort my wife to our room, then I will meet you in the lounge.' Handed their key by the concierge, who wished them good night, he turned to Caseley as they walked upstairs.

'Pawlyn will have learned more about the situation here. And I daresay you will welcome a little solitude. I'm aware of the strain you're under, Caseley.'

She looked at him and quickly looked away. What strain was he referring to? Grief? Their fractured marriage? Her part in the task ahead of them? All were draining, all demanded strength she didn't have. Laughter and tears made her throat tight.

'Thank you,' was all she could manage.

He unlocked the door and pushed it open. The lamps had been lit and were casting a soft, welcoming glow. The bed had been turned down.

'Translating for me with the Sheikh and Sheikha, then this evening's dinner party, will have left you exhausted. You must be longing for sleep.' Giving her a gentle push he remained on the threshold. 'If I take the key with me I won't have

100

to wake you to let me in.'

Relief and gratitude warmed her smile. 'Thank you.'

A muscle jumped in his jaw. 'Goodnight. You won't be disturbed.'

Everything about him disturbed her. 'Goodnight. Jago.'

For a moment neither moved. Caseley sensed a new tension in the air. Would he–? Should she–? But the moment passed, the gulf between them too wide. As she turned away he quietly closed the door.

She undressed quickly and put on a nightgown. After washing her face she unpinned and brushed her hair before braiding it into a loose plait.

Turning out all but one of the lamps she climbed into bed. The fresh sheets were cool, the mattress and pillows soft. Thoughts and images tumbled through her mind, so much to think about. She slid into sleep.

Chapter Eight

When Caseley opened her eyes it was morning. At home she often woke during the night and prowled the house, ravaged with sorrow, tortured by anger, loneliness and a sense of having been abandoned. During the voyage that pattern had been broken, first by exhaustion, then by the ceaseless movement of the ship.

This morning she felt calmer. Nerves frayed by

the importance of translating for Jago had been soothed by the balm of sleep, the comfort of his proximity, and the knowledge that whatever happened while they were here she would not have to face it by herself.

Then she realised she was alone. His side of the bed was cool. She listened but heard no sound from the adjoining bathroom. She sat up quickly. Her feelings towards him were painfully confused, yet when he wasn't there she missed him. Her gaze fell on a folded note on the nightstand.

Gone to the harbour. Will return in time to escort you to breakfast. As ever, Jago.

She stared at the phrase *As ever.* He had used those same words in his note of condolence after her father died on the day that they returned from Spain. He told her later that with so much unsettled between them, so many questions still needing answers, he had not dared speak of love. Instead he had chosen those words hoping to reassure her that his feelings for her had not changed and never would.

Was that why he used them now? Despite the hurt, she loved him still. How could she not? He had been – was – her world. He had awakened her as a woman and given her two precious sons. He was an integral part of her life, of her.

But the day the boys died their marriage changed for ever. There was no going back. But what lay ahead? Emotionally, as well as physically, she was in unknown territory.

She washed and, leaving her lilac gown lying on the ornately carved wooden chest, put on a clean shift, drawers, stockings and her white kid boots, then her corset, camisole, flounced petticoat and a tiered skirt of white spotted muslin.

Sitting down, already uncomfortably warm, she brushed her hair and twisted it into a coil high on her crown to allow air to the back of her neck. Lastly, she put on the white, long-sleeved, swallow-tailed jacket trimmed with a sash and bow of holly green ribbon.

She had just fastened the last button when she heard the key turn. The door opened and her heart gave an extra beat. *He was back: she was safe.* He placed his hat on top of another tall chest, concern in his gaze as he smiled.

'Good morning. How are you?'

'I'm very well, thank you.'

'I'm truly glad to hear it. Are you ready to go down?'

She nodded. There were shadows under his eyes and the crease between his brows had deepened. About to ask him if everything was all right, she held back. Of course it wasn't.

'What?' he said as she walked out into the passage. He might be tired, but he missed little.

Caseley waited while he locked the door, keeping her voice low as she replied. 'I was thinking that in a few days we will be leaving for the desert with £20,000 of England's gold to persuade people, whose loyalties are unknown, to fight against Egyptians who simply want the right to govern their own country.'

'This is the world of politics,' he said dryly. 'For all its unpredictability and physical danger I prefer the sea.' He cupped her elbow as they walked downstairs.

'What are your plans for this morning?' she asked.

'Why? Is there something you wish to do?'

'The hotel has a laundry service–'

'Of course, you want to collect our washing from *Cygnet*.'

'You should have woken me.'

He shook his head. 'You needed sleep.'

'It would have spared you a second visit to the harbour.'

'It's no trouble, Caseley. We'll go directly after breakfast. Then I must call in at the Consulate. A note was waiting when I went down this morning.'

The sun was already hot, the air only slightly cooled by an on-shore breeze as they took a calèche to the port. As they drew closer, gulls soared and wheeled overhead with mournful cries. Caseley was reminded of Bonython's yard by smells of coal smoke, sawn timber, boiling pitch and rope.

The crew paused to greet her then returned to their repairs and cleaning. Jago remained on deck talking to Nathan while she went below and gathered their dirty linen, stowing it all in a pillowcase. Then she folded his work shirts and her navy skirt and jacket into another.

'Do you want to come with me?' he asked as they headed back towards Midan Muhammad Ali.

'Thank you, but I think not. Sir Douglas will prefer to see you alone. I'll deal with this,' she indicated the two stuffed pillowcases at her feet. 'You haven't forgotten Miss Collingwood is taking me to Sheikha Sabra's villa this afternoon?'

She could not read the look that crossed his

face. 'No, I haven't forgotten.'

He escorted her into the hotel and handed the pillowcases to the concierge, who instantly summoned a servant. As their laundry was borne away with promises of careful handling and swift return, Jago returned to the waiting calèche. Collecting the key, Caseley went up to their room.

During their absence the bed had been made, the bathroom cleaned, and fresh towels hung on the rails. Her lilac gown had vanished. She tugged the bell-pull. A servant reassured her it would be returned the following morning.

Though she appreciated the efficiency, it meant she had only the dress she was wearing which was very plain for a visit to the Sheikha. Still, fretting would not bring it back any sooner.

Removing her jacket, she dipped her facecloth in cold water and bathed her face, throat and the back of her neck. Allowing the water to evaporate on her skin, she sat down at the table and began a letter to Rosina. After assuring her they were safe and well, she described the people she had met and everything she had seen since their arrival.

Rosina would share the letter with Liza-Jane and Ben, and they would be fascinated by her descriptions of the different clothes, buildings, food and people. She had completed two closely written pages when she heard footsteps in the passage.

She turned on her chair as the door opened and Jago strode in, coldly furious.

'Sir Douglas is demanding that *Cygnet* should carry the family of a banker friend of his to Cyprus.'

'But you can't–' She stopped herself.

'Of course *I* can't. He's well aware that we leave for Cairo in two days. He proposes I allow the mate to take command in my absence.'

'Do you doubt Nathan's ability?'

Jago shook his head. 'Not at all. Though being a man short will make it a demanding voyage.' His rage released, he was already calmer. 'I don't like it. But as Colonel Arabi has ignored calls to stop reinforcement work on the forts along the waterfront, at least *Cygnet's* absence would remove her from potential danger. And the banker is offering a substantial sum.'

Caseley remained silent. He was talking to clarify his thoughts. The knowledge that she was valuable to him in business as well as their domestic life had drawn them closer. He had talked more to her since they embarked on this journey than in a long time. Had he tried? Would she have heard?

A wave of misery gathered and broke. She wrenched her thoughts away from a path too painfully familiar.

'Caseley? Are you–?'

She made herself look up, made herself smile. 'I'm fine.'

As the words left her lips she sensed the change in him: a slight but definite withdrawal. Was it relief? Her denial of anything wrong avoided a scene that might have become uncomfortable, emotional. Or had she missed an opportunity?

This wasn't the time. But when was? Did he know she knew about Louise Downing? Would he not have said something? Why would he? Perhaps he considered it none of her concern. How

106

could he think that? She was his wife. Theirs had been a marriage of love, not an alliance made for money or property.

She had believed them united, two become one. But how could she hold that thought with secrets and deceit driving a wedge between them? She dragged her attention back to the present.

'What will you do?'

He raked a hand through his hair. 'Go and tell Nathan. While I'm on board I'll plot his course for *Cyprus*. He can use the sea-berth in my day room. The banker can have the sleeping cabin. His wife and ch – family must cope as best they can in Nathan's cabin. Even with unfavourable winds the voyage should take less than a week.'

'Will you have lunch first?'

'I'll have something on board. What about you?'

'I'm not hungry.'

'I'll ask the concierge to arrange for something light on a tray. Don't fight me, Caseley,' he warned as she opened her mouth. 'If you wish to enjoy your afternoon with Miss Collingwood and the Sheikha, you will need your wits about you. You will do better if you have eaten. I don't want to be worried about you.'

How could she argue? He held her gaze until she nodded.

'I'll see you later.' He left for the harbour and *Cygnet*.

Caseley sat down again and picked up her pen. But instead of writing she stared into space, her thoughts in turmoil. *I don't want to be worried about you.* How was she to interpret that? He had not wanted her to come, yet never failed to show consideration. She should be grateful. Indeed she was.

Was it merely good manners? A gentleman by birth, he had been raised to treat women with courtesy, and she was his wife. Yet how was he able to focus on professional demands as if – as if he had put their tragedy behind him? Logic might say that was the only thing to do. But logic took no account of grief. Looking forward felt like betrayal. Yet looking back was torture. A knock on the door jerked her back to awareness.

The servant brought in a tray containing a plate of flatbread, cubed goat's cheese, fresh dates, fat green grapes and a glass of fresh orange juice. The bread was still warm, crisp outside, soft and fragrant inside.

Adjusting to so much that was new and strange was demanding. She owed it to both of them to build up her strength. Having insisted on coming she had no right to add to his burdens. He was in Egypt for a purpose, one of national importance. Now *Cygnet* was leaving Alexandria under Nathan's command. She knew Jago had complete faith in the mate. But it was a concern he could have done without.

She ate as much as she could, and felt better for it. After washing her hands she continued her letter, finishing it as a servant knocked and told her Miss Collingwood was downstairs.

Caseley put on her bonnet, locked the door and went downstairs.

'There you are,' Antonia said. Over her draped and tiered skirt of apple green silk she wore a matching light jacket with three-quarter sleeves with frilled cuffs. A small hat decorated with satin ribbons and silk flowers perched on her upswept hair.

She looked Caseley up and down. 'White does not become you. It makes you look awfully pale, apart from your hair, of course. To be honest, you look like a lighted candle. I intend no offence, Caseley, but you really should have worn something more fashionable. Still, it's too late for you to change now. I don't want to keep Sabra waiting.'

'No, indeed,' Caseley agreed quietly. She was already uncomfortably warm in her multiple layers of clothing. Handing the key to the concierge, who wished her a pleasant afternoon, she followed Antonia out into the hot afternoon.

'It'll be a bit of a squeeze, I'm afraid,' Antonia said as they reached the caliche, and Caseley realised they were sharing the carriage with Antonia's telescopic tripod and two polished wooden boxes.

'Which of these holds your camera?' Caseley asked, stepping carefully over them into the hood's shade.

'The smaller one; the other contains spare plates. I hope you won't mind me saying I was surprised that Sabra invited you to her villa. You may not realise how privileged you are.'

Recognising jealousy, Caseley automatically tried to defuse it. 'Then I have you to thank. Without your exhibition I would not have met her. I was as surprised as you. I feel honoured.' Her smile and soft words pacified Antonia. 'Where does she live?'

'On the edge of the Greek Quarter. It has the most beautiful properties in the city. She must be exceptionally wealthy.'

Caseley wasn't sure if the undertone she detected was envy or resentment. She looked round. 'Where are we now?'

'The street ahead used to be called the Canopic Way. At the eastern end was the Gate of the Sun and at the western end, the Gate of the Moon. Isn't that romantic? You see that mosque?' she pointed. 'Alexander the Great was supposedly buried underneath it. But he may actually have been buried in the Greek necropolis. My favourite part of the city is the souk. The shops have some lovely jewellery.' She sat back. 'So, tell me, which of my photographs did you like best?'

Caseley knew what was expected of her. 'You have a remarkable talent, Antonia.' In that at least she could be totally honest. 'However, if I may choose only one then it must be the portrait of Sheikh Imad.'

Antonia nodded. 'He refused to sit and would allow me only moments to take the picture. I'm sure I could have done better if I'd had longer.'

'I must disagree. I don't think you could. I know nothing about photography. But what appealed to me about that picture was the fact that it *wasn't* posed. You captured him just as he turned his head. It was the perfect moment. I doubt you could ever repeat it.'

As Antonia stared at her, Caseley felt her stomach tighten. Then pride and delight softened Antonia's expression and suffused her face with radiance.

'I *knew* it was good. Here we are,' she said as the calèche drew up outside heavy wooden gates set in a high white-painted wall.

110

They climbed out. As Antonia took coins from a small purse and paid the driver, Caseley reached in and picked up the tripod. Antonia grasped each of the boxes by the single brass handle set into the lid.

By the time they reached the gate, it was silently swinging open on greased hinges. They walked into grounds of cool green grass, banks of vivid flowers and groups of tall palms very different from the oaks, elms and beeches back in Cornwall. One servant closed the gate and another waited to escort them to the villa.

Two storeys high, dazzling white in the afternoon sunshine, the house had a flat roof, a portico entrance and tall upper windows with narrow balconies of wrought iron.

Walking through the garden they passed a splashing marble fountain. The sun shining through falling droplets created a miniature rainbow. Pergolas supporting cascades of purple bougainvillea provided shade for marble benches.

Carnations, geraniums and roses added bright colour and in the background the slender branches of a weeping willow bowed gracefully to trail like long skirts on the cut grass.

Entering the house they walked through a cool, airy space with a tiled floor. Caseley glimpsed white-clad servants disappearing through archways. Their guide stood aside and bowed.

'Bienvenue, mes chère amies.' Wearing a loose, flowing robe of emerald and turquoise, with a golden silk scarf covering her dark hair, Sabra came towards them.

Expecting a formal greeting, Caseley was surprised when the Sheikha took both her hands and kissed her on each cheek.

'What a pretty gown,' she smiled. 'So simple, yet elegant.'

'Thank you.'

Relief coursed through Caseley. She hadn't caused offence. As Sabra kissed Antonia her gaze met Caseley's, telling her the Sheikha understood Antonia rather better than she realised.

'Come,' she continued in French, beckoning Caseley. 'Let us be comfortable while Antonia sets up her camera.'

Caseley followed her into another room across Persian and Indian rugs to a divan piled with cushions. Additional divans sat against the other walls with hexagonal brass-topped tables at either end.

A servant brought in a tray containing a silver coffee pot, thimble-sized cups, and a plate of honey and almond pastries and set it on a low oblong table in front of the divan.

Antonia had taken off her hat and was setting up her tripod.

'You have a beautiful home, ma'am,' Caseley said.

Sabra inclined her head, acknowledging the compliment. 'In private you may use my name. Yours is unusual.'

Caseley nodded. 'It was my mother's maiden name, suitable for a son or daughter.'

Sabra's nod told Caseley no further explanation was necessary. 'You are a long way from your home.'

'True. But, fortunately, I am a good sailor and

112

have been privileged to accompany my husband to other countries.'

Sabra's brows lifted. 'Do you not have children?'

Caseley had known the question would be asked at some point. She was not yet thirty. A woman with a young family would be at home with them. *If only*– Grief pierced, sharp as a blade. She drew a breath and swallowed the fist-sized lump in her throat. 'I did. I had two beautiful sons. They died.'

She waited for the condolences she had come to dread: sympathy, claims of similar loss, being told they had gone to a better place.

Sabra tilted her head and gave a slight nod. 'You were fortunate.'

Caseley heard Antonia gasp and saw her mouth fall open in shock. 'It's all right, Antonia. I recognise the point the Sheikha is making.' She returned her gaze to Sabra. 'I was fortunate. I had Philip for five years and James for three. They were a joy. They died the same night.'

Antonia had turned away and was attaching the camera to the tripod.

'An accident?'

'Putrid throat. There was an epidemic in the town.'

Sabra touched Caseley's hand and spoke softly. 'I mourn your loss. And I envy you.'

Caseley met the other woman's dark gaze. 'Envy me?' She was too startled to be offended.

'You were blessed with something I will never know. I cannot be a wife so will never be a mother.' She moved one shoulder in a gesture meant to indicate acceptance. But in her eyes

113

Caseley glimpsed rage and despair.

'Please don't think me impertinent, but as you have shared this confidence, may I ask – can nothing be done?'

Sabra gave a bitter smile. 'Something was done.' She paused as if gathering her thoughts. 'All young Muslim girls are cut, down–' she gestured briefly. 'This is traditional in our culture so we cannot feel pleasure and will be faithful in marriage.'

Struggling to hide her horror, Caseley was overwhelmed by memories of Jago's lovemaking. With patience and tenderness he had kindled passions she had never suspected, ignited sensations more powerful and consuming than anything she could have imagined. Busy and apart during the day, at night they had come together to explore each other and learn. He had been profoundly moved by her response – first shy, then eager – to his kisses and caresses. She had found joy and pride in her power to arouse him.

Had he done those same things with–? She slammed a mental door and focused on Sabra.

'But – forgive me, I don't understand. If others marry, why can't you?'

'I suffered a severe infection. The result was scarring that meant – that made it impossible for me to–' Below the proud, calm face Caseley saw Sabra's throat work. Though more than twenty years had elapsed, grief and anger were still strong.

Caseley knew – who better? – that words held no comfort. Silently she turned her hand over and clasped Sabra's. The Sheikha was right. She had indeed been blessed. She had known a man's love. She had felt her babies grow inside her, had

114

given birth to two fine, healthy sons and nursed them at her breast. Though her loss and sorrow sometimes felt too great to bear, at least she had known joy.

Pressing Caseley's fingers, Sabra withdrew her hand. Inhaling deeply, she smiled. 'I am more fortunate than many. My wealth allows me freedom and my position gives me power. But, because my life is different from most other women's, they are wary of me. I think you too will have found that.'

It occurred to Caseley that she was thousands of miles from home, talking to a woman whose life bore no resemblance to hers. Yet somehow they shared a bond.

She nodded. 'Yes, I have. Because I am no longer a mother, women who used to be friendly avoid me. Perhaps they don't know what to say. Some have been sympathetic. Yet I also sense criticism. Other children survived, why didn't mine? Do they imagine I have not asked myself that question a dozen times a day? I don't *know* what more I could have done. But perhaps there was something–' She broke off, grief threatening to choke her.

'Do you have the power of bestowing life and death?' Sabra demanded.

'No,' Caseley said, startled.

'Then stop blaming yourself.'

Opening her mouth to argue, Caseley closed it again. Sabra's ordeal meant she understood. She had had to come to terms with a situation outside her control, one that had changed her life and denied her a woman's reason for being – motherhood.

'Sabra, I hate to interrupt but the light is going. Would you prefer to leave the photographs to another day?'

In the Sheikha's brief glance Caseley read tolerant amusement.

'After you have gone to such trouble to set everything up? Certainly not.' Sabra rose from the divan. 'Where do you wish me to stand?'

Caseley followed them out to the portico, staying out of the way and watching as Antonia positioned Sabra, then adjusted the folds of her robe and headscarf.

Ducking under the black cloth covering the camera, she called instructions, exposed the plate, and emerged, flushed and pleased.

'What did Mr Blaine think of your exhibition?' Sabra asked as Antonia inserted a fresh glass plate into the frame.

'Spencer relies on my father for his opinions. As he has been too busy at the Consulate to come and see my photographs, Spencer has remained silent on the subject.' She took another picture. 'Which is a great relief, as it spares me the pain of biting my tongue while he pontificates on matters on which he is completely ignorant. I care for only one person's opinion – apart from yours, of course.'

She carried the heavy camera back inside. 'We were so caught up in arrangements for the trip into the desert I had no opportunity to ask Sheikh Imad for his reaction. He must have told you though, Sabra. You were talking for ages. What did he say?'

'He thought your photographs were remarkable and that you have considerable ability. I'm sure he will have said as much to you.'

'Yes, he did. But I thought – I hoped he might have said something more to you.' Desperation tightened her voice. 'Why else would he have come?'

'He and I had several appointments last evening. Alas, our conversation was more of politics than the pleasure of viewing your photographs.'

'But he must have liked his portrait?' Antonia insisted. 'Caseley said it was the best of the entire exhibition.'

'Madame Barata shows shrewd judgement,' Sabra said, and Caseley knew the Sheikha understood how she had been manipulated. 'Antonia, you should know by now that Sheikh Imad takes his tribal responsibilities very seriously. For all his wealth and power he is a modest man. So though he admired the skill of the photographer, and no doubt told you so, he will say little about his image. To do so would be vanity.'

'I don't understand that,' Antonia huffed out a breath.

'Which is why, as your friend, I advise you to look among your own people for–' she paused for an instant and, seeing Antonia's mouth compress mutinously, Caseley held her breath, '–for future portraits,' Sabra finished, neatly avoiding a potential argument.'

'Politics,' Antonia snorted. 'My father and Spencer talk of little else. It's so boring.'

Impatience crossed Sabra's face. 'The future of this country will be decided in coming weeks. The English have brought order to Egypt's finances, for

117

which we must be grateful. But the Egyptian people do not want to be governed by a foreign power.'

'But the Khedive–' Antonia began.

'The Khedive is a weak man determined to be on the winning side by playing British, French, the Nationalists and the Sultan against one another.'

'How do you know that?' Antonia was curious.

'Because I know him. He is my cousin.'

Impatient to tell Jago, Caseley was suddenly startlingly aware how, immersed in her grief, and the anger and blame that went with it, she had shut him out, leaving him isolated. Was that why he had volunteered for the long winter voyages to Canada? Was that why he had turned, not to her, but to his former mistress?

Chapter Nine

The calèche arrived outside the hotel, drawing up behind another already there. Stepping down, Caseley saw Jago and Hammer lifting out a trunk.

'Thank you so much, Antonia. It has been a fascinating afternoon.'

'You and Sabra certainly found plenty to talk about.' Petulance coloured her voice. 'I don't know why you had to whisper. I felt quite excluded.'

'Speaking for myself, I was anxious that our chatting did not disturb your concentration. I imagine you have an idea in your mind of how you want a picture to look?' She had assumed the Sheikha lowered her voice because they were speaking of matters that Antonia, unmarried and a non-Muslim, would know nothing about. But nor had she lowered her voice until Sabra's revelation. It had been an extraordinarily intimate confidence to share; yet so had hers. She felt as if she had taken a step forward, as if her burden of grief was a fraction lighter.

Antonia nodded. 'There is far more to taking a good photograph than most people realise. Anyway, I'm glad you enjoyed yourself.' Her smile widened, grew warmer. 'Just think – tomorrow we leave for Cairo. The city is sweltering at this time of year. I hope you will not find the heat too much.' Instructing the driver to go, she waved then sat back under the shade of the calèche's hood.

Caseley walked towards Jago.

'I don't like it,' Hammer was saying. 'Jimbo and I should be going with you to look after that gold.'

'You know that's not possible,' Jago replied. 'Nathan needs you to sail *Cygnet* to Cyprus. Besides, having you two along as guards would insult the Sheikh.'

'How's that then?'

'It would imply he's unable to guarantee the safety of his guests and their property.'

Catching sight of her, Hammer raised a crooked forefinger to his forehead. 'Af'noon, missus. All right, are 'e?' Jago turned. His glance was searching and Caseley knew he was seeing more than she might have wished.

'Hello, Hammer. I'm very well, thank you.'

119

'Did you have a pleasant afternoon?' Jago enquired.

'It was certainly interesting. Shall I ask the concierge to send servants to help with the trunk? Have a safe trip, Hammer. Please pass on my good wishes to the rest of the crew.'

'Thank 'e kindly, missus. I'll tell 'em.'

After setting the trunk down near the window, the servants left. Clean laundry had been placed in three neatly folded piles at the foot of the bed.

Jago shrugged out of his coat, crossed to the table at which Caseley had written her letter, and poured fruit juice from the glass jug into two crystal tumblers. He handed one to her and sat on the lid of the trunk. Caseley perched on the chair.

'What happened?' The gentleness in his voice made her eyes sting. She didn't want him to be gentle. She couldn't be angry when he was kind. Yet she was weary of rage and grief. Her breath caught on a sob. She disguised it by clearing her throat and bent her head to stare blindly at the juice.

She swallowed. 'Sabra told me–' looking up, she was jolted by the devastation on his features. It was gone in an instant, leaving her wondering if she had imagined it.

'Sabra told you?' he prompted. His raised glass hid the lower half of his face.

'That the Khedive is a weak man who is determined to be on the winning side by playing the English, French, the Nationalists and the Sultan off against each other. How does she know this? Because the Khedive is her cousin.'

He was silent and she knew he was weighing up

120

all the possible ramifications. Then he raised his glass in salute. 'You are – invaluable. But surely you did not talk politics all afternoon? I cannot imagine Miss Collingwood bearing that with patience.'

Caseley drank. The juice was sweet and tart and slid down her dry throat like soothing nectar. 'You're right. She has little concern for anything except what interests her.'

'What does interest her?'

'Sheikh Imad. Sabra tried with great tact to warn her off. But Antonia is deaf to anything she does not wish to hear.'

'What is your opinion of the Sheikha?'

'I like her. She knows her position is unusual, especially for an Egyptian woman. Her wealth and status give her freedom to live as she chooses.' Caseley drank again. 'She envies me.'

Jago leapt to his feet. 'Envies you?' He frowned, incredulous. 'If she had any idea–'

'She does,' Caseley broke in. 'She was surprised that I had accompanied you and asked did I not have children. Please, will you sit down?'

Lowering himself onto the end of the trunk he leaned forward, elbows on his knees, turning the glass in his fingers. They were barely a foot apart. 'I'm sorry. Go on.'

'I told her I'd had two sons but they had died.' Saying it made her want to rip her clothes and howl. But hearing the words come from her mouth was another small step towards accepting that it was not a nightmare from which she could wake. It was real and all the tears in the world would not change it.

121

'She envies me because I have experienced something she never will.' He raised his eyes to hers and waited. She knew him as a ship's master who drove his ship and his crew hard, demanding instant obedience, yet never asking of them anything he would not do himself. She also knew him as a man of deep emotion and infinite patience.

Caseley moistened her lips. 'All Muslim girls go through a – a procedure. Sabra said they are cut.' She felt heat flush her face. 'It is done so they cannot feel pleasure and will remain faithful in marriage.' His expression had hardened to an unreadable mask. But the horror she saw in his eyes made her glad she had told him. She wanted him to understand.

'Something went wrong and she was left with scarring that meant–' Caseley swallowed. 'She cannot be a wife and will never be a mother.'

Muttering a curse, Jago jumped to his feet and prowled the room. 'She told you this to win your sympathy?'

Caseley watched him. 'If she did, I willingly give it. But I don't think that was her motive. Her situation makes her an outsider, as I am. Losing my mother, my limp, working for my father – it made my life very different from those of the girls I grew up with. And now – a mother without children – I am even more so. This afternoon was only the second time I have met her. Yet there is a bond – it is hard to explain.'

A knock on the door made them both turn. Jago took a folded paper offered by the servant, who bowed and disappeared down the passage. Closing the door, he unfolded the note.

'It's from Robert Pawlyn. He has just arrived back from Cairo and has news he believes I should know.'

'Invite him to dine with us. Unless you would prefer to see him alone?'

'I would not. I value your opinion. You often notice things I might dismiss as unimportant or irrelevant. The more information we have before leaving for the desert, the better.'

While Caseley bathed, Jago dashed off a note and took it down to the concierge for a servant to deliver.

Cool and fresh, Caseley redid her hair, then put on a clean shift and her newly laundered lilac gown. Servants emptied the bath and brought large copper cans of clean water. Jago was in the bath when there was another knock on the door.

A servant stood outside. Begging her pardon for the intrusion he told her Miss Collingwood was downstairs and needed to speak with her most urgently.

Caseley followed him down. Antonia was pacing the foyer. Seeing Caseley as she descended the final few stairs, Antonia hurried forward. Before she could speak, Caseley took her arm and steered her past the reception desk and curious gaze of the concierge into an empty lounge.

'You have to do something!' she burst out as Caseley closed the glass door.

'Why don't we sit down and you can tell me what has upset you?'

Antonia drew herself up. 'Don't patronise me!'

Caseley flinched. 'That was not my intention. I am simply concerned that your hasty arrival and

123

obvious distress might provoke gossip.'

'You're right.' In another of her lightning changes of mood, Antonia touched Caseley's arm. 'I should not have spoken so. But how can I be calm when my whole future is at stake?'

Caseley sat down on the nearest chair and gestured to the one beside her.

Reluctantly Antonia sat, then leaned forward to confide, 'My father has learned of the bad feeling between Sabra and the Khedive.'

'How?'

'From Spencer, who else? Horrible little man. Though how he would have heard... Still, I daresay such information could not remain secret for long. The point is my father has decided I am not to visit the Sheikha any more, which is ridiculous when only days ago he was praising the usefulness of the connection. He says my unconventional behaviour and choice of friends are causing people to question my loyalties. What people? Most of the English have gone. He must mean Maud. I never liked her. Now he announces that he wants me to marry Spencer. He says it will put an end to gossip. Well, I won't. Nor can he make me. But Caseley, he is forbidding me to attend the desert wedding. You must ask your husband to speak to him. I can't miss it. I just can't.'

Battered by this impassioned torrent, Caseley leaned forward and touched Antonia's knee. 'Try to be calm–'

'Calm?' Antonia's voice climbed an octave. 'Have you any idea what–?'

'Hush, Antonia.' Hearing herself use the same

tone she had used to discipline her sons, Caseley felt her heart stutter. 'Do you want the hotel servants spreading your private business all over the city?'

'No, of course not. But–'

'You are upsetting yourself for no reason.'

'How can you say that?'

Ignoring Antonia's muted shriek, Caseley continued evenly, 'You could remind your father that my husband is acting on behalf of the British government, so he must go with Sheikh Imad to meet the tribal elders. Jago needs me with him because I speak French but he doesn't. Neither of us speaks Arabic, but you do. That being so your presence is vital to the mission. As Mr Pawlyn speaks both those languages it might be better if you do not mention his presence in the party. But that must be your decision.'

Antonia's tension drained away, her anger and anxiety softening into a relieved smile. 'Of course. That's perfect. I have to go because Captain Barata needs me.'

'And I will welcome your company, not simply as another Englishwoman, but to advise me on protocol when we meet the Bedouin women.'

'But I don't know anything about Bedouin life.' Seeing Caseley's surprise, Antonia lifted one shoulder. 'Why would I? Sheikh Imad's education means he is practically a European.'

Recalling the Sheikh's adherence to cultural rules forbidding him even to shake hands with a woman, Caseley doubted that. But she decided it was more diplomatic not to comment.

'My own father had very strong views and

125

never hesitated to voice them,' she told Antonia. 'So I sympathise with your situation. My advice would be not to argue. Tell him you understand his concerns. But as a diplomat and Sir Charles's deputy, he will surely want to do whatever is necessary, regardless of his personal feelings, to persuade the Bedouin to take England's side.'

Antonia clapped her hands. 'That's perfect! I should have thought of it myself. But if he says anything more about me marrying Spencer–'

'You tell him you appreciate his anxiety–'

'For himself and his reputation, not my happiness.'

Caseley ignored Antonia's bitter words. 'However, as the desert trip is of national importance, would he not agree that personal matters ought to be set aside until your return?'

Antonia nodded quickly. 'He cannot argue with that. Oh, that is such a relief. I'd better get back. Thank goodness I came. You have helped put it all in perspective. I'll see you tomorrow.'

Jago was putting on his coat as Caseley re-entered their room. 'Where did you go?'

'Downstairs. Miss Collingwood arrived in a highly agitated state. She and her father have fallen out. He said she cannot attend the Bedouin wedding and wants her to marry Mr Blaine. She wanted you to speak to him – to her father, not Mr Blaine.'

'And say what?' He adjusted his cuffs.

'That as neither you nor I speak Arabic, but she does, we need her. I thought she might be able to help me with advice on Bedouin culture.'

'Of which she knows nothing.' He was scathing.

126

'What makes you say so?'

'Observation.' Impatience compressed his lips as he shook his head. 'I do not like you being drawn into Miss Collingwood's dramas.'

'I did not ask for it.'

'I know that. But be wary, Caseley. It is in your nature to be kind. I would not like to see you taken advantage of.'

She wished she could tell him he was imagining things. But from what she had seen of Antonia's erratic emotions, she didn't think he was.

As they left their room. Robert Pawlyn emerged from his. Exchanging greetings, they walked downstairs together.

In the candlelit dining room tables were laid with crisp white cloths and napkins, gleaming glassware and silver cutlery. Jago held her chair while she sat, and she looked around while he and Pawlyn discussed wines. Not many tables were occupied. Caseley wondered if this was because so many people had left the city. Used to country hours and shipboard mealtimes they were eating comparatively early. Perhaps the other guests – if there were any – preferred to dine later.

While the wine was poured and a fragrant clear soup served, Pawlyn asked after Antonia. Caseley told him of their visit to the Sheikha's villa. She described the airy comfort of the house and the colour and tranquillity of the garden. To no one but Jago would she ever speak of the confidences she and Sabra had shared.

When the waiter left, Pawlyn told them how anti-foreigner and anti-Christian feeling was creating an atmosphere of increasing tension.

'Cairo is a powder keg,' he said quietly. 'All it needs is a spark to light the fuse. The ruling Turco-Circassian elite view the nationalist cause with contempt. They cannot or will not accept that their oppression and misrule are responsible for the surge of support for Colonel Arabi. Sir Auckland Colvin, the English Financial Controller, is absolutely furious. He expected his draft budget to be adopted. But the Egyptian government has its own ideas so they ignored it. Now he is vowing that if the Nationalists should ever come to power he will do all he can to ruin them.'

'Wasn't he against any armed intervention by England?' Jago asked.

Pawlyn nodded. 'He *was*. Now he's in favour of it. He claims to have the correspondent of the *Pall Mall Gazette* in his pocket. The paper will print whatever he wants in return for exclusive information. This is the newspaper read by most English MPs and they are being given a distorted picture of the situation here in Egypt.'

The Sheikha said as much,' Caseley said.

'How would she know?' Jago asked.

'The *Pall Mall Gazette* and the *Times* are telegraphed back to Cairo,' Pawlyn explained, 'and translated into French, English and Arabic. Egyptians are bewildered, hurt and furious at the bias and outright lies being printed.'

He fell silent as their soup plates were cleared and the fish course was served. 'Europeans make a grave mistake in assuming they are intellectually superior to every other race,' he said when they were once more alone.

'Peasants working in the fields are not capable of

governing themselves.' Jago pointed out. Caseley recognised his tactic of offering an opinion he didn't necessarily hold in order to provoke a response.

'Are farmers in rural England or the slum-dwelling poor in cities who work in factories any more able?' Pawlyn replied. 'Don't they rely on their countrymen who have the benefit of education to govern on their behalf and in their best interests? Why then should it be any different here?'

'You make a fair point.'

'Will you excuse me?' Caseley rose from her chair. Both men immediately stood. 'I need to pack.'

'Shall I–?' Jago began.

Shaking her head, she touched his arm lightly. 'Please, stay and enjoy your coffee.' She knew they would talk more freely without her there, and she needed some time alone.

Chapter Ten

The following morning Caseley was sitting in front of the mirror. She had released her hair from its loose braid and was brushing it out when a momentary faintness made her head swim.

Resting the brush in her lap she closed her eyes and willed it to pass, dimly aware that the splashing in the adjoining room had stopped. She tried to draw in a deep breath, but the rigid cage of her corset made it impossible. Her shift was damp

129

and uncomfortable against her skin. Outside it would be hot, and Cairo would be hotter still.

'Caseley?'

She started, and met Jago's gaze in the mirror. 'Good morning. I won't be long.' Putting down the brush she gathered her thick hair into a twist on top of her head. Exposed to the air, her neck felt cooler. She could do this. She was stronger than she looked, stronger than she felt.

'There's no rush. Pawlyn has ordered three calèches for nine o'clock, so we have plenty of time for breakfast.'

The thought of food made Caseley's stomach lurch. She swallowed hard and drew another slow breath. *Calm. Be calm.*

'Are you all right? You're very quiet this morning.'

She had to pull herself together. He could not afford to be distracted by concern about her.

She put all her effort into a convincing smile. 'Having Mr Pawlyn in the party will be very useful.'

'His fluency in French and Arabic will take the pressure off you.'

'Yes.' Caseley stood up, shook out her skirts and buttoned up her lilac jacket. In one way it was indeed a relief. At the same time it made her feel redundant. She gave another bright smile; saw his eyes narrow.

'Caseley–'

'We ought to go down. It won't do to keep everyone waiting.'

He caught her hand. 'You must tell me if–'

I'm scared? How selfish would that be when he

needed to focus on the task ahead? How much atten-
tion and understanding could he spare when his mind
was already engaged elsewhere? He might say he
wanted her to confide, but he didn't, not really.

'I'm just a little nervous, that's all.'

'It would be strange if you weren't.' He drew her hand through his arm. 'Is it the train?'

She nodded, grateful to be offered a ready-made excuse.

'Pawlyn is a seasoned traveller. He will smooth our path.'

Forty minutes later, they stood in the shade of the portico while servants loaded their luggage and the trunk containing the chest of gold into calèches.

Antonia had arrived with her tripod and camera cases. She rode with Caseley in one carriage. Jago and the trunk were in another. Pawlyn was in the third with the rest of the luggage. Leaving the hotel, the carriage turned onto a wide boulevard that would take them to the train station.

Antonia's gown was a ruffled and swathed confection of pale blue silk with satin trim, and a small bustle worn with a matching hat. Her cheeks were pink, her eyes bright with excitement.

'I can't believe we're actually on our way. I've looked forward to it so much. I scarcely slept last night. You're very quiet this morning. I see you took my advice. That is a much more suitable dress, though I'm not sure about that colour with your hair. I can't wait to see Sheikh Imad! It's going to be such an adventure. I plan to take lots of photographs. Are you ever going to speak?'

Tempted to point out she'd had little opportun-

131

ity, Caseley smiled. 'I was enjoying your pleasure.'

Antonia gripped her gloved hand. 'This is my opportunity, Caseley. Being with Sheikh Imad, away from my father and Spencer, we'll have time to talk and–'

'I don't think–' As Antonia glared at her Caseley wished she had kept silent.

'What don't you think?'

'That the Sheikh will have the free time you are hoping for.'

'Why not?'

'He'll be an important guest at the wedding.'

Antonia waved a dismissive hand. 'I'm fully aware of that.'

'So he will be expected to spend time with his relations and friends. He will also be having meetings with the elders of the tribe to discuss the political situation.'

'I daresay. But there will be interludes when he is free and we can be together,' Antonia said confidently. 'Why else would he have invited me?'

He didn't invite you. You pleaded. It was Sabra who persuaded him. Caseley clenched her teeth to stop the words before they spilled out.

'I'm sure you mean well, but really you're worrying over nothing. You don't know Sheikh Imad like I do.'

'As you say.' Anything Antonia did not wish to hear she simply ignored.

A few minutes later they drew up outside the station. Fronted by lawns, flowerbeds and a fountain, the long imposing building of dark red and cream brick had arched windows and a massive central portico with fluted columns supporting

132

more tall arches.

Pawlyn took charge as a dozen porters swarmed around the calèches. He chose six and dismissed the rest. Jago escorted Caseley and Antonia and they were soon on the platform, tickets bought, watching the porters load the trunk, their luggage, and Antonia's camera equipment into a baggage compartment at the end of the third class carriage.

Their first class carriage was built of teak and had a footboard running the full length of the deep-buttoned dark red upholstery, a matching carpet and glass windows with shutters.

After paying off the porters, and speaking to the guard, Pawlyn took his seat beside Antonia, opposite Caseley and Jago.

'The journey will take about four and a half hours,' he told them. 'There will be several stops to allow people to board and leave, also for–' he hesitated and the tips of his ears turned pink. 'For passengers' comfort and, of course, for food.'

Caseley had never been on a train and was surprised by the richness of the furnishings. A loud hissing and a violent jolt made her clutch instinctively at Jago's arm. The train started moving.

'I fear you will find it a lot less comfortable than a ship,' Pawlyn smiled at her. 'The springing is very harsh. Also the carriages are linked by loose couplings which make the ride rather jerky.'

Caseley nodded, still waiting for her heartbeat to slow to normal.

'Egypt was the first country in Africa to have a railway system,' he continued. The kindness in his eyes told her he recognised her unease and was trying to take her mind off it. 'By 1877 there was a large network of main lines. But in the entire twenty-five years of its operation, the national rail company had never produced an annual report. The result was a financial nightmare. This was only one of Khedive Ismail's many projects designed to make Egypt more European. Instead, his wild spending and even wilder borrowing plunged the country deep into debt.

'Two years later the Sultan ordered Ismail to abdicate in favour of his son, the present Khedive. On June 30th 1879, a long baggage train left Cairo for Alexandria. It was packed with pictures, furniture, dinner services, rare carpets, bronze and silver candelabra, and plates of solid gold inlaid with jewels. Everything was loaded onto Ismail's steam yacht and taken to Italy, where he is living in comfortable retirement.'

Recalling his description of poverty-stricken Egyptians barely able to afford seed for the next year's crops, Caseley shook her head. 'That doesn't seem right.'

'It isn't,' Pawlyn agreed.

'Oh, *please*,' Antonia begged, 'no more politics.'

Seated by the window, Caseley was surprised at how quickly the city gave way to dusty sand and bare rock. Then she began to see areas of cultivated land surrounded by embankments, criss-crossed by narrow channels.

She watched a man swing a long pivoted pole with a leather bucket on one end and dip it into a canal leading off from a river.

'Is that the Nile?' she asked.

'One of its tributaries,' he explained. 'The river is low at the moment but in a week or so it will start to rise. By September it will fill the delta and canals and enrich the land with all the silt it carries.'

The squares of land were filled with crops: vibrant green wild clover, rows of broad beans and onions, fields of Indian corn and plantations of date and banana palms.

Men in loincloths or ragged blue cotton robes pulled up between their legs and tucked into a cord tied round the waist were working barefoot in the fields.

'The swing bucket is called a *shaduf*. Over there, the vertical waterwheel driven by an ox, that's a *saquia*.'

'They may not have much money, but at least they have plenty to eat,' Antonia indicated the fertile plots.

'No,' Pawlyn corrected gently. 'The fellahin work for landowners who employ overseers. All the crops are sold. The men you see working eat only maize bread, beans and goat's milk or goat's cheese. Meat is a rarity for them.'

Caseley remembered the fish, chicken and beef they had eaten at the hotel and the Consulate.

As they headed inland the temperature increased. Even though the carriage had a double roof open at the sides to allow heat to escape she was hot, clammy and uncomfortable. Perspiration prickled her forehead and upper lip. She rested her head against the padded seatback and closed her eyes. But that made the jerky swaying even more noticeable. She felt queasy and a knot of tension was forming at the base of her skull.

'Are you unwell?' Jago murmured.

135

'Just hot.' Turning to him, she smiled. 'I much prefer travelling by sea.'

After a fifteen-minute stop during which they drank tea and made use of the facilities, Caseley felt better.

'At Kafr el-Zayyat,' Pawlyn said when the train was under way once more, 'the line used to cross the Nile by means of an eighty-foot float car. But in May 1858 a special train carrying Prince Ahmad Rifaat fell off the float into the river and he was drowned. Robert Stephenson, who was Egypt's first railway engineer, replaced the car float with a swing bridge nearly sixteen hundred feet long.'

'How do you know all these things?' Antonia asked, surprised.

'I'm a journalist. I'm also naturally curious. I want – no, I need – to know as much about the country as possible if I'm to do my job properly. For instance, did you know that the Bedouin speak the oldest and purest form of Arabic? And they have a love of poetry and songs. Storytelling and recitation of old poems is a popular pastime in the evenings. Anyone – man or woman – who shows a talent for creating poetry is greatly respected.'

Four and a half hours after leaving Alexandria, they arrived in Cairo. The train pulled into the station with a squeal of brakes, hissing clouds of steam and the acrid smell of soot.

Jago got out first and turned to offer Caseley his hand. Gripping it tightly she stepped down onto the platform. People surged around them. An anxious group of Europeans disembarked from the other first class carriage, summoned porters and pushed their way towards the entrance.

On the platform barefooted men carried shallow baskets of fruit, dates and golden rings of baked dough. Wealthy Egyptians wearing ankle-length sleeveless coats of blue, black or ochre over long white robes, their heads covered by spotless white turbans or head cloths held in place by thick black cords, moved along the platform followed by veiled women in head-to-toe black.

A water-seller carried a large chased-metal jug on a leather strap, with a small handleless cup attached to it by a long chain. The air was pungent with the smells of smoke, spices, rotting fruit and sweating humanity.

Caseley's grip tightened and Jago turned to her. 'Don't worry, I won't lose you.' His gaze held hers.

You already have.

The thought sprang within her, unbidden and horrifying. She thrust it away. 'It's a little over-powering.'

One corner of his mouth quirked upward in a wry grin. 'A little?' He guided her through the crowd towards the luggage van. Quickly, Pawlyn organised the porters and they followed their baggage out of the station building into blinding sunlight, heat and noise.

Stalls crowded together piled high with fruit and vegetables, mounds of spices, folded lengths of cloth, sweet pastries and cooked food. Peddlers shouted, beckoning towards loaded trays hanging from a strap around their necks. Donkeys tottered by, so heavily laden that only their long ears, faces and hooves, no bigger than

137

eggcups, were visible.

Caseley watched, awed, as a string of camels stalked past, stately and disdainful. Once again her head was swimming. Not just from the heat but from the impact of so much that was new and strange.

'Come on, Caseley,' Antonia said impatiently from a calèche.

'Go with her,' Jago said quietly. 'I'll be right behind you.'

Sabra's house was in a quiet street. Three storeys high, the house had a box-like structure made of louvered wooden slats with adjustable openings attached at the front of the second storey.

'What is that?' Caseley asked, pointing, but Antonia had turned away and was beckoning to the doorkeeper.

'It's the window of the women's quarters,' Robert Pawlyn came to her side. 'You will see them on nearly every house. The design provides excellent ventilation and views of the street while ensuring the privacy of those inside.'

The doorkeeper admitted them into an airy portico, leading to a lobby. The spicy smell of cooking drifted out through an archway. Another servant, wearing a white skullcap, spotless white robe and sleeveless red jacket directed more servants to bring the luggage and led them up a shallow stone staircase to a large reception room.

As they walked in, Sabra came forward, hands outstretched.

'Ma chère Madame Barata,' she said in French. Clasping Caseley's hands, Sabra kissed her on both cheeks. 'I am so happy to see you again, and

138

to welcome you to my house.'

'I – we – my husband and I are very happy to be here.'

'And relieved to be off the train, I imagine. Even a camel is more comfortable, as you will see for yourself.' Gently pressing Caseley's hands she released them and turned to Antonia.

While Sabra greeted Antonia, Caseley quickly repeated what the Sheikha had said. His gaze on the two women, Jago gave a brief nod, murmuring, 'Thank you.'

Sabra offered her hand and he bowed over it. Then he stepped back to allow Pawlyn to take his place.

'Your refusal to accept the English government's claim that Egypt isn't capable of running her own affairs may cost you dearly, Mr Pawlyn,' Sabra said. 'Should you not be supporting your government's position?'

As they were still speaking French, Caseley was able to whisper a translation to Jago. How would she manage if they switched to Arabic? Even as the thought occurred she realised Sabra's courtesy would not permit that while she and Jago were present.

Pawlyn tipped his head to acknowledge her point. 'There are more than enough correspondents doing that, ma'am. In my opinion, the job of a journalist is to report both sides of a situation.'

'In these difficult times some would call that treason.'

'As an Englishman I believe in the principle of free speech. As a journalist I hold truth more important than political expediency.'

Sabra smiled. 'You are either very brave or very foolish.' She turned from him. 'Sheikh Imad has sent Bedouin clothing for each of you.' She signalled another servant, who brought the neatly folded garments first to Caseley then Antonia, then to the men.

'You each have an ankle-length long-sleeved *thobe,* which simply means garment. The long, sleeveless, open robe is an *aba* and can be wrapped loosely across the body while sitting or riding.'

A length of lightweight black cloth to cover Caseley's head was embroidered in tiny red cross-stitches, whereas the stitching on Antonia's was blue.

'The red embroidery signifies you are a married woman,' she explained before Caseley could ask. 'And now you will be shown to the guest rooms.'

'Ask her where you will be,' Jago murmured to Caseley, taking the folded garments and leather sandals the servant placed in his arms.

'In the women's quarters upstairs,' Sabra replied to Caseley's enquiry.

'Tell the Sheikha I am honoured by her kindness in inviting us into her home, and have no wish to offend. But I would appreciate it if we could remain together.'

Even as Caseley's heart soared, painful memories lurked like assassins. She shut them out. That was then. This was now.

Chapter Eleven

Sabra's gaze remained on Jago while Caseley translated. Caseley knew that, despite his courteous choice of words, he expected his request to he granted.

'But of course, Captain Barata,' Sabra agreed at once, the perfect hostess. She gave quiet instructions to the servant in Arabic.

'A meal will he served in an hour. I ask that you all come down dressed in your Bedouin garments. Tonight is an opportunity for you to get used to them.'

Caseley translated quickly. Jago bowed to Sabra. 'Please tell the Sheikha I am most grateful.'

Pawlyn was shown to his room, along a passage on the same floor.

'If you will go with Anwar, Captain? Madame Barata will join you as soon as I have explained to her and Miss Collingwood certain details of how their robes should be worn.' Her polite nod dismissed him and she looked to Caseley, who quickly translated. Jago bowed and followed the waiting servant up a further flight of stairs. Caseley turned to focus on what Sabra was saying.

'Though some Bedouin women veil their faces, many do not unless strangers enter their camp.'

'Sabra?' Antonia interrupted. 'Do you think Caseley's hair might be a problem? I have heard that the Bedouin are superstitious and regard red hair as a sign of the devil. They think the same of blue eyes.'

How strange she should know that, Caseley thought, *yet know so little of Bedouin life and customs*.

Sabra smiled. 'As Caseley's eyes are green I do not think we need be alarmed. As for her hair, it is not the shade most people think of as red, but coppery-bronze. Besides, it is customary for a married woman to wear an additional scarf folded into a broad band tied across the forehead.' She turned to Caseley.

'You will find one with your robes. If you loop the long scarf under your chin and tuck it into the top of the band, your hair will be completely hidden. I see no cause for concern.'

Caseley wanted to believe Antonia's critical remark was well-intentioned. But she was also aware Antonia was jealous of Sabra's friendliness towards someone who was a newcomer to Egypt with no connection to the resident English community.

She picked up her new clothes. 'Please excuse me. I need time to practise.' Leaving Antonia with Sabra, she followed a waiting servant up a second staircase. Indicating a door, he bowed.

'I trust you will find everything you need, madam,' he said in perfect French. 'But should you require anything at all, please ring the bell.'

'Thank you.'

He bowed again and silently retreated.

Closing the door behind her, Caseley looked around. The room was spacious and airy. As at the hotel, the large bed was covered, not with the blankets she was used to at home, but with a thick, soft quilt. She lifted one corner and was surprised at its lightness, then realised the quilt, mattress and pillows, all covered with crisp white cotton, were stuffed with feathers.

A large chest of dark wood with a carved lid stood at the foot of the bed. In one corner was a tall, vase-shaped hamper made of woven palm fibre. Two elegant chairs upholstered in rose pink velvet flanked a hexagonal table inlaid with mother-of-pearl. Their bags sat on top of the trunk that had been placed against the wall.

Compared to their bedroom back home the furnishings seemed sparse. But the louvred slats blocked the sun's glare and air flowing in cooled the room. Where was Jago?

Laying the neat block of folded garments on the bed, she peered through an archway and saw a room with a porcelain slipper bath half full of water on which rose petals floated, and a wooden stand with several towels folded on it.

Through another arch was a smaller cubicle. Relief made her smile as she saw a smooth stone seat on stone supports, beneath which was a large removable earthenware pot with sand in the bottom. Beside it, against the wall, were two more pots. One contained sand, the other water. After a moment's uncertainty she guessed the sand was an alternative to ash from the cooking range. Was it the custom here to use water instead of the squares of newspaper they relied on aboard *Cygnet*?

Back in the bedroom she crossed to a door in the opposite wall and found herself in a room identical to hers.

143

Beyond an archway she heard splashing. After a moment, Jago came out. Naked to the waist, he was wiping his bearded face and the back of his neck with a towel. His hair was wet and tousled. She glanced away, oddly shy, but still saw his broad shoulders and the dark hair that covered his chest and disappeared beneath thin white cotton trousers tied with a drawcord.

'There's a separate lavatory as well as the bathroom.'

She nodded. 'My room has the same.'

He grinned. 'Luxury compared to *Cygnet's* facilities.'

'I won't hear a word against *Cygnet's* facilities,' Caseley said. 'Though I do miss a bath.'

'Go,' he smiled. 'Enjoy it while you can.'

Returning to the bedroom she took a clean shift from her bag, scooped up the garments and leather sandals from the bed, and went to the bathroom, hanging everything over the rail as another need took priority.

A few minutes later, she eased hot feet out of her ankle boots then stripped off her stockings and layers of clothing. Tugging the clinging shift away from damp skin she pulled it over her head and dropped it on the pile, then stepped into the tepid sweet-scented water.

Bending her knees she slid down so it covered her shoulders and released a blissful sigh. She wished she could wash her hair. But even in this heat it would take too long to dry.

After soaping and rinsing she stood up, stepped out onto the cool stone tiles, and dried herself.

She unfolded the purplish-black garments. Over

her clean shift she put on the loose, long-sleeved *thobe,* then the sleeveless open robe trimmed with red and gold braid. Slipping her feet into the sandals she scooped up her discarded clothes and returned to the bedroom.

As she entered, Jago turned and they studied each other. Over the white cotton *thobe,* his *aba* was the colour of sand. Held in place by a thick black cord, a length of white cloth covered his hair, the long ends hanging down on his chest.

'You look – different,' she blurted. It was like looking at a handsome stranger.

'I was thinking the same.'

Laying her discarded clothes on top of the carved chest she sat on the bed, but immediately got up again and moved to the louvred window.

'What is it?'

She turned to face him, forced the words out. 'I think – perhaps it would be better if I didn't go.'

His features tightened but his voice remained calm. 'Why?'

'The last thing I want is to cause trouble.'

'Why should you?'

'The Bedouin have a superstitious fear of red hair. They consider it–' she stopped.

'Unlucky?'

As his gaze went to the thick coil high on her crown she was struck by a sudden vivid memory. The night of their first voyage together after their marriage they had gone down to his day cabin. Closing the door, he had kissed her with slow thoroughness. Then, reluctantly lifting his mouth from hers, he had taken the pins from her hair and, as the coil unwound, caught the tumbling

145

wavy mass and buried his face in it.

She wrenched herself back to the present. 'Worse. A mark of the devil.'

'The princess told you this?'

'No, Antonia did.' His brows lifted but he remained silent. 'I think she was warning me I would need to be careful. But Sabra said that if I cover my head the way married women do, no one will see my hair.'

'Then surely you have nothing to worry about? Caseley, I can't leave you here.' *She had insisted on coming.* He didn't say so. He didn't need to. 'If you've changed your mind, I'll take you back to Alexandria and you can stay at the hotel until *Cygnet* returns.'

'I haven't changed my mind. And you can't take me back. You need to reach the tribe as soon as possible. It was– I just thought you ought to know.'

'Now I do. It's of no account. How do you like your new clothes?'

'Very much. They feel strange. But it's such a relief to be free of–' *Corsets and tight bodices and petticoats.* 'Restriction.'

'They suit you.'

He pulled off the black cord and head covering and dropped them on the bed. 'Are you ready to go down?'

In the hall they met Pawlyn. Dressed like Jago, he was also bare-headed. A servant led them into a comfortable room furnished with low divans against the wall and many large cushions on a floor covered by a richly patterned carpet. Sabra greeted them.

'Ah, my apologies, gentlemen. I should have

146

asked you to wear your head cloths. Please do so for breakfast in the morning. The quicker you become used to them the more comfortable you will be.'

Caseley translated for Jago, ignoring Antonia's impatient sigh.

'Tonight,' Sabra continued, 'you will eat as the Bedouin do. In the camp, men and women eat separately. But Captain Barata and Mr Pawlyn must remain with us so they may learn what to do.'

They sat in a circle on a beautiful Persian carpet over which a cloth had been spread. A servant brought in a large platter of steaming rice and vegetables topped with pieces of cooked meat, and placed it in the middle of the cloth. A basin, pitcher and fresh towels were set to one side.

Caseley looked for plates and cutlery but saw neither.

'It is customary in small groups for food to be presented on a single large dish, from which everyone helps themselves. At the wedding there may be several different dishes. Eat with your right hand only,' Sabra said. Caseley translated for Jago. 'This is important. The left hand is considered unclean.' Caseley thought back to the pot of water in the small room upstairs and realised she had guessed correctly.

'Pinch a little rice together into a small lump and lift it to your mouth.' Sabra demonstrated.

'You make it look so easy,' Caseley said.

'With practice everything becomes easy,' Sabra replied. 'You will see.'

Jago waited, glancing sideways at Pawlyn. When

147

no one moved he reached towards the platter and picked up a cube of meat.

'That's cheating,' Caseley murmured as she concentrated on gathering the sticky spice-fragrant rice into a ball.

'As soon as you have picked up the rice,' Sabra directed, 'turn your hand over. Your palm will form a cup and catch anything that falls.'

This time Caseley did better. It felt awkward and completely wrong. But she was in a different country with different rules of etiquette.

Antonia got her rice halfway to her mouth when it crumbled out of her fingers and she caught it in her left hand. 'This is ridiculous. We aren't Bedouin. Surely they won't expect–'

'Miss Collingwood,' Sabra cut in, 'if Sheikh Imad was invited to dinner at the Consulate, how would you react if he put his plate on the floor and ate with his fingers? Would you be embarrassed that he didn't know what was expected of him?'

'But that's–'

'Different?' Sabra's tone was cool.

Colour flooded Antonia's face. 'I beg your pardon.'

Releasing the breath she had been holding, Caseley murmured an explanation to Jago, winning a glare from Antonia, who clearly thought she shouldn't have told him what had been said.

She was surprised that, despite being smitten with the educated, multi-lingual and dignified Bedouin Sheikh, Antonia had not bothered to understand the etiquette of his people.

As the meal progressed, Caseley found she was able to carry food from platter to mouth without dropping any. Her movements lacked Sabra's neatness but at least she would not offend their Bedouin hosts.

She glanced at Jago, and the image of him sitting cross-legged on the rug wearing the clothes of a different race and adapting to different manners sent a quiver through her.

This man was her husband, had fathered her sons. Yet this past year he had become a stranger. His manner had been courteous, pleasant, and protective. But he had withdrawn from her. *As she had from him...*

In the way of all men, Jago and Robert Pawlyn were silently competing to be the first to succeed at eating neatly with their fingers.

Jago had loved the boys and been hugely proud of them. Though her days had been full, she had missed him during his long weeks at sea. Had he missed her? He never said so. Why would he? The arrival of children had changed both their lives as motherhood kept her at home.

Men seemed more able to *accept* and move on. For her, the deaths of her children had been devastating. But their loss was more bitterly poignant because of the chasm that yawned between her and Jago. 'Caseley?'

Jago's voice, low and quiet, brought her back.

She looked up with a start. 'I'm so sorry. I was–' *Grieving.* 'Concentrating.'

Sabra smiled. 'You are making good progress. Now I must tell you about the Bedouin camp. It will be very large with many *bayts*–'

'Forgive me, Sabra,' Caseley interrupted. 'What is a *bayt*? I don't recognise the word.'

149

'Of course you don't. It is I who should apologise. It is a Bedouin tent.'

'What is she saying?' Jago asked softly. Pawlyn opened his mouth but closed it again without speaking.

Appreciating his tact, Caseley translated quickly. Jago trusted her, she knew, but he loathed being at a disadvantage.

'There will be many *bayts*,' Sabra went on, 'because relatives of both the bride and the groom will have come a great distance to attend the wedding. Each *bayt* is home to a married couple, their children, the parents of husband or wife and perhaps a brother or sister of the bride. Family ties are strong and older relatives are always looked after. Inside the *bayt* there is a public area where men meet and guests are received. Fabric walls keep the rest exclusively for the women.'

'Why are women never seen?' Antonia asked. 'There are always Bedouin men on the streets of Cairo and Alexandria, but never any women. Are they hidden away?'

Impatience crossed Sabra's face. 'Not hidden, Miss Collingwood, protected. Among the Bedouin, men and women are considered equal. But certain tribes are known to be hot-blooded and quarrelsome. Disputes over land or grazing or water rights can quickly become violent. Violence is always kept away from the camp because women are valued and respected.' She paused to allow Caseley time to translate, then continued.

'You would be wrong to assume that because they take no part in public life, women count for little. The reverse is true. They are highly esteemed. The Bedouin have a saying: "Men can get nowhere without a woman and women can be no one without a man". Though a woman derives her status from her husband, he relies on her to safeguard his honour through her responsibility for their *bayt*, the household and domestic animals, raising their children and hospitality to guests.'

After translating for Jago, Caseley turned to Sabra.

'Though Bedouin live in tents in the desert and we live in a house overlooking the harbour in a Cornish town, it sounds as if the responsibilities of family life are not so different.'

Sabra nodded and Caseley saw approval in her smile. 'Hospitality is an unbreakable rule for the Bedouin. If a traveller arrives at a camp and touches the tent pole, the family must welcome him and his animals and anyone with him. This applies even if he is an enemy. The traditional greeting "Peace be with you", which is returned, ensures his safety. He may stay for three days and nights and will not be asked for payment. The teapot or coffee pot is constantly refilled. Food is provided, so is fodder for his animals. In return, the guest is expected to be generous with conversation and pass on all the news he has heard on his travels. This is how families who must constantly move to find new grazing can keep informed of what is happening.'

As servants moved around the group, one carrying the basin, another the ewer, to carefully pour water over greasy fingers then offer the towel, once again Caseley told Jago what had been said.

'I hate this,' he muttered.

'I'm sorry–'

'No, I don't mean... You are doing your best. I know that, and I'm grateful. It's just – I dislike intensely the fact that it's necessary.'

As tiny cups of bitter coffee and small sweet cakes were served, Sabra told them how several *bayts* might travel together; an extended family linked by lineage or marriage.

The meal ended. Hoping she would remember everything she had learned, Caseley thanked Sabra and wished her and Antonia good night. As she walked upstairs with Jago, rubbing the back of her neck where intense concentration had tightened the muscles, exhaustion broke over her like an Atlantic wave.

As she entered the bedroom she realised the clothes in which she had travelled from Cairo had disappeared. The servants must have taken them away to be laundered. Jago's coat, trousers and shirt had also vanished.

As Jago disappeared through the arch she took her nightgown and went into her bathroom. Exchanging the dark robes for her white cotton nightgown, she washed her face and hands and cleaned her teeth in the fresh water that had been brought while they were downstairs.

Returning to the bedroom she laid her robes on the chest, and sat on the edge of the bed. As she removed pins, her coiled hair unwound and fell down her back. She picked up her comb.

Jago padded in on bare feet wearing his nightshirt. The long, loose white cotton had a plain round neck slit to the chest. It resembled his robe

152

apart from the cuffed sleeves.

No, it didn't. His robe would be seen in public. Only she saw him like this.

He held out his hand for the comb. 'May I?'

His request made her eyes sting. She didn't know whether to be glad that he wanted to or sad that he felt he needed to ask. Yet whose fault was that? How could she forgive what he had done? But if she could not, what future did they have?

Not trusting herself to speak she handed him the comb. Sitting behind her he drew it carefully through the thick waves.

'What is your opinion of Antonia Collingwood's connection with the Sheikh?'

Relieved and grateful for conversation that was not personal, she thought for a moment. 'I am not sure there is one. Her interest in him is plain. His manner towards her at the hotel was courteous. He allowed her to take that photograph. But his dignity and reserve make him difficult to read. I'm astonished that she has lived here all her life yet knows so little of Bedouin customs.'

'You shouldn't be. She sees everything in terms of how it affects her. Be careful, Caseley. She is jealous of you.'

Caseley turned her head quickly, wincing as the comb caught and pulled her hair.

'Be still,' he murmured, gently disentangling the comb.

'I cannot imagine why she should be. What makes you say so?'

'Observation. With Sabra, I'm reserving judgement.'

'Jago, we are strangers to her yet she welcomed

153

us into her home.'

'Exactly, and I cannot help wondering why. I do not question her generosity, only her motives. She is a woman of many faces.'

Startled by his remarks, she was shaken by the realisation she couldn't instantly dismiss them. What he'd said echoed thoughts she had felt ashamed of, even as they occurred. Having been open about her dislike of her cousin, Khedive Tewfiq, perhaps it wasn't altogether surprising for the Sheikha to show interest in new English arrivals, especially as the English currently controlled Egypt's finances.

Now they were alone there was so much that needed saying. But Caseley didn't know where to start. She was exhausted, her energy sapped by the heat and travelling. Questions clamoured and anxiety nagged. The silence stretched. Then, too tired to worry any more, she let it all go. They were here. He had asked to share her room so she would not be alone in a strange place. For now that was enough.

When he had finished he dropped the comb on the quilt then, surprising her yet again, divided the thick fall of hair and quickly plaited it into a loose braid. As she turned to thank him he started to get up. Without conscious thought she laid her hand on his arm, then quickly withdrew it. She didn't want him to leave. But Louise Downing's triumph still haunted her, still hurt.

She couldn't – she wanted – she didn't know what she wanted.

He pushed back the quilt, lay down and drew her down beside him. 'You're safe, Caseley. Go to

154

sleep. We have an early start tomorrow.'

He heard her quiet sigh. Within minutes her breathing had deepened as exhaustion claimed her. Through the layers of fine cotton that separated them he could feel her body's warmth. He breathed in the unique scent of her skin and a hint of summer roses.

God, he missed her. Ached for her. As her husband he had every right to use her how and when he wished. Yet he could not, would not. More than once, frustration and need had tempted him to press. But fear held him back: fear that she would acquiesce from duty, not desire. Fear she would turn her face away, denying him her mouth and her steady open gaze. Fear that if he used her in such a way something precious and fragile would be irreparably broken.

Experienced with women, he understood the value of patience. Their wedding night had been a long slow journey of delight that had given joy and profound pleasure to them both. He wanted that again. He wanted his wife, the only woman he had ever loved, would ever love. Rather than risk widening the distance between them he would wait for her to come to him.

Louise had been a willing source of relief. She knew the rules and he was financially generous. But it was Caseley he thought of; Caseley he longed for.

His nerves were twitchy and his gut felt full of rocks. But he could wait. He would wait. She had overridden his objections and insisted on coming. That gave him hope.

Chapter Twelve

Stirred and aching for her, Jago got up before Caseley woke. He forced himself to leave, returning to his bathroom. He opened the door to a quiet knock and found a servant with two large ewers of water, hot and cold.

Washed and dressed once more in her robes, Caseley pinned up her hair and covered it with the scarf. Tying the folded band across her forehead, she drew one end of the scarf under her chin and tucked it into the top of the band.

Hanging her towels over the rail she went back into the bedroom. Jago was dressed and waiting for her. This morning he wore his head cloth, held in place by the doubled black woven cord. One end of the white cloth hung to his chest. He had slung the other across his chest and over his other shoulder.

He was both familiar and a stranger. Once again she felt a quiver deep inside as his gaze raked her from head to foot.

She moistened dry lips. 'Can you see my hair?'

He shook his head. 'Pawlyn was telling me yesterday that among the Tuareg it is men, and not women, who cover their faces. In some tribes only a husband may see his wife's hair. I find that rather appealing.'

Caseley recalled the previous night and his

156

gentleness with the comb.

'You always liked my hair,' she murmured, aware only after the words were out how much sadness and yearning they held.

'I still do. Are you ready?'

'Almost.' She moved around the room, wrapping her toiletries in the dry towels she had brought, quickly folding then rolling their nightwear and packing it all into the large striped cloth bag Sabra had provided. She placed it next to the small iron-bound chest containing the gold.

They started down the stairs. 'I'm glad you are here,' he said. Her spirits soaring, she glanced at him as he continued. 'Without you to translate for me I'd be completely in the dark.'

'I'm sure Mr Pawlyn would–'

'No doubt he would. And will, once we reach the Bedouin camp. But I prefer – you have an eye for detail. Our home is testament to that. You notice things, especially about people.'

'Are you expecting trouble?'

His hand rested briefly on her shoulder, a gesture of reassurance, and she welcomed it. 'No. As Sheikh Imad's guests we are under his protection. Yet it would be foolish to discount the possibility that others know the real reason I'm there.'

'How could they?'

'News travels fast in Falmouth. Why should it be any different here, especially with so much at stake? I may be seeing threats where none exist. But it will do no harm to be cautious.'

As they reached the bottom of the stairs a servant appeared and led them into the room where they had eaten the previous evening. Sabra, An-

157

tonia and Robert Pawlyn were already there sitting on the carpet. Pawlyn scrambled to his feet as Caseley walked in with Jago behind her. As greetings were exchanged, Caseley saw Antonia's gaze dart from her to Jago and glimpsed envy.

Antonia saw a man and his wife coming to breakfast after a night spent together. Was she imagining herself with the Sheikh? Did she not realise that an image could be misread, that assumption was not reality?

Everyone sat. A platter of still-warm flatbread and others of cold roast mutton, white crumbly cheese, grapes and dates were brought in and set on the carpet. They were offered tea or coffee.

Everyone helped themselves; tearing the soft bread into bite-sized pieces.

Caseley helped herself to tiny chunks of cheese. It was creamy and mild. 'S – ma'am,' she corrected quickly as she remembered that Sabra only used their first names when no men were present. 'What cheese is this?'

'Feta, it is made from sheep's milk.'

Startled, she reminded herself that at home she happily ate cheese made from cow or goat's milk, and decided to think only of the taste, which was delicious.

'How far is it to the camp where the wedding will be?' Robert Pawlyn asked. Caseley translated for Jago.

'Perhaps three days' journey,' Sabra replied. 'Sheikh Imad is providing camels for us.'

Antonia glanced up. 'Not horses?'

Sabra shook her head. 'In the desert horses are reserved for men. I have kinsmen in Sinai who

158

breed Arabian horses famous for their speed, agility and courage. But for our journey camels are better. Sheikh Imad will bring fine beasts. He is a Tarabin, one of the royal tribes, and owns a superb camel herd.'

While she ate, Antonia adjusted the folds of her robe. 'I will need an additional camel for my photographic equipment. I did tell Sheikh Imad.'

'Then you may be sure he won't forget,' Sabra said.

Trying to remember all Sabra's instructions so she would not offend her Bedouin hosts or disgrace herself and Jago, Caseley was careful to use only her right hand to carry bread and small pieces of cheese to her mouth. Glancing up, she saw Jago watching her. 'Is something wrong?' she asked quietly.

'No.' He kept his own voice low. 'It's just – I thought I knew you. Instead–' he shook his head. 'You constantly surprise me.'

'Perhaps you expected too little.'

As surprise widened his eyes she bent her head to her meal. Of course she had changed. After what had happened, how could she not have?

Yet, mired in her grief, it had not occurred to her that he, too, must have been altered by what had happened. How ironic that it had taken a voyage to Egypt for them to recognise that neither was who they had been before. Yet the bond between them, though stretched, frayed and tenuous, had not broken.

Last night she had not expected to sleep. But a combination of exhaustion and the reassuring warmth of Jago's body close to hers had tumbled her into deep dreamless oblivion moments after she closed her eyes.

When she woke it was morning and she was alone. Panic had brought her upright, heart racing. Then she had heard him in the adjoining room.

On the way downstairs he had asked for her help. Now, though apprehension and excitement churned in her stomach, she made herself take a handful of fresh dates and a few grapes. With a long demanding day ahead, she would need all her strength.

A short while later they were preparing to leave. The servants had brought down their bags and the small, heavy chest. The trunk would remain here until their return.

Sabra joined them. She was carrying cloaks of thick black felt with colourful embroidery around the edges and armholes. She handed one to Caseley, who thanked her.

Taking hers, Antonia laughed. 'Sabra, it is summer, anyone who can has left Cairo to escape the heat.'

'That is true. But desert nights are bitterly cold. You will be glad of this extra layer.'

Soon Sheikh Imad arrived and greetings were exchanged. Antonia's smile was suddenly brighter. She laughed and fluttered, every gesture seeking attention.

As Jago rolled her cloak and put it into the soft bag, Caseley recognised his impatience. It was a shame Antonia had no close female relative to guide her. She'd had Rosina Renfree. Her childhood nurse had stepped into the terrible gap left

160

by her mother's death, supported her with love and patience and become a treasured house-keeper. Rosina would have given Antonia a set-down she would never forget. But it was not her place to criticise, nor would her advice be welcome.

Fighting sudden homesickness Caseley pulled herself together. Without Sheikh Imad and Sabra, Jago's task would be impossible. At the camp he would have Robert Pawlyn to translate for him. But they would be confined to male company.

Caseley knew that Cornish wives often had considerable influence over their husband's decisions. Did this apply in Bedouin society? Thanks to Sabra she would have a privileged glimpse into a very different way of life. But would anything she observed help Jago?

Sheikh Imad motioned a servant forward. The man bowed and offered first Jago then Robert Pawlyn a neat parcel of fabric. When opened, these proved to be long, sleeveless coats of heavy, dark material bound with red and silver braid, not unlike those Sabra had given her and Antonia.

Jago quickly asked Caseley how to say thank you in both French and Arabic, and repeated the words to Sheikh Imad with care and sincerity.

The Bedouin nodded. Jago re-folded and rolled the coat, adding it to the bag. Then it was time to go.

Leaving the cool, airy apartment for outside was like walking into an oven. Caseley was deeply grateful to be free of her corset and all the additional close-fitting layers required by European fashion. Yet she felt acutely self-conscious in her loose robes and head covering, as though she had come outside in her nightgown. But, as similarly dressed women passed along the street without so much as a glance in her direction, it occurred to her that she was virtually invisible. After nearly a year of sidelong pitying looks the relief was enormous.

Six camels knelt, their legs tucked under them, in the shade of tall date palms. A length of silver chain joined the braided halter to a single rein. Two white-clad servants with blue head cloths wound like turbans and a silver dagger in the red sash at their waists each held the reins of three camels.

The camel saddles were unlike anything Caseley had seen. Covered by several tasselled blankets woven in diamond patterns of black, red, gold and blue, they had a short round post front and back.

A little distance away more camels knelt. One carried Antonia's two camera boxes half-covered by fodder sacks. Two more were laden with additional fodder sacks and water pots in nets of plaited fibre. Caseley watched as more servants, similarly dressed but without daggers, hung the bags containing their clothes, tied together by the handles, over other camels' backs. Each beast had a long-barrelled gun wrapped in cloth suspended from the front saddle post.

That the men were armed and could provide protection was reassuring. That it might be necessary caused a tightening in her stomach.

The gold chest was placed in a fibre sling and hooked over Sheikh Imad's saddle, next to a leather gun scabbard.

'Hold on tight as the camel gets up,' Robert Pawlyn advised her. 'It's quite a lurch: back, forward and back again. But once they are on their feet and you get used to the sway it's a very comfortable way to travel.'

A servant brought a low wooden stool for Caseley to stand on and she hitched herself onto the blanket-padded saddle. Sabra came to her side. 'Hook your right leg around the post and put your left foot in the stirrup. You will feel more secure.'

Caseley settled herself, arranged her robes, then caught her breath and grabbed the front post as the camel suddenly heaved itself up.

'All right?' Jago asked.

'Fine.' Caseley looked down and wished she hadn't. The ground seemed a very long way away.

Jago nodded. 'Well done.' He spoke so only she could hear.

'We haven't started moving yet.'

Antonia gave little yelps as her camel rose to its feet making them both glance across. Sheikh Imad was talking quietly to Sabra and didn't look round.

'I expected her to have more sense,' Jago said, making no effort to hide his scorn.

'In what respect?'

'Pretending feminine weakness is the least likely way to win his admiration,' shaking his head he went to his camel.

He was speaking of Antonia, but were his words a warning to her as well? She knew this was not a holiday trip. He had an important job to do and nothing must be allowed to interfere.

Caseley straightened her back. Never in her life

163

had she pretended feminine weakness. She had no intention of starting now.

With everyone mounted they set off. The Sheikh's bodyguards led, Sheikh Imad, Pawlyn and Jago were next, followed by Antonia, Sabra and Caseley. The baggage camels were on leading reins held by two servants and two more armed guards brought up the rear.

As Antonia chattered to Sabra, Caseley was reminded of the magpies in the oak tree in the back garden of her home on Greenbank. What would Rosina and Liza-Jane say if they could see her now? How much she would have to tell them.

An unexpected stab of grief stopped her breath. She fought it off.

'Madame Barata? You are unwell?' Sabra had dropped back beside her.

The princess's use of her title and married name made Caseley flinch. She looked up expecting contempt or impatience, but saw only concern. Though her eyes still stung, she managed a smile. 'No, ma'am. I – a brief discomfort. It has passed.'

In front of Antonia, who was adjusting her head cloth, Caseley saw Robert Pawlyn riding between Jago and Sheikh Imad, turning one way then the other as he interpreted.

Sabra nodded. 'You came to Egypt by ship. Were you seasick?'

'No. Fortunately, I am a good sailor. I love being at sea, even in a storm.'

Sabra laughed. 'Camels are the ships of the desert. Now you know that you can relax and be comfortable.'

'I would feel more confident if I knew how to steer.'

'Later I will ask one of the servants to find you a stick. Not to beat,' she added, reading Caseley's expression. 'Light tapping on the neck or shoulder will make it turn.'

'As my camel seems perfectly content to follow those in front I will not interfere.' She looked around. 'What are those enormous buildings?'

'Egypt is a very old country. It has had many rulers. As is the way of men,' Sabra's tone was dry, 'each wanted to be remembered. The mosque of al-Azhar is nearly a thousand years old, though it has been much altered over the centuries. It was Saladin who built the mighty citadel and part of the city walls.' She indicated buildings on a hill behind a massive encircling wall of stone. 'He was very clever and created bent-entrances, putting two in the walls and three in the citadel.'

'For what purpose?'

'To delay any army trying to storm its way in.'

Caseley pointed to a huge square building within the complex, topped by two slender minarets and a double dome. 'And that?'

'The mosque of al-Nasir Muhammad.'

'How old is it?'

'More than five hundred years.'

She looked forward to telling Jago later. Watching Sabra move forward to help Antonia, who seemed to be having trouble with her camel, Caseley realised she had been so absorbed in what Sabra was telling her, she had relaxed and was swaying easily with the movement of the animal beneath her.

Before long they had left the city and the cacophony of braying donkeys, hawkers shouting to attract buyers, the richly dressed, the rag-clad beggars, grinding wheels and jingling harnesses of calèches, and the babble of different languages. The smells of rotting fruit, dung and smoke from charcoal fires receded.

It was still hot and the breeze whipped up fine dust that caught in her throat. She lifted the edge of her head scarf over her nose and was instantly more comfortable.

As they passed a small group of flat-roofed mud houses she saw women dressed in dusty black cotton and blue beads carrying pots to a well.

Soon they were climbing along a narrow, stony track between rocky crags. The day wore on and grew hotter. Heat shimmered above the rocks and Caseley felt increasingly thirsty.

Rounding a bend they gazed down onto what looked like a dry riverbed. Though deep and narrow, it was flat. As her camel picked its way down the steep, stony path Caseley leaned back and closed her eyes. She quickly opened them again, preferring to see where she was going. She left the rein loose and trusted her camel.

At the bottom they stopped. As a servant caught the halter and tugged, Caseley's camel dropped to its knees then folded its legs underneath. Lifting her leg over the saddle post she slid stiffly down, her legs shaky. A few moments of stretching and flexing loosened her up. Jago came over.

'Did you enjoy your first camel ride?'

'I did. If I sound surprised, it's because I am. I was very nervous when we set off. Being perched so high with nothing to hold on to was – terrifying.'

His smile flashed white and wry in his bearded face. 'You looked as if you had been born to it.'

His compliment sent a rush of pleasure through her and she felt her face warm. 'Sabra was telling me about some of the ancient buildings. Listening to her I forgot to be scared and that helped me relax.'

'You make it sound easy.' His self-mockery, admitting to her what he would deny to anyone else, reminded her how close they used to be.

She had told him things she had never spoken of, even to Rosina. He had revealed secrets of his own. Out of sharing those revelations had grown a bond she treasured, believing it unique and unbreakable. No matter how distant his voyages or how long he was away, she had believed she was as often in his thoughts as he was in hers. She had trusted their love, their marriage, him.

She knew men strayed. Living in the same house as Rosina and Liza-Jane, who knew all the town gossip, how could she not? But never once had it crossed her mind that Jago might.

Her throat painfully raw with unshed tears she turned away, swallowing hard. She would not cry. That would provoke questions she could only answer with lies because the truth was too private and painful.

She had seen what happened to betrayed wives who complained about their husbands' actions. They forfeited their dignity, only to be scorned and blamed. As if a man's decision to break his marriage vows must be his wife's fault. Besides, tears would make her appear weak. Though battered by grief and wounded by loss, she was not weak. She would take a breath, then another. Her heart would continue to beat, and she would go on living.

'When you get used to it, it is not so hard,' she said.

Sabra called, beckoning them towards food the servants were laying out, and the moment passed.

Caseley crossed the dusty ground, aware of Jago close behind.

Chapter Thirteen

Seated in shadow cast by a jutting rock, they ate a picnic lunch of bread, cheese and dates. Sheikh Imad, Jago and Pawlyn sat a little way away, talking in low voices.

Antonia kept looking across, visibly irritated. 'They're not being very sociable.'

'For Captain Barata and Mr Pawlyn this journey is not a social occasion,' Sabra reminded.

Dragging her gaze from Jago, Caseley saw two of the bodyguards sitting one on either side of the group, their backs to the cliff. The other two, each carrying a gun, had positioned themselves high in the rocks so they could see anyone approaching from either direction.

Two of the servants were walking away, apparently searching the sandy wadi floor.

'Sabra?' Because the three of them were alone,

Caseley was comfortable using the Sheikha's name. 'What are they looking for?'

'Wood.'

'Here?' Antonia's voice rose in disbelief. 'There isn't even a blade of grass, let alone a tree.'

'True,' Sabra agreed. 'But rain does come, though it is unpredictable, sometimes very little, sometimes too much. Then this bare ground is covered with grass, flowers and small bushes.'

'That must look very beautiful, though it's hard to imagine right now.' Shielding her eyes, Caseley looked up. The sky wasn't the cornflower blue of a summer sky at home. It had the brutal glare of hammered steel.

'After the rain sinks into the ground, the vegetation quickly dries out.' Sabra nodded towards the returning servants, each now carrying an armful of scrub and twigs. She spoke to one. Dropping his armful he pulled two dry brown palm fronds from the pile. Taking the dagger from the scabbard on his belt he stripped off the ragged leaves, then handed the long, flexible stems to Sabra, bowed, and picked up the scrub again.

Sabra offered one of the sticks to Antonia and the other to Caseley. 'Gentle tapping,' she reminded.

'Thank you.' Caseley wasn't sure she would dare use it, but it would have been discourteous to refuse.

The men stuffed most of the scrub into the nets. With the rest they lit a small fire, boiled water, and brewed tea sweetened with hard sugar cracked off a cone and flavoured with torn mint leaves. Served in small, thick glasses, it was surprisingly refreshing. Then aware of a need that had become more pressing during their meal, Caseley turned to Sabra.

'I need to– Where should–?'

'I was about to suggest it.' The Sheikha led her and Antonia a short distance back down the wadi to privacy among the rocks.

Out of the shade the heat was intense, radiating off the rocks and burning her head and shoulders. Caseley was grateful for her loose robes. Covering her from head to toe, they were more modest than the fashionable figure-hugging gowns well-dressed Cornish women were wearing. The loose layers allowed air to reach her body and offered a freedom of movement she wasn't used to. They were, she realised, ideal for this climate.

As they walked back to the camels she saw the three men returning from the far side of the track and guessed they had answered a similar call.

'Can we not wait for an hour or two, until the sun is lower?' Antonia asked.

Sabra shook her head. 'We still have some distance to travel and Sheikh Imad will not wish to arrive late.'

'Surely he could arrive whenever he wished.'

Sabra shook her head. 'To do so when his party includes strangers would insult his hosts.'

Once again, Caseley was surprised by Antonia's lack of understanding. It couldn't be deliberate rudeness. She wouldn't want to jeopardise her friendship with Sabra or Sheikh Imad. Perhaps because they were at ease in European company, she had never thought it necessary to learn what Egyptians or Bedouin considered polite. How could she not realise, that far from excusing bad manners high rank made courtesy imperative, not least because it set an example.

As the remains of the meal were quickly packed away, one of the servants helped Sabra onto her camel then turned to assist Antonia. Another approached Caseley. He bowed then bent forward, linking his fingers. She put her sandaled foot into his cupped hands and he boosted her up onto the saddle.

She quickly hooked her leg around the post and slid her other foot into the stirrup. She was still adjusting her robes when the great beast lurched to its feet, with a sound between a bray and a roar. She grabbed the front saddle post and nearly dropped her stick.

'You need to be quicker, Caseley,' Antonia called from her own camel. 'There are no doctors here if you fall off and hurt yourself.'

'I'll remember next time.'

'She has a gift for stating the obvious,' Jago said as he came to Caseley's side.

'It is a fair point. I'm sure she means well.'

'Don't count on it. The heat isn't too much for you?'

'No. I'm so grateful to the Sheikha for making sure we were – are – properly dressed for it.'

'I would have liked to ride and sit with you, but–'

'You and Sheikh Imad have much to discuss. It's a blessing you have Mr Pawlyn to translate. The Sheikh has beautiful manners, but I don't think he would have been comfortable with me as your interpreter. Everything has worked out for the best. You need not worry about me.'

His gaze held hers, intent. 'You ask the impossible.' Summoned by Pawlyn's shout, he returned to his camel.

Watching him go, Caseley waited for her heartbeat to settle. He did care. She wanted to believe it. But doubt whispered: *with such an important task to fulfil he will not want distractions.*

As soon as the men were mounted the party set off.

The wadi wound between tall rocky cliffs that crowded in on both sides. They walked from deep shadow to glaring sunlight and back. The heat was like an oven. Conversation became too much effort.

Moving easily with the swaying gait, Caseley changed both rein and stick to her left hand and raised her bent leg to free wadded layers of cotton. She was instantly more comfortable. Her gaze fell on the tasselled blanket with its diamond pattern of red, black and gold covering the padded saddle. Who had made it? How long had it taken to weave?

Her camel smelled warm and musty, like hemp rope. It was the colour of caramel. So, too, were Antonia's and Robert Pawlyn's. Sheikh Imad and Sabra's camels were pale cream, and Jago's golden brown.

As her camel turned its head she saw its eyelashes were over an inch long. She really would have so much to tell Rosina and Liza-Jane. Shying away from thoughts of home, she looked at the rocks. In a deep, damp crevice the green leaves of a tiny plant provided an unexpected flash of colour in a landscape of grey, ochre and brown.

Her camel swung its head again. She tapped its shoulder with the stick, then held her breath. Its ears twitched then it stalked on, facing forward. She smiled to herself and felt ridiculously proud.

Soothed by the rhythmic swaying her mind drifted. It was a relief not to think, to simply *be*. Hours passed.

Eventually, the narrow ravine widened. Behind the rocky hills she could see higher crags and peaks. Wide shallow channels of grey sand and gravel that reminded her of streambeds marked the wadi floor. As the sun sank lower, the harsh quality of the light softened and the furnace-like heat began to diminish.

At last Sheikh Imad called a halt. Caseley waited while a servant made her camel kneel. She slid down with a groan of relief and arched her back.

Returning from a much-needed comfort break among the rocks, she saw a fire had been lit and the last of the riding camels were being unsaddled then hobbled so they could not stray.

The servants unpacked fodder from the nets and poured water from large clay jars into a bowl, taking it to each camel in turn.

'What about us?' Antonia complained. 'Surely the camels can wait?'

'No, they are always tended first,' Sabra said. 'We treat them well because without them we would die. We could not walk to safety. It is too far and there are few wells in this part of the desert. Besides, these animals are from Sheikh Imad's own herd and very valuable.'

As the servants started unloading the pack

camels, Antonia hurried across to supervise the removal of her camera boxes and tripod. Suddenly Caseley was aware of Jago beside her. Though she had spent the afternoon looking at his back, seeing his bearded face beneath the loosely draped white head cloth sent a jolt through her. Meeting his gaze she felt a tug of attraction all the more startling because for an instant she was seeing, not her husband, but a stranger.

'Caseley? Is the heat–?'

'No, no.' She pulled herself together. 'I'm glad we've stopped, though. Have you got used to your camel?'

'You were right. It does feel like being on board a ship.'

Caseley saw Sabra beckon. 'I think it's time to eat.'

As they walked towards the fire she saw two woven striped blankets had been laid on the ground a short distance apart. The Sheikh and Robert Pawlyn were sitting cross-legged on one. Sabra stood by the other, speaking to one of the bodyguards.

'It seems we are to be separated again,' Jago murmured.

'Sabra wants to make us familiar with Bedouin customs so we will feel more comfortable.'

'And do you? Feel comfortable?'

Seeing his concern she answered honestly. 'I am beginning to, though everything is very new and strange. I'm glad I came. I won't let you down, Jago.'

His features tightened as if in pain, then he smiled. 'I hope I may see you later. But–'

'I won't expect it. How are you getting on with the Sheikh?'

'He wears courtesy like armour. Yet his questions show an open mind and make me hopeful he will be able to persuade the elders to our side.'

'Surely the gold will help?'

Jago shrugged. 'The tribe is already wealthy, so who knows? Pawlyn is invaluable and not only for interpreting. Without his knowledge of Arab manners and the way they do business I might have caused grave offence.'

Looking past him she touched his arm lightly. 'You should go. The Sheikh is waiting.'

'I'm glad you're here.' Without waiting for her response, he left.

Caseley watched Antonia try to place herself near Sheikh Imad but Sabra diverted her. As Caseley lowered herself to the blanket she could hear the two servants muttering their disapproval. Should she warn Antonia? No. Rather than taking heed, she would be more likely to take offence.

One of the servants came over with a water jar and a small bowl. Caseley watched Sabra rinse her dusty hands, press them to her face and the back of her neck, then use the edge of her scarf to dry her fingers. When he came to her she did the same.

Sitting cross-legged and leaning in to take food from the large platter in the middle, she glanced across and saw Jago watching her. He raised an eyebrow. Touched by his concern she nodded to reassure him.

Unlike Antonia she did not mind separation from the men. With so much still unresolved between her and Jago, sitting apart eased her turmoil. Yet she found his presence reassuring.

The lavender sky deepened to purple. Dusk was brief and darkness sudden. Beyond the dancing firelight the blackness was dense. The moon rose, almost full, and in its cold, pale light the gritty dust glistened like powdered diamonds.

The temperature had dropped sharply and she shivered.

'You are cold,' Sabra said.

'You did warn us,' Caseley smiled. 'I just didn't expect the change to be so sudden.'

One of the servants came over with the three cloaks and laid them respectfully between Sabra and Caseley.

'*Shukran,*' Caseley said, smiling her thanks as she reached for hers. Startled, the man nodded and melted into the darkness.

'I didn't know you spoke Arabic,' Sabra said, sounding surprised.

Caseley stood, shook out the folds and wrapped the cloak around her before sitting down again. 'I don't. Well, only a little. Hardly anything. After we picked up Mr Pawlyn at Gibraltar I asked him to teach me a few words.'

'Why?' Antonia demanded. 'You'll only be in Egypt a few weeks.'

'I know. But it seemed only polite to be able to say please and thank you. I didn't know then that I would have the privilege of attending a Bedouin wedding. So I'm even more glad I made the effort.'

Caseley was offered mint tea or coffee. Knowing the coffee would be thick, strong and gritty, she chose tea.

After the heat and dust of the day's riding she would have loved a bath. At home she took such comforts for granted. Here water was precious and never wasted. She could not even unpin her hair. That reminded her of Jago wielding the comb with slow, soothing sweeps. *I'm glad you're here.*

The meal finished, they settled down for the night using the camel saddle blankets as pillows. Two guards moved away to take the first watch.

The ground was hard but that wasn't what kept Caseley awake. Wrapped in her cloak she lay on her back, gazing up at a black velvet sky strewn with countless stars.

Reliving the day's journey through bare rocks, stony paths, dry river beds and desert heat, she thought of small fields of long grass or golden wheat bounded by stone hedges; moors of yellow gorse and purple heather; wooded valleys, soft breezes and the sparkling waters of the Carrick Roads.

In the early years of their marriage she had sailed with Jago to other countries. But pressure of schedules meant there had never been time to venture beyond the ports. This journey was different. Not only because of all she was seeing and experiencing, but because here, away from all the reminders, the pain was not so raw.

For months grief had ripped at her with sharp, jagged teeth. Tonight it was a dull ache, a deep bruise. But with relief came guilt. It was too strong to fight. All she could do was wait. A constant background presence, it surged and ebbed like a tide. While her attention was engaged it would build unnoticed then suddenly break over her, leaving her abandoned, devastated, castaway.

With a lifetime's practice of hiding tumultuous emotions behind a calm façade, she did her weeping in the privacy of her bed. There was no privacy tonight. Her eyes burned and her throat ached. But she could not, must not, weep tonight.

Jago had asked for her help and she had promised it without reservation. But Robert Pawlyn's language skills far surpassed hers. The Bedouin women would speak Arabic, not French, so she would have no idea what they were saying.

I'm glad you're here.

Working together when they were first married they had learned much about each other. Life had changed after the boys were born. New joys gained had been countered by a loss of closeness, due to frequent separations and the demands of their busy lives. She yearned for the man she married, but not at any price.

It was tempting to regard any intimate connections he formed outside their home as not her concern. Plenty of women took that view. But she couldn't. If she did, she would lose part of herself.

Eventually, exhausted, she slept.

The next day followed a similar pattern. Using her stick, she guided her camel away when it crowded Sabra's and was warmed by the nod of approval. When they stopped for the midday meal Jago came over.

'Have you noticed how quiet it is?' she asked.

'You mean apart from the camels growling and Antonia's prattle?'

Caseley's giggle surprised them both. 'Yes, apart from that. The camels' feet make no noise, not like horses. The saddles creak a bit. But mostly there's just the sound of the wind.'

'Quite a contrast to Cairo and Alexandria.'

'It reminds me of *Cygnet* at night. The wind in the rigging, the hiss of water against the hull.'

'Why at night?'

'Because during the day Martin is crashing pans in the galley shack, you or Nathan are calling sail changes, and Hammer and Jimbo bicker like a couple of old women.'

Jago's eyes gleamed as he laughed. 'You're right. I'm so used to it I don't notice.'

When they set off again, Sabra moved her camel to ride beside Sheikh Imad. Antonia would have joined them but one of the bodyguards positioned himself between her and them. With Jago and Pawlyn already deep in conversation, Caseley urged her camel up to Antonia's by tapping its rump gently with her stick.

'Have you ever visited a Bedouin camp before?'

'No. Why would I? Sheikh Imad's life is not in the desert, it is in Cairo and Alexandria.'

'Surely he will make visits to his people if only to take them news of political developments?'

Antonia shrugged. 'Perhaps. But I doubt he would stay long.' After a few beats of silence she turned to Caseley with barely-suppressed excitement. 'I am hoping to be introduced to some of his relatives.'

'It is a great honour to be–' About to say *invited*, Caseley remembered that their journey was being made at Jago's request. 'Allowed to attend such an important family occasion.'

'This is my chance to show Sheikh Imad how

179

well I would fit into his life.'

'Might you not find it difficult to adjust to constant travel without the conveniences you take for granted in the city?'

'Surely you cannot imagine he lives as a nomad?' Antonia's expression reflected her astonishment. 'Of course he doesn't. But even if he did have to spend some time in the desert, he would have a luxurious tent and scores of servants to take care of domestic details. I was my father's hostess for years until Maud Williamson got her claws into him. I am perfectly aware of the demands of protocol.'

'I don't doubt that for a moment. You could probably host a dinner party of English diplomats and their wives with one hand tied behind your back. But didn't the Sheikha tell us that in Bedouin society the lives of men and woman are more separate?'

Antonia didn't try to hide her impatience. 'Sheikh Imad is highly educated. He speaks several languages and moves in government circles. Naturally, he will attend family weddings and such. That he takes time to do so reflects well on him. But he will be more comfortable in the city than the desert. You must take my word for this, Caseley. I have a great deal more experience than you, who knows nothing of Egypt.'

Caseley realised further discussion was pointless and might cause a quarrel. She would not risk embarrassing Sabra or Sheikh Imad.

'You're right. I know very little. I am learning more each day, but there is such a lot to take in. If I offended you, I am truly sorry.'

180

Her irritation dissolving like morning mist in sunshine, Antonia smiled. 'Perhaps I spoke hastily. I confess I am a little nervous. Sheikh Imad has been very different since we set off, not himself at all.'

'That's hardly surprising,' Caseley said gently, anxious not to provoke. Until he has spoken to the elders he won't know if they will accept the British Government's proposal, or what demands they might make if they do.'

Antonia thought this over. 'You could be right. May I ask how long have you been married?'

'It will be eight years in December.' During those years she had changed from a girl into a woman; been blessed with countless joys and suffered devastating loss. She and Jago had shared thoughts, concerns and secrets in total trust. His betrayal had rocked her world.

Antonia nodded. 'That's a long time. So you may have forgotten what it feels like to be in love.' The sympathy on her face told Caseley she was serious.

Torn between laughter and tears, tempted to retort that she had known love Antonia could not even begin to imagine, Caseley lowered her gaze. 'Oh, I think I can remember.'

Chapter Fourteen

Late that afternoon they reached a small oasis with date palms, scrubby bushes and a well protected by a rough wall.

The riding camels were quickly unsaddled. Using a leather bucket on a rope, one of the servants drew enough water to fill a shallow basin in the rocks. The camels crowded round and the basin was refilled several times.

When they had drunk their fill they were led away and their halters tied to a rope between two of the trees, where a mix of scrub and fodder had been tossed down.

Two guards remained on watch. The other two watered the pack animals. Robert Pawlyn carried Antonia's camera boxes to a flat space away from the well and the animals. She set up the tripod.

A fire had been lit and Caseley breathed in the scent of wood smoke.

A servant brought over a full water pot. Watching Sabra rinse her hands, face and feet before replacing her sandals, Caseley did the same. Though the palm trees and well indicated a permanent source of water, it was still used sparingly.

She had just replaced her sandals when she saw Sheikh Imad and two of his bodyguards disappearing around a bend in the wadi, all three carrying rifles.

'Where are they going?' she asked Jago as he

joined her.

'Hunting. How are you?'

'Hot, tired and I would love a bath. But I am comfortable on my camel now.'

'I'm going to see if I can find some wood. I need to find my land legs. Would you like to come?' As she nodded, Jago continued, 'Miss Collingwood wants to take photographs and requires Pawlyn to carry her tripod.'

'I don't think he minds.' Caseley bent to pick up a lumpy, desiccated chunk.

'Here, let me.'

She passed it to him, then found another piece among the rocks. Sabra told us that when there is heavy rain it carries a lot of debris. But–' She looked back down the wadi.

'What?'

'She also said water is scarce here in the Eastern Desert. There aren't many wells. So those that there are will be visited regularly, by Bedouin passing along on their way to wherever they are going.'

'Yes. So?'

'So they will do what we are doing, gather fuel for their cooking fire to make what they are carrying last longer.'

'What is worrying you, Caseley?'

'We have just gathered an armful. It can't have been here long or other people would already have picked it up.'

Realisation softened his expression. 'You believe there may have been a recent flood?'

She nodded.

'If that is so, then surely the chance of another one occurring any time soon must be very small?'

Caseley smiled, shaking her head as she relaxed. 'You're right. I should have thought of that. It's just–' Suddenly her throat closed on a choking lump. She dare not speak; afraid her voice might betray her. She lifted one shoulder and turned away, pretending to look for more wood.

'Everything is so different?'

She nodded. It was easier to agree. It was also true. But wearing strange clothes, riding a camel, eating with her fingers and sleeping on the ground were nothing compared to the upheaval inside her when she was with him.

A shot rang out, making her jump as it echoed off the rocky heights. She whirled to meet his sombre gaze.

He smiled, but she could see it cost him effort.

'That's probably Sheikh Imad with dinner. We had better go back.'

A few minutes after they arrived and Jago dropped the wood beside the fire, the Sheikh returned, with one of his guards carrying the carcass of a small gazelle over his shoulder.

While the servants skinned, gutted and butchered the carcass, stones were heated in the fire. The joints were wrapped in date palm leaves, then placed on the stones and covered with hot embers. Soon the smell of roasting meat drifted over their camp and Caseley felt her stomach cramp.

For months she had eaten at Rosina's insistence. On the boat she ate because after her collapse she needed to regain her strength and, after their arrival in Alexandria, to maintain it. Hunger felt strange.

She sat on her saddle blanket beside Sabra. 'Sheikha, how should I greet the women in whose tent we'll be staying? Mr Pawlyn taught me to say *as-salaamu-aleikoum*, and to respond to anyone who greets me with *wa-aleikum as-salaam*. I know please is *min fadlak*, and thank you is *shukran*.'

Sabra patted her hand. 'That will do very well. Few English take the trouble to learn. Miss Collingwood and Mr Pawlyn are unusual.'

Antonia beamed at the compliment and sent Caseley a triumphant look that said *I told you so.*

The meat was tender and delicious. They ended the meal with mint tea and dates.

'I do like these,' Caseley said, taking another.

'The date palm is a truly miraculous tree,' Sabra said. 'As well as being tasty and nutritious, dates can be used as medicine.'

'How?' Caseley asked.

'Dates, figs, raisins and hibiscus are boiled in water. When the liquid is strained and cooled it is drunk as a remedy for congestion in the chest. Empty fruit bunches are dried and used as brooms. The leaves can be used as fences or woven into baskets, and the beaten stalks are turned into rope.'

'It was branches from the date palm that Christians placed on the roadway when Christ entered Jerusalem,' Antonia announced to Caseley's surprise.

'On Easter Sunday we were given crosses made out of dried palm leaves,' Caseley said. 'But I never knew they were from date palms.'

That night, in spite of the hard ground, she slept deeply. But waking soon after sunrise, with a dull headache, she felt grimy and unsettled. The servants were up, moving quietly about, tending the camels and rekindling the fire.

Seeing one returning from the well with two water pots, Caseley pushed her arms through the slits in her heavy cloak, grabbed her soap, face-cloth and comb from the striped bag, and hurried to intercept him.

'*Min fadlak?*' she pointed to one of the pots, speaking softly, anxious not to disturb the others. 'I won't use much.' He shook his head and shrugged, clearly not understanding. So Caseley held up her hand showing her forefinger and thumb with an inch between them. 'Only a little,' she repeated in French.

Shaking his head again he passed her the pot, bowed, and left. She crossed to the rocks. The air was still chilly.

Removing her cloak, headband and scarf she washed her face and neck. As she shivered, she reminded herself of the heat that would beat down on them as the sun climbed higher.

Aware that Sabra or Antonia might appear at any moment, she pulled her arms free of her sleeves and, still covered by the loose black garment, washed as much as she could reach. Goose-pimples rose on her skin and she clenched her teeth to stop them chattering.

Quickly combing her hair, she repinned the coil then replaced her scarf and tucked one end into the headband. With her soap and facecloth wrapped in the towel, she returned to the camp. Her headache banished by the cold water, she felt calmer. *She could get through this one hour at a time.*

186

'Where have you been?' Antonia demanded.

'To the rocks. I took some water with me and had a wash.'

'Sabra's over there somewhere. Weren't you cold?' Antonia hunched her shoulders.

'Yes, but it was worth it. I'll just go and refill the pot.'

'That's what the servants are for.'

'They have enough to do and I don't mind.'

'Really, Caseley–'

She walked away, aware it was rude – but her fragile balance could not bear any more of Antonia's criticisms or complaints. Glancing across, she saw Jago rolling up his thick coat as he talked to Robert Pawlyn.

Breakfast was fresh bread and dates. Offered coffee, she smiled and shook her head.

'Don't you like it?' Sabra asked.

'I love the smell. But–' One hand went to her tender stomach. 'For me it is too strong.'

Sabra beckoned one of the servants over and murmured to him. Bowing, he left.

Caseley looked across and saw Jago watching her. Seated between him and Sheikh Imad, Pawlyn said something and he turned away to respond.

The servant returned and offered her a glass of milk. It was warm and frothy.

'All Bedouin drink camel's milk,' Sabra said. 'It is very good for the digestion.'

From the corner of her eye Caseley saw Antonia's nose wrinkle. She raised the glass and sipped. 'It tastes – different, but very pleasant.' She emptied the glass in a few swallows and saw

Sabra nod approval. Better still, her stomach, so tender on waking, now felt soothed.

Twenty minutes later, water jars refilled, dung collected in bags to be dried for fuel, and camels re-saddled, they set off. Caseley looked back at the remains of their fire, the only sign they had been there.

It was late morning when, to her great relief, they stopped for a comfort break.

'What kind of arrangements will there be at the camp?' Antonia asked as she, Sabra and Caseley returned to their camels.

'At some *bayts* women dig a pit a little way from the tent and screen it with a blanket of woven palm leaves. Men find privacy among the rocks. They do this away from women, so you need not fear embarrassment.'

The horror on Antonia's face made Caseley glad she was familiar with *Cygnet's* bucket-and-chuck-it simplicity.

'I didn't expect it to be quite so – basic,' Antonia whispered as Sabra left them to speak briefly to Sheikh Imad.

What did you expect at a temporary camp in the desert? Caseley knew better than to ask. 'It's only for a few days.'

'I daresay you will be quite content,' Antonia sniffed. 'But I am used to modern conveniences. Our apartment in the Consulate had piped water *and* flushing lavatories.'

Caseley had heard Robert Pawlyn telling Jago that Khedive Ismail had employed an army of civil engineers to install piped water, gas and a sewer system in the European quarters of Alexandria

188

and Cairo. But for the vast majority of Egyptians in both cities there were no such luxuries.

'Then you will appreciate them even more when you return home,' Caseley said lightly, and walked away to her camel.

Two hours later, after picking their way down a path through a rocky canyon, they emerged onto a flat, gravelly plain. A third of it was already covered by a sprawl of brown tents.

Caseley's first impression was of heat, dust, noise, and the combined smells of dung fires, coffee, roasting meat and animals.

On the far side in a gully, a clump of date palms and women carrying pots indicated a spring or well.

She started as half a dozen grubby, dust-streaked children burst from a gap between two tents, shouting and laughing as they vanished behind another. She saw older boys carrying fodder or armfuls of wood and scrub. Slim girls carried water pots or babies on their hips. One swung a toddler who shrieked with delight.

Her vision splintered and the wrenching pain in her chest stopped her breath. She had been so focused on Jago's mission she had forgotten this would be a gathering of families. She blinked hard, wiped her eyes with the end of her scarf, and sat straighter on her camel.

'What's the matter?' Antonia whispered.

'Nothing. It's just the dust.' *She must not embarrass Jago.*

Their arrival had been noticed. As Sabra moved her camel so she was behind Sheikh Imad and his bodyguards, women quickly covered their noses and mouths with their scarves. Those whose hands were full turned their heads away.

'That's hardly a warm welcome.'

At Antonia's peevish remark, Caseley sucked in a breath. 'I think it's because we're strangers,' she whispered back. She had insisted on coming. Now she must cope.

Sheikh Imad and his entourage preceded Jago and Pawlyn across the space, heading towards a large tent at the front, where men sat on rugs in a semi-circle around a fire with two brass coffee pots.

Stopping a short distance away they made the camels kneel, then dismounted. The men rose to their feet as the Sheikh approached.

Sabra halted further back and as Caseley slid down and surreptitiously flexed her back and shoulders, she saw Imad greeted with bows and a kiss on each cheek from the men. The Sheikh introduced Jago and Pawlyn. When the elders offered their hands to be shaken, Caseley released the breath she hadn't realised she'd been holding.

The Sheikh indicated the waiting women. As the elders looked across, Sabra bowed her head politely. Caseley quickly did the same. The man to whom Imad had been speaking gave a brief nod, and Sabra turned away.

'Come.'

'Where are we going?' Antonia asked.

'To meet our hostess.' Two young men ran to take their camels and Sabra led Caseley and Antonia round the side of the tent.

Raised on numerous poles braced with ropes, and high enough even for Jago to stand upright, the tent was made of strips of woven camel hair. Inside, a wall of heavier fabric separated the men's area at the front from this part. More hangings with zigzag patterns divided the women's quarters into separate rooms. Some of the hangings were pinned back to allow free passage of air and Caseley glimpsed rugs, small chests, folded blankets and decorated cushions.

An awning, formed from one tent wall propped on two poles, offered welcome shade for several women seated near a fire burning in a shallow pit. Amid the embers stood three large stones, on which rested a large flat metal plate. Beside them were water pots, pewter mugs, a long-necked brass coffee pot, a large bowl and several small sacks.

The women looked up. Seeing strangers they immediately covered their faces. But as Sabra greeted the older woman in the centre, Caseley saw recognition then pleasure. Quickly on her feet, with the others following, the woman greeted Sabra with delight and kisses. Aware she was being studied, Caseley smiled and nodded politely as they murmured among themselves.

Beckoning Caseley and Antonia forward, Sabra introduced them. Antonia gave the Arabic greeting and received the response. Caseley knew her own attempt sounded clumsy and didn't mind the half-smiles when the women responded.

Their dusty black robes had red cross-stitching like hers. Like her, they wore the folded headband with one end of their scarves tucked into the top. Wide sleeves were rolled halfway up brown forearms, and two had a length of fabric tied around their waists like a sash.

The woman who had greeted Sabra jabbered away in Arabic. Sabra thanked her. She turned to Caseley and Antonia. 'I have to go and visit other *bayts*. You may come if you wish.'

Caseley appreciated Sabra's invitation, but did not want to intrude. 'May I stay here? I would like to help if that would be permitted?'

Sabra's brows climbed. 'You're sure you want to?'

'Oh yes. As we will be eating here it seems only fair to contribute in some way. If they don't mind.'

Sabra spoke to the woman, who looked from her to Caseley and back.

'Caseley, we are guests,' Antonia hissed in English.

'Yes we are, and Bedouin laws of hospitality guarantee us food and a place to sleep. But we're not family. Nor were we expected.'

Caseley turned and saw Sabra watching. 'Did I do wrong?' she asked in French. 'I didn't intend any offence.'

'None is taken,' Sabra said. 'In fact, you could not have acted more wisely.'

Sitting down again, the woman gestured to the space beside her. Caseley sat on the woven cloth and folded her sleeves back. Tearing a piece of dough from the large lump in a metal bowl, the woman swiftly and expertly flipped it between her palms into a flat oval then slapped it onto the hot metal plate.

'Sheikha, will you ask her if I may wash first?' Caseley lifted her grubby hands.

Sabra pointed. 'Take it from the pot. But only use a little.'

Aware of being watched as she tipped water into her palm, Caseley rubbed her hands, used a little more to rinse then, having no towel, dried her hands on her skirt.

'Honestly, Caseley,' Antonia sighed. 'Is this how you live at home?'

Forcing a smile, Caseley replied in English. 'We're a long way from the city, Antonia. Surely you realised life out here would be different from what you're used to?'

'I certainly didn't expect this. You can play housewife if you wish. I must go and fetch my camera.'

Sabra spoke to their hostess who glanced at Antonia and shook her head. Sabra asked something else. Caseley didn't need to understand the language to recognise the answer as a definite no.

The woman indicated the flour sack and waited for Caseley to dip her fingers in and spread a little over her palms. Tearing off two more pieces of dough, she gave one to Caseley and kept the other for herself.

Copying the woman's quick hand movements, Caseley achieved a flattened ragged circle. The woman nodded, smiled, and pointed to the metal plate.

'Bravo,' Sabra smiled. Leaving the tent, she called to Antonia who had stopped to look for someone. *Sheikh Imad.* Caseley watched them for a moment then was nudged and returned her attention to the dough.

She was glad to have something to do. The women were bound to talk among themselves. Perhaps her willingness to make herself useful

193

would filter back, make the elders better disposed towards Jago. She mocked her presumption.

Antonia clearly disapproved of her offer. Why couldn't she see that English conventions didn't apply here? Had she been willing to spend an hour or two helping prepare food, the woman might have responded to her differently.

Offering help, which had been readily accepted, generated goodwill that might benefit them in other ways. She'd have expected Antonia to recognise that. How ironic that her focus on her photography had blinded her to the wider picture.

As she concentrated, gaining confidence and speed, the pile of cooked flatbreads grew. When the woman glanced at her, nodding approval, Caseley wondered why Sabra had not told her their names. She pointed to herself with a floury forefinger.

'Caseley.'

The woman shrugged and shook her head.

Caseley tapped her chest, leaving a floury fingerprint. 'Caseley.' Then she indicated to the woman and raised her eyebrows.

'Ah.' The woman's frown cleared. Nodding, she pointed at herself. 'Fayruz.'

'Fayruz,' Caseley repeated and won a smile.

Fayruz spoke to the others then told Caseley their names. Caseley thanked her, looking at each woman as she repeated. 'Rashida, Zainab, Noor.'

Sabra returned with Antonia. Behind them, the servants put down her camera boxes and tripod then disappeared. As the women stood, in recognition of the Sheikha's rank, Caseley scrambled to her feet.

'How are you getting on?'

'Very well. I have learned how to make and cook flatbread and we now know each other's names, though I'm not sure of the relationships.'

'Excellent,' Sabra's smile held approval. 'Rashida is Fayruz's mother, Noor is her divorced sister, and Zainab is her daughter-in-law.' She spoke to Fayruz, who led her to one of the partitioned areas. Sabra beckoned Caseley and Antonia. 'This is where we will sleep. Sheikh Imad's servants are bringing our bags and camel saddles.'

Taking Fayruz's arm, Sabra walked with her to the awning, talking quietly.

'It's not very big,' Antonia grumbled.

'There's plenty of space for three,' Caseley whispered. 'Considering we weren't expected, Fayruz is showing great hospitality.'

'They have to. It's one of their rules.'

Caseley clamped her mouth shut. Though Antonia was right, she was missing the point.

'What am I supposed to do with my camera boxes?'

'Stand one on top of the other in that corner with the tripod propped upright between them and the tent pole. Or,' she continued as Antonia opened her mouth to argue, 'you could lay the tripod down flat, make a pad with your saddle blankets and use it as a pillow. We'll manage, Antonia. We have to. We are of no importance. Sheikh Imad is here for the wedding of his cousin, and to persuade the elders to listen to my husband.'

Antonia's eyes had widened in surprise. 'You're right. It's just–'

'Shall we see if our blankets and bags are here

195

yet? If we make things comfortable now, we won't be stumbling around in the dark.'

As she led the way out, Caseley's overriding emotion was relief that she would not have to sleep wearing her scarf and headband to keep her hair hidden.

The following morning, after a breakfast of goat's milk yoghurt sweetened with a little honey, dates and camel's milk, Caseley went with Fayruz to the latrine, then to the spring-fed well. She washed her hands and face, dried them with the end of her scarf, and took the pots as Fayruz filled them.

As they walked back to the tent Caseley noticed that though the camels were penned in one area, they were tethered in separate groups. Men moved among them, talking as they stroked the huge beasts with easy familiarity.

During the day more people arrived. Once again, Sabra was greeted with kisses and deference. After courtesies were exchanged she introduced Caseley and Antonia.

Having managed to get her tongue around the Bedouin dialect, Caseley had been quietly practising her greetings and responses. Her efforts were met with surprise and pleasure.

As the women dispersed to meet others and set up their tents, Antonia announced that she was going to take some photographs of the trees at the well.

'As women and children will be there that would not be wise,' Sabra said. 'Take some of the animals or of the landscape. It has a stark beauty few ever see.'

'But–'

'Upsetting our hosts will end Captain Barata's mission and reflect badly on Sheikh Imad.'

Flushing, Antonia marched away carrying her camera box and tripod. Caseley took her place beside Fayruz and settled to making flatbreads. At one side of the awning a tripod of curved poles had been erected and a goatskin suspended between them.

She watched Zainab carefully pour a large pot of fresh goat's milk into the skin at the neck end. When she had emptied the pot of milk, she blew air into the skin several times then quickly tied the neck closed with a leather thong. As she moved away, one of the young girls sat down and began to shake the goatskin to and fro to separate the curds from the whey.

Later, returning from the latrine, she saw Jago walking from the camel pen with two of the elders and Richard Pawlyn. Her heart leapt.

Seeing her, he murmured something to Pawlyn who spoke to the elders. They nodded and she saw their teeth flash in their dark faces as they waved Jago away.

'It seems a long time since I've seen you,' he said as he reached her. He started to lift his hand, then withdrew it without touching her. 'Are you comfortable?'

She nodded. 'Fayruz is very kind. We have part of the tent to ourselves. How are discussions going?'

'Slowly. Many people must have their say, and there are constant interruptions and diversions. I'm not sure which way it will go.' He studied her, suddenly intense. 'I wish–' Then his mouth twisted and he shrugged. 'I should get back.'

He returned to Sheikh Imad's uncle's tent where Pawlyn waited and the discussions resumed.

'The elders are angry that Turco-Circassian landowners are encroaching on tribal land,' Pawlyn quietly translated. 'Some believe this is a good reason to take the gold and give their backing to the English. But others question whether the English would respect their traditional rights any more than the current ruling class does. They want to know what assurances you can give.'

'None,' Jago muttered. 'I have no authority to make promises on such matters. Don't translate that. It makes us look weak. Just wait.'

The elders talked among themselves some more, then one looked across and asked a question.

'He wants to know why they should support the English.'

Jago bowed politely before replying. 'Tell him that the English have created financial stability in a country whose own rulers had brought it to the brink of ruin. Britain has a major shareholding in the Suez Canal, and British trade is vital to Egypt's economy. The relationship between the two countries is important to both, and of benefit to both.'

Pawlyn translated. While the elders were talking, two left and three more arrived. They were greeted and offered coffee. While they were informed of discussions so far, several of the men began talking among themselves.

Used to accepting responsibility and making quick decisions, Jago kept his features expressionless as he fought growing impatience.

An hour later, with nothing resolved, youths brought over huge platters of spiced rice and goat meat.

All over the camp men were cooking their own food and eating together. Despite being used to all-male shipboard life, it seemed strange to him that men and women of an extended family, sharing the same tent, should live so separately and independently of each other.

When not at sea, his happiest times were those spent with Caseley, discussing their future plans, the business, the boys. But all that had been *before*.

This past year had been... A shudder rippled through him. Quickly disguising it by shifting as if to make himself more comfortable, he murmured '*Shukran*' as a dark-eyed youth handed him a tiny cup then filled it with freshly brewed cardamom-flavoured coffee.

'Now it is time for stories,' Pawlyn whispered.

'What kind of stories?'

'Historic tribal raids and epic battles.'

As one of the elders spoke, the others fell silent, listening intently. As Pawlyn translated, Jago was caught up in the tale. After two more stories Imad gestured to Jago. Through Pawlyn one of the elders asked if he had taken part in battles.

'My battles have been against the sea.' Urged to continue, he described a fierce storm, the sea streaked with foam torn from breaking waves by a wind that screamed like souls in torment as it shredded canvas and tried to drive the ship down into the dark ocean depths. They watched him closely, listening to Pawlyn's translation.

'Every time I leave harbour and set out on another voyage, I recite the seaman's prayer, "God be kind to me. Your sea is so wide and my boat is so small".'

As Pawlyn finished, Jago saw a lot of nodding and more coffee was poured.

'After I started it occurred to me that some of these men may never have seen the sea,' he murmured to Pawlyn.

'That doesn't matter. You described a battle. Better yet, it is a battle against the elements, testing your courage as well as your skill. You made a good impression.'

'Let's hope it may weigh in the discussions.'

Pawlyn was watching the two elders opposite. When they rose, the others did too.

'Up,' Pawlyn muttered and Jago stood. 'There'll be no more discussions tonight, at least not officially. The wedding celebrations are about to begin. We are invited to the groom's father's tent to watch intricate designs being painted on the groom's hands and feet with henna. It's an important tradition.'

Refusal was out of the question. So when Sheikh Imad beckoned Jago bowed politely to the elders, then followed.

'Henna symbolises beauty, good fortune and good health,' Sabra explained as she led them into the bride's mother's tent, where women from both bride's and groom's families had gathered to help decorate the bride's hands and legs.

'I don't understand why I can't take photographs,' Antonia grumbled. 'We're all women.'

'Yes, but we're not family. We're very privileged to be invited.'

'We can't see anything. It's too crowded.'

Caseley was content to remain near the entrance where it was cooler and less noisy. 'I understand you being disappointed.'

'No, you don't,' Antonia snapped. 'You have no idea. You're not artistic. You're just a housewife, happy making endless piles of bread.'

Caseley thought back to the months she had run her father's business during his final illness, keeping her efforts secret from everyone, including him. She recalled the day that Jago, a man used to controlling everything in his life, handed her total responsibility for refurbishing the house he had inherited, the house that was now their home. He had trusted her to hire and oversee tradesmen and left the choice of colours, fabrics, carpets and furnishings to her. When it was finished he had approved the result, saying he had expected nothing less.

Antonia moved away through the press of teasing, laughing women. Sabra watched her go.

'She's upset,' Caseley explained.

'Indeed.'

'It's – things are not as she hoped.'

'They are what they are. She had no right to expect differently. And you? Are you disappointed?'

Caseley smiled at her. 'How could I be? I have met such kindness. Being welcomed into the tent, permitted to help prepare food. Antonia mistook that for a menial task, not something expected of a guest. In England she would be right, but not here. Here it is a gesture of acceptance. I find that humbling.'

'Yet she was born in Egypt. You have been here less than a month.'

Caseley shrugged. 'I suspect my upbringing was very different from hers.'

'Be glad of it.'

Chapter Fifteen

The following morning, after breakfast, Caseley went with Sabra and Antonia to the bride's father's tent which had a black roof and striped side cloths.

A coffee hearth had been scooped out of the dusty ground in front of the men's area. Coffee pots, a stone mortar and pestle for grinding coffee beans and cardamom seeds, and a roasting pan were lined up to one side of the fire. There were rugs on the ground and camel saddles to lean against.

Already the breeze carried the aroma of roasting meat from a cooking fire near the groom's father's tent, where a number of young men were busy with knives and cooking pots.

The women's area of the tent was already crowded. Caseley followed Sabra who was easing her way through a press of women, all talking and laughing. Though she understood only the occasional word, Caseley guessed this was a rare and welcome opportunity to catch up with family news.

Finally, she was close enough to see the young bride. Wearing a dress of red silk, richly decorated on the front and down the sleeves with cross-stitching, she was seated on a large, embroidered cushion. Her eyes were outlined with kohl and around her throat hung several large silver pendants studded with amber, turquoise, coral and pearls.

Standing on either side of her, two women dipped their fingers into pots held by helpful friends. Spreading the salve over their palms they smoothed it onto the bride's head, then combed it through her long hair.

'What's that?' Caseley whispered to Sabra.

'Herbal mixtures to make the hair smell nice.'

The women began braiding the bride's hair into many shiny plaits.

Another woman came forward with a tiny pot of golden powder and dabbed some on the bride's ears, cheeks and neck.

'Powdered saffron,' Sabra said, before Caseley could ask. 'It is very expensive and indicates the family's wealth.'

In front of the bride, more jewellery, folded clothes and a small, carved chest were displayed beside woven blankets, cooking pans and utensils, dishes, small tea glasses, coffee and tea pots.

The sun was high and, though the tent walls had been rolled up to allow air to circulate, the crush of women made it uncomfortably stuffy.

Caseley touched Sabra's arm. 'Will you excuse me? I need some air.'

'I'll come with you.'

'Please don't. This is an important occasion

and you should be with your family and friends.'

'I'll take her,' Antonia said, grasping Caseley's arm and pushing her towards the opening.

'You didn't need to leave.' Outside Caseley drew a deep breath. Though the intense summer heat of Cairo was tempered by altitude, it was still very warm.

'I'd had enough anyway. I'm sure they were talking about us.'

'Why would they? This is probably the biggest family gathering in months. It's also for a wedding. That's far more important than us.'

'There's Imad!' Antonia's irritation vanished.

Looking across, recognising Jago, Caseley felt her heart lift. It seemed such a long time since she had seen him.

As Antonia raised her arm to wave, Caseley grabbed it.

'What are you doing? Let me go.'

Releasing her at once, Caseley said, 'He will not thank you for attracting attention.'

'For heaven's sake, Caseley. What makes you such an expert?'

Had Antonia learned nothing here?

Jago acknowledged her with a nod, then spoke to Sheikh Imad who looked across.

Caseley remained where she was. If they were on their way to further discussions, Jago would not have time to talk. But Antonia wasn't willing to wait and was already hurrying towards them. After another brief exchange, Jago left the Sheikh. Caseley went to meet him.

'I'm sorry if we distracted you.'

'You are always a welcome sight.'

She wanted so much to believe him. 'We have just visited the bride. She looked beautiful, and a little overwhelmed. Obviously I could not understand what was being said, but it looked as if everyone was offering her advice. It was very crowded and noisy so I came out for some air.'

'Miss Collingwood doesn't appear to be enjoying herself.'

'She's upset because she hasn't been permitted to take photographs.'

He made no attempt to hide his impatience. 'Why would she expect otherwise?'

Anxious not to waste this brief time together, she asked, 'Are you making progress?'

'I believe so. Formal discussions have finished until after the wedding.' She followed his glance towards groups of men making their way from the outlying tents of recent arrivals towards a large *bayt*.

'All the important leaders of the tribe are gathering at the groom's father's tent to drink tea and coffee, offer their congratulations, and present gifts to the bridegroom and his father. Then we will be eating. I'm told that after the marriage ceremony the bride will be taken to her new husband's tent and won't be seen for the rest of the celebrations.'

'After so much preparation and so many people I imagine she will welcome some quiet time.'

'You never liked crowds.' He brushed her cheek with his fingertips. Unexpected, it stopped her breath. 'Are you finding it very difficult?'

'Less than when we arrived. Fayruz and her family have been very kind. Though in some ways things are very different here, in others – people are people wherever they live. They care about their families, enjoy a wedding, love their children–' she cleared a sudden thickness from her throat. 'I've learned a lot, even a few words of Bedouin dialect, though my efforts sound as if I have a cough.' She looked across to where the Sheikh stood, as still as a rock, while Antonia talked and gestured. Jago followed her gaze.

'Is she giving you trouble?'

Caseley hesitated. 'Not exactly. It's just – she doesn't seem to realise that our behaviour here reflects on Sabra and Sheikh Imad.'

'You would be welcome anywhere.'

Spoken as a simple statement of fact, his words warmed her more than any flowery compliment. 'You should go.'

'Later I will leave the Sheikh to talk privately with the tribal leaders. Will you meet me?'

'Where?'

'I'll find you.'

When the food was ready – rice cooked in broth and goat meat simmered in a spiced yoghurt sauce – the young people of the two families carried platters first to the tents of the bride and groom's fathers, then to other nearby tents. As always, men and women ate separately. Sitting with Sabra and Antonia, Caseley heard lively conversation and laughter from every part of the camp.

'When will the ceremony take place?' Antonia asked.

'After the meal. It is very brief, just a formality,' Sabra said. 'The bridal contract was arranged some time ago in front of witnesses and Sheikh Imad's uncle.'

After the meal, platters and dishes were gathered up, the fragrance of fresh coffee filled the air, and trays of honey and almond cakes were passed around.

Then everyone followed the bridegroom's family walking in procession to the bride's father's tent, singing songs accompanied by a one-stringed violin and drums.

The women of the bride's family had displayed all the gifts given to her by the groom's family on several blankets spread on the ground at the front of the tent. The guests proceeded past, adding their gifts. The most important was a female camel and her calf. Others were three sheep, two nanny goats with kids, sacks of rice, engraved platters and money.

'The bride and groom give their promise separately,' Sabra whispered. 'They do not see each other until he takes her to his tent.'

Caseley thought back to her own wedding, standing with Jago as they made their vows. She couldn't watch any more and edged away from the chattering women as a handsome camel with a decorated halter and tent-like structure over the saddle was led forward. The bride was helped onto the saddle, the cloth folded around her like curtains, and she was led away to her new husband's tent surrounded by the women of both families singing and clapping.

A small boy stood by himself; left behind as the women crowded round the bride's camel. He couldn't have been more than three, the same age as her younger son James had been when... Caseley felt a tearing wrench in her chest.

His little face puckered, his eyes widening in panic as he realised his mother wasn't coming back. He started running towards the women, tripped over a stone and fell flat on his face.

Caseley was already running, her limp making her ungainly. After an instant's shock he struggled to his feet, howling in shock and pain. But his shriek was lost beneath the women's high-pitched ululating cries.

She scooped him up, cooing comforting words he couldn't understand. Gradually his screams subsided to hiccupping sobs as he peered at the blood on his scraped knee. Telling him what a brave boy he was, she dabbed away his tears with one end of her head cloth then wiped the blood from his grubby knee and kissed it better.

He stared at her, his brown eyes awash, tears tracking down his dusty face, small chin quivering. She wiped his eyes again then brushed the end of the cloth lightly against his nose. He smiled and pushed it away. She tickled him gently and started to put him down. But he clung, arms and legs tightening around her.

So she limped to and fro with him on her hip, holding one grubby little hand in hers as she sang the lullabies she used to sing to her boys. He tucked his head between her neck and shoulder and the weight of the little body in her arms breached the carefully built dam. Memories overwhelmed her. A sob made her chest heave. Anxious not to frighten him, she bit hard on her bottom lip, too hard, and tasted the warm saltiness of blood.

Hearing Sabra call her name she turned to see a group of women approaching. One hurried forward and the little boy reached out.

Caseley handed him over and quickly dashed away her tears. She ran her tongue over her lip, felt the soreness and swelling. 'He fell. Please–' she cleared her throat. 'Please tell her I meant no harm.'

'She knows that,' Sabra said as the women murmured among themselves.

'What have you done?' Antonia demanded. 'Why is your lip bleeding?'

'I bit it,' Caseley said. 'It's nothing. Will you excuse me?'

'Where are you going?' Antonia demanded.

'For a walk. The noise – I have a slight head-ache.'

'Come,' Sabra cupped Antonia's elbow and drew her away.

Caseley walked to the well. She could still feel the weight of the toddler in her arms, the warmth of his little body against hers. Her babies. Her beautiful sons. The pain was unbearable. She scooped up cold water. Pressing wet hands to her burning face she fought the sobs that would wreck her if she gave in to them.

She bathed her face again then dried it with the end of her scarf. Her lip throbbed. Seeing a young man coming towards the well, she moved away towards the camel pen and paused to look at the regal animals.

Some stood, others had their long legs tucked beneath them and gazed about with stately disdain as they chewed, their jaws working one way then the other. Several of the females had long-legged, curly-coated youngsters with them.

She had to go back. To stay away any longer, especially on a day of celebration, might appear discourteous. Her breath shuddered in her chest. Her face felt tight and her eyes stung. But they were dry.

She started walking towards the camp then stumbled as she saw Jago with Antonia pressed against his front. She froze, light-headed with shock.

'*No.*'

The sound of her own voice startled her. She whirled around and walked away.

'Caseley!'

Ignoring his roar she carried on walking. She heard running footsteps. Her arm was grasped. Violently she wrenched free.

He caught her shoulder, turned her towards him. 'God in heaven, what happened to your lip?'

'You care?'

He stiffened. 'Of course I care.'

'Oh please.' Sick at heart she turned away. But he moved round to face her.

'Tell me what you think you saw.'

'I know what I saw.' Her contempt was withering.

'No, you don't. I know you to be fair and just. So please, allow me to explain.'

Caseley looked away, hugging her arms across her trembling body. Desperate to escape, she had nowhere to go.

'Antonia came out of the tent, clearly upset. I

210

was coming to meet you and mistook— She rushed over and threw herself against me. She was sobbing. I grasped her shoulders to prise her loose. That is what you saw. If you ask her she will tell you the same. She must because it's the truth.'

'Why did Antonia throw herself at you?'

'I don't know. I didn't ask. Nor do I care. I left the gathering to come and meet you. I had no interest in anything else.'

'Did Louise Downing fling herself at you as well?' As the words tumbled out, propelled by intolerable anguish, she saw his shock. 'Did she cling so tight that you were unable to shake her off?'

'That meant nothing.' His voice was harsh.

'It certainly meant something to her. She flaunted her conquest in my face with pride and a pitying sneer. If I count for so little–'

'Don't say that! You could not be more wrong.' He grasped her upper arms, his fingers biting into her flesh, and she glimpsed desperation. 'You are everything to me.'

'I wish with all my heart I could believe that.'

'You can, you must.'

'No, Jago. Your words are worthless if your actions betray them. You say I am fair and just. So if you were driven to find comfort elsewhere I must take some of the blame.'

His bitter laugh made her flinch. *Comfort?* I wanted escape, oblivion. I did not seek comfort. I deserved none. When you needed me I was not there. By the time I got home our sons were buried. You had faced it all alone. Never in my life have I felt so useless. You never spoke a word of reproach, but you had withdrawn from me. I have to live the rest of my life knowing I let you down. How could I comfort you? What had I to offer?' Anguish roughened his voice.

Scalding tears spilled down her cheeks. 'You could have held me. Let me rage and weep, at God, fate, my failure to save them. Had I not cared for them well enough? Were there other treatments, other medicines we could have tried? If I had done all I could why did our boys die when others lived?'

He released his bruising grip and gathered her into his arms. 'Oh Caseley, my dearest–' His voice cracked.

'I was so tired and nearly out of my mind with grief. Yes, and fury. But you were at sea. You didn't know. I did blame you for not being there, even though I knew it was unjust. I could have borne it better had you been with me.'

'I wish you had told me.' His voice was unsteady as he drew her closer, his bearded cheek warm against hers.

'I wanted to. But you were very distant and I was so afraid–'

He raised his head. 'Of what?'

'That you blamed me.'

'How could you ever think so?'

'You never reached for me.'

'I ached for you. But it felt selfish. I wanted to give you time.'

Relief loosened painful knots of tension. 'Oh, Jago.'

Tilting her chin he covered her mouth with his

own, lightly, tenderly, careful of her sore and swollen lip. She felt his quickened heartbeat beneath her palm and knew her own matched it. The sharp crack of a gunshot made her start violently.

'Don't be frightened. Sheikh Imad warned that this is the traditional way the groom lets everyone know he has – that his bride is now his wife.'

'You are teasing me.'

'Indeed I'm not.'

'Goodness. How very–'

'Public?' Jago murmured.

Holding Caseley's hand against his chest, Jago rested his head against hers. She felt his breath warm on her cheek. 'Do you remember when I said you amaze me, and you replied that perhaps I expected too little? You're wrong. I relied on you totally and took you for granted.

'Every time I went away on a voyage I never doubted that you would manage everything in my absence. The image of you that I carried in my mind and my heart gave me strength. Because I had complete faith in you I expected to return and find things the same as when I left. And they were, except the boys were bigger and had learned new things they couldn't wait to show me.

'I was so glad to see you, to be with you again, that regardless of any problems in the business or the yard all was well in my world. You would give me all the news and–' one corner of his mouth tilted in a brief smile, 'a list of matters requiring my attention.' He was quiet for a moment. 'Did you miss me?' The unexpected wistfulness in his tone tugged at her heart.

'Every hour of every day. But it would have

been cruel of me to say so and cause you to worry. You were relying on me. I could not let you down.' Her breath hitched. 'Only I did.'

'No, no, no,' he said softly. He kept his arm around her shoulders as they crossed the stony ground to some low rocks. Daylight had faded to purple dusk and the full moon rose in a rapidly darkening sky. From the camp came the sounds of music, singing and laughter. In the pens sheep and goats bleated and the camels grumbled.

'Rosina, Liza-Jane and Ben were wonderful.'

'So I would expect. I never doubted that all of you did everything you could.' He was silent for a moment. 'You were so fortunate, being with the boys every day. Each time I came back from a voyage they had changed. I imagined them sailing with me when they were older. I had plans to show them the world...' His voice faltered.

Caseley clasped his hand between hers. 'I'm so very sorry.'

'For what?'

'Shutting you out. I was–' *Destroyed*. 'I did not give you the comfort you deserved and should have expected.'

He raised her hand and kissed it. Then he tilted her chin and gently kissed her mouth. He raised his head and in the cold, silvery moonlight his eyes were dark and bottomless. 'Caseley, I–'

She silenced him with a finger against his lips. *Now.* She would face it now. 'I wanted to come to Egypt with you because I don't know who I am any more.'

He started to speak but she wouldn't let him, covering his mouth with her fingertips. 'Please,

214

Jago, let me finish. I have been an outsider since I was twelve years old. I was with my mother in the pony-trap when it overturned and she was killed. Everyone sympathised with my father over the loss of his wife, and with Ralph and me for losing our mother. But I lay awake every night reliving the moment the birds flew out of the hedge and scared the pony. I kept thinking of all the things I might have done.'

Jago shook her gently. 'It happened in seconds. You could not have prevented it. Besides, you were badly injured yourself.'

'I know. But I lived and my mother died. Then when the boys– I wished it had been me. I would willingly have given my life in exchange for theirs.'

'Stop!' His grip tightened painfully. 'Don't say that. I cannot bear–' He started to pull her close but she pressed her palms flat against his chest.

'Wait. Please, you must listen.' She moistened dry lips, fighting to hold her voice level. 'Since the boys died I have been talked about and avoided. When – when Louise Downing made a point of letting me know that you both were once more–'

She broke off, a shaky breath hissing between her teeth.

'I love you, Jago. More than you know. And I always will. But I can't go back to my life as it was. I won't share you. I would sooner leave.'

'And go where?'

'I don't care.'

He eased back. 'So I must choose?'

'It is only a choice if she is important to you. You said she wasn't.'

'I know what I said. You are my wife. You

215

promised obedience.'

'And you promised fidelity.'

Anger then astonishment crossed his face. 'Are you threatening me?'

'I deserve better than to be laughed at or pitied.' Gently detaching herself, she walked away. *What had she done?*

Chapter Sixteen

Jago watched her go, angry, unsettled and afraid. No woman had ever controlled him. How could she say she loved him then talk of leaving? She could not leave. She was his wife. She had a duty– *Duty?* Even as the thought formed it appalled him. She was not a possession, or one of his crew. He could not lose her. Not now. Not ever. He had loved his sons. But she completed him. With her he was a better man. Without her...

He could not imagine his life without her in it.

He had always followed his own star. Women had come and gone from his life. He was a seafarer and sailors ashore took pleasure wherever it was offered. But by birth he was a gentleman. So, lightskirt or lady, he treated them well – and instantly forgot them.

Louise had been a convenience. Their previous liaison had spared him the usual dance that led – inevitably – to mutually satisfying consummation. Only there had been no satisfaction, merely fleeting relief.

He had missed Caseley. Cynics claimed all cats were grey in the dark. For them, perhaps. Not for him. He knew the scent of her skin, the texture of her tumbling hair. He knew the sound of her breathing when she slept, and the catch in her throat when he stroked her.

This journey had shown him her courage. It had reinforced his love for her, his desire to protect, his passion and his need for her. Until her he had never *needed*. Need implied weakness. It made him vulnerable and that scared him. Her accusation that his behaviour shamed him cut deep. It stung and angered because it was true.

Louise had been determined to gain his attention. First she had sent a letter of condolence to the office. Then she had begun meeting him in the street as he walked the length of the town between Greenbank and Bonython's Yard on Bar Road. He had quickly recognised the encounters as contrived rather than chance.

Caseley's desolation, the knowledge that he had failed her when she needed him most, had crucified him with guilt. He could not reach her. But if he had, what comfort could he have offered? What did he say to a loving mother whose sons had died in her arms?

He would have given his life for his boys. Instead theirs had been snuffed out far, far too soon. Caseley had been inconsolable. And he, on whom they all depended, could not retrieve what had been lost nor mend what was broken. So he had sought escape.

He despised himself. Louise might have pushed herself at him, but he had taken advantage of her.

Telling Caseley that Louise meant nothing to him was the brutal truth. He had done nothing unusual. More than half the businessmen in Falmouth had connections outside marriage. Most of the wives knew. But, provided a husband was discreet, they were willing to look the other way.

Not Caseley.

Her defiance shouldn't have surprised him. She had defied convention in so much else. But it had wrong-footed him, and he had reacted as any proud man would when challenged. He was master in his world. Though he listened to his crew and to Toby, the yard foreman, all decisions were his, and his word was law.

But in truth she was right. She did deserve better. From this moment, Louise was out of his life. There would be no others. He wanted – needed – only Caseley.

On this journey her acceptance of demanding conditions had amazed him. He had taken at face value her reassurance that she was comfortable with the Bedouin women because it left him free to focus on discussions with the elders.

This evening, for the first time since – in nearly a year, both of them had bared their souls. Realising how much she meant to him was terrifying.

Returning to the tent where he was staying, he looked for Pawlyn and felt his muscles tighten at the frown on the journalist's face.

'What's wrong?' he asked quietly. 'I thought we were hopeful of agreement.'

The journalist looked up. 'I suspect – actually, I'm almost certain, that hope is as much as we will achieve. You will have to decide whether it is

218

worth leaving the gold here as a token of good faith. Though to take it back with us–'

Jago was already shaking his head. 'We can't. It would be an open admission of failure, and might even be seen as an insult. I'm very aware that few people know we are here. I won't do anything that might jeopardise the safety of – of any of our party. Is that what was worrying you?'

'No, though naturally I am disappointed not to be able to claim unqualified success, especially after all our efforts. The truth is my mind was on something else. Your mission is not the only matter being discussed at this gathering.'

Emotionally exhausted, Caseley slept deeply, undisturbed by the singing and chatter. When she woke soon after sunrise she lay for a few moments, surprised by her calm. Perhaps she was simply numb after such violent emotional upheaval. At last the truth was out. A weight had been lifted. Now it was up to him.

Three hours later, after shaking out rugs and blankets, she watched Zainab open a cloth containing a lump of salted milk solids then break off chunks, roll them into balls and set them on a tray to dry in the sun.

'They are called jameed,' Sabra explained. 'They will keep for a year without spoiling.'

'How do you use them?'

'Break them up and soak the pieces in water overnight. In the morning give the mixture a brisk stir, then it is ready to be added to meat and broth for a yoghurt-based sauce.'

Sabra left, and Caseley took her place beside

Fayruz. She was flipping dough between her palms when Antonia hurried over.

'Caseley, come and sit for me. Please?' she added.

Dusting flour from her hands, Caseley stood up. She held up her splayed fingers to indicate five minutes then realised Fayruz wouldn't know what she meant.

'How do I say in Arabic that I will be back very soon?' she asked, listening carefully while Antonia, openly impatient, rattled off the phrase. Caseley repeated it as best she could. Fayruz nodded, her smile fading as her gaze switched from Caseley to Antonia, then returned to the dough.

'I cannot imagine why you do it.' Antonia headed towards her camera set up on its tripod by the rocks.

'No,' Caseley agreed. She would never tell anyone that after her conversation with Jago she desperately needed an anchor, and found it in sharing domestic jobs with women who accepted her presence as they moved about the tent or chatted around the fire. She felt less of an outsider among Fayruz's family than she had during dinner with Maud Williamson at the Consulate.

Antonia directed her to a rock then crouched to rearrange her robes into graceful folds around her sandaled feet. 'Cover your face so only your eyes are showing.'

Caseley didn't move. 'You want people to think I'm a Bedouin woman?'

Antonia waved the question aside. 'They will think what they want. We both know you aren't. But if you don't cover your face you look like a

220

European dressed for a masquerade. Sitting among the rocks with your face veiled and camels in the background, the image is so much more evocative. Please, Caseley? The women won't help and there's no other way for me to get a photograph.'

Reluctant, but recognising what it meant to Antonia, Caseley drew the fine fabric of her scarf over her nose and tucked it into the band above her temple.

'That's perfect. Sit very still while I take the lens cap off. Now.'

Holding her breath until Antonia had put the lens cap back on, she released the scarf.

'Being here for the wedding will have helped focus Imad's thoughts on our future,' Antonia confided as she took the plate from the camera and slotted it into the box. She looked up. 'Don't you think?'

'I'm sure he's had a great deal to think about.' Caseley couldn't give the encouragement Antonia wanted. The Sheikh's attention was more likely to be on politics and family matters, but to suggest it would only cause ill feeling. Nor would Antonia believe her.

She caught her breath as her heart gave an extra beat at the sight of Jago and Robert Pawlyn coming towards them.

Pawlyn beamed with pleasure as Antonia waved and smiled. 'Robert, I'm so glad to see you. Please will you ask the elders if they will permit you to take a photograph of them? Obviously they won't allow me to do it. I can't even photograph the women.'

221

His smile faded as he realised her warm greeting had a price. Caseley watched as disappointment gave way to acceptance.

'It would be a waste of time.'

'How do you know unless you try?'

'Antonia, I've spent the past three days with these men. Because they are nomadic, meetings like these can happen only rarely. A lot must be discussed and decided in a short time. It's a simple matter of priorities and implies no disrespect to you.'

Caseley suspected he was being less than truthful out of kindness. She could see Antonia fighting tears of sheer frustration as she huffed out an impatient breath.

'I know it's not the same,' he went on, 'but what about taking one of me?' He gestured at his dusty robes. 'I never imagined seeing myself dressed like this. I would very much like a memento of this trip. Then perhaps I could take one of you. Come on, I'll help you move the camera. Where shall we set it up?' He went to pick up the tripod. Antonia hurried after him, pointing and calling instructions.

'He's more patient than she deserves,' Jago said.

'She believes Sheikh Imad is about to declare himself.'

'To her?'

Caseley nodded.

'You aren't serious.'

'I am. It's so sad.'

'What is?'

'That she yearns for Sheikh Imad while Robert Pawlyn yearns for her. He's not blind to her faults but seems able to see past them.'

'Indeed,' Jago's expression was cold. 'Then he has better vision than I.'

Caseley changed the subject. 'This morning's meeting?'

'Interesting.' His expression was grim. 'As some of the visiting elders only spoke dialect the Sheikh translated it into Egyptian Arabic so Pawlyn could keep me informed of what was being said. As a final persuasion Imad condemned Egypt's Turco-Circassian ruling elite as having no honour. Honour is more important than wealth to the Bedouin. He is usually so formal and diplomatic. Yet this morning he spoke with barely-controlled loathing. I suspected there had to be a personal reason.'

'And was there?'

Jago nodded. 'During a break for coffee I asked him through Pawlyn. He was quiet for so long I thought he wasn't going to answer. Then he told us that a Turco-Circassian officer had raped the daughter of one of his uncles.'

Shock made Caseley gasp.

'That's not the worst of it.' His mouth tightened. 'She was then killed by her father and brothers.'

Caseley's hands flew to her mouth. '*What? Why?*'

'To erase the stain on the family honour.' He kept his voice low. 'I know this is a different country with different codes of behaviour, but even so–' He shook his head. 'Apparently Imad was fond of his cousin and at the time of the ... attack, marriage discussions were taking place between their families. I asked what was done about the officer. Imad had hoped for justice from

223

the Khedive. But none of the officers would admit even knowing what had occurred. So his uncle organised a night raid. The officer was seized and brought to a desert camp for *Bisha'a*.'

'What's that?'

'The accused must lick a metal spoon that has been heated in a fire then rinse his mouth with water. A burned or scarred tongue is proof that he lied. Only one particular elder can order this and he was away. But the officer had dishonoured the girl, her family and the tribe, and had to be punished.' He paused, glancing away.

'What happened to him?'

'He was tortured then Imad ended his life.'

The brutality of it shocked her.

'I shouldn't have told you–'

'I'm glad you did. As you said, things are different here. That officer's attack on a defenceless girl led to her being murdered by her own family. He chose to do what he did. She had no choice at all. I cannot like the thought of torture, but his life for hers is justice.'

Jago touched her hand. 'I was sure you would understand.'

'One of Sheikh Imad's bodyguards is coming.'

'I must go.' He hesitated. 'Caseley, last night – I should have told you–' His gaze held hers. 'There is no choice for me. It's you. It always was, always will be.'

Her heart leapt, relief made her legs weak, and she pressed a hand to her chest, watching as he joined Pawlyn and they returned to the meeting.

'You're looking very serious.' Antonia shortened the last of the tripod's telescopic legs, turned the securing wing nuts then fastened the leather strap that bound them together.

Caseley gathered her scattered thoughts. What had passed between her and Jago was private. She would never share it, not even with Rosina. 'I've just heard something shocking.'

'Tell me,' Antonia demanded, laying the tripod on top of the camera box then straightening up.

Caseley repeated what Jago had told her.

Visibly startled, Antonia was silent for several seconds. 'Well, it seems to me the officer got what he deserved.'

'I agree. But there is another aspect to be considered. Do you not see?'

Antonia drew herself up. 'For goodness' sake, Caseley. Stop being so mysterious. Just say it.'

'What kind of honour demands a woman's death for something not her fault, something she could not have prevented? This code is completely different from everything you are used to–'

'Yes,' Antonia waved her to silence. 'But it is *desert* culture. Of course Imad must show respect for the old traditions when he visits. It is his duty as a prince of his tribe. But this is not how he lives, or where he lives. He owns properties in Cairo and Alexandria.'

'That has nothing to do with–'

'No,' Antonia cut across. 'You have said your piece. Have the courtesy to let me say mine. I will give you the benefit of the doubt and assume you have my best interests at heart. Though if you really cared about my happiness you would be more supportive. All I ever hear from you are warnings. Anyone would think you do not want me to be happy.'

The words landed like blows. 'No! You misunderstand me. That is not at all—'

'Yes, you suffered a grievous loss,' Antonia continued, not listening. 'I'm sure you had the sympathy of everyone you told. But you must accept that I know far better than you do what is best for me.'

Everyone you told. As if she had been begging for sympathy, when nothing could be further from the truth. As raw anger stirred, Caseley fought it down. Her intention had been to spare Antonia embarrassment. But she was wasting her breath.

'You're right,' Caseley said quietly. 'I should not have spoken.'

Antonia couldn't hide her surprise. Then satisfaction smoothed away her frown and lifted the corners of her mouth. 'We'll say no more about it. I'm sure you meant well.'

'If you'll excuse me, I'll go back to the tent.'

'Aren't you bored with baking?'

'No, I enjoy it. With so many extra guests, Fayruz is glad to have help.'

'Go ahead if it makes you happy. I can see we were brought up with very different expectations. Carry this for me, will you?' She handed Caseley the tripod, then picked up the camera box.

When they reached the tent, Caseley put the tripod down beside the fabric wall and lowered herself onto the rug beside Fayruz, who smiled warmly at Caseley's murmured *'As-salaamu aleikum,'* and returned the greeting.

Reaching for the pot of water, Caseley poured a little into her palm and washed her hands,

226

wiping them dry on the end of her scarf. Reaching to pick up a lump of dough she felt a sudden tug. Her head was jerked back and both scarf and headband wrenched off.

There was a collective gasp and all chatter stopped as her reddish hair was exposed.

'Oh dear, I'm so sorry. I tripped.' Antonia moved on into the sleeping area.

Two women pulled their children away and made signs Caseley guessed were intended to ward off evil. Rashida scolded them. As more joined in, taking sides, the noise level rose.

Face burning, heart pounding in shock, Caseley twisted round to pick up the scarf and headband lying behind her.

Adding her voice to the argument, Fayruz gestured for Caseley to cover her head with the scarf while she quickly refolded the band and tied it in place for her.

She wanted to believe it was an accident. For Antonia to have done such a thing deliberately– Her entire body burned. Shame suffused her at having deceived them. Yet what else could she have done? The colour of her hair was outside her control, an accident of birth. She was the same person they had accepted, welcomed. But many who had smiled in welcome now glared in suspicion.

Caseley saw Sabra arrive from another tent with more women, who clustered around the tent opening. The Sheikha asked a question and the babble erupted again. They were speaking Arabic so Caseley could only guess at what was being said. Antonia emerged and shrugged, brushing it off as a simple accident.

Scathing and angry, Fayruz and Rashida made their opinion of her very clear. Antonia flushed.

Head down, her face hidden, Caseley edged backward then slipped out of the tent. Sabra found her sitting on a rock watching the camels.

'Miss Collingwood has caused more harm to herself than to you.'

'It doesn't feel like that.'

'Bedouin women are not stupid.' She raised her hand before Caseley could speak. 'I know you do not think them so. My point is that they have experienced your politeness, your willingness to help. They allowed you to prepare food with them and watched you comfort a child.'

'But that wasn't enough to overcome—'

'You do them an injustice. Fayruz, Rashida and Zainab spoke strongly for you and others were persuaded.'

'Many were angry.'

'You will leave soon, so why does it matter?'

The question jolted Caseley. 'I suppose I – I should have liked them to remember me kindly.'

'What others think of you is not your concern. Have you enjoyed your visit?'

'Oh yes. I had no idea what to expect. But it has been an amazing experience. One I will never forget.' *For so many reasons.*

Sabra slipped her arm through Caseley's. 'I am glad. Come, we will return to the tent. It will soon be time to eat.'

Caseley held back. 'Are you sure I will be welcome?'

Sabra's brows rose. 'You are with me.'

It was not the reply Caseley hoped for. But if

the Sheikha's patronage deflected any residual ill feeling, the remainder of the day and evening would be more pleasant for everyone. They were, after all, still celebrating the wedding.

She looked across the encampment. Outside the tents groups of elders were seated on the ground, around several cooking fires tended by young men. Boys hurried back and forth with armfuls of thorn and sacks of dried camel dung to feed the flames.

Jago was there with Sheikh Imad and Robert Pawlyn. But from this distance she could not pick him out from among all the others.

They reached the tent behind several others who had just arrived. Caseley withdrew her arm from Sabra's. 'If you don't mind, I'll stay back here.' She indicated a spot against the side wall. 'This is an important occasion for the ladies of the bride and groom's families, and you are a guest of honour. Just being part of it is a privilege for me. Besides, after what happened earlier I would prefer not to be noticed.'

Sabra studied her for a moment, then nodded. 'Your modesty does you credit.'

Knowing the compliment was undeserved, Caseley watched as Sabra was drawn into a group of women. She looked for Antonia and saw her on the far side of the tent opening, talking animatedly to the woman beside her. The woman gave her head a brief shake, then got up and moved away to another group.

Antonia's smile froze and she glanced round, adjusting her scarf in an attempt to mask her embarrassment.

Sighing, Caseley raised her hand to catch Antonia's attention. Though she would have preferred to sit by herself, had it not been for Antonia pressing Sheikh Imad for an invitation she would not even be here. Maybe Antonia wouldn't come over.

But she did, dropping onto the sand beside Caseley, just as three older women and a pretty younger one arrived from another tent. The older women, clearly pleased, were talking excitedly. The younger one smiled shyly, glowing with happiness.

Other women got up and went to greet them, then clapped and squealed with pleasure.

'What's happening?' Caseley asked.

'An engagement has been arranged,' Antonia said. Then her colour drained away, leaving her face ashen and slack with shock. 'No,' she whispered, stunned and stricken. *'No!'*

As two women glanced round, Caseley quickly got up, dragged Antonia to her feet and pulled her out of the tent. In all the excitement no one noticed them go.

'He can't – he wouldn't–'

'Lean on me.' Caseley put a supportive arm around her. 'We'll go to the well.' Hearing laughter and the sounds of celebration drifting across from the men's camp she realised.

'The engagement, is it Sheikh Imad?'

Antonia moaned. 'Why did he let me think–?'

Caseley said nothing. She had not seen him do or say anything to give Antonia cause for hope. *He had allowed himself to be persuaded to include herself and Antonia in the party.* That had been Jago's doing, because he had not wanted to leave her behind. From that single thread Antonia had spun a vivid tapestry of a future together.

'You saw.' Stopping suddenly, Antonia seized Caseley's wrists. 'You must have noticed how he looked at me. He can't want this. He is being pressured–'

Caseley stood still. Surely Antonia knew better than to imagine Sheikh Imad would bow to pressure from anyone about anything? 'I'm so sorry.'

Antonia's expression reflected her agony. 'I thought– I was sure–' She flung Caseley's hands away and her face contorted as she swiped at the tears that streamed down her face. 'Go on, then. Tell me you were right all along and I've made a complete fool of myself.'

They reached the well. Caseley lowered the leather bucket, heard it splash and drew it up again as Antonia slumped down onto a stone. 'Bathe your face and wrists.'

'That's supposed to make me feel better?'

'No. But it will calm you and erase the signs of your weeping. Do you want their pity?'

'No!' Dipping one end of her head cloth into the water Antonia wiped her face and the back of her neck. Caseley did the same and the cool, wet cloth felt blissfully refreshing.

'I can't go back.'

'To the tent?'

'Where else?'

'Yes, you can. If you show courage and dignity–'

'Dignity?' Antonia gave a short, scathing laugh. 'Oh yes, you'd know all about that. What is dignified about doing the work of a servant? What dignity did you show, crying over a child that isn't even yours?'

Caseley's heart thumped painfully as Antonia strode away. She closed her eyes. Antonia had lashed out because she was upset and embarrassed. Even if she was right, and Caseley had compromised her dignity, she could not regret it for she had gained far more than she'd lost. An arm encircled her shoulders.

'There you are.' Jago's voice was gentle, his face thunderous. 'I see Miss Collingwood has heard the news.'

Caseley nodded. 'I – we–' She couldn't get any more past the lump in her throat.

'Come, my love.' He drew her away, walking her slowly towards Fayruz's *bayt*. 'Go and eat now. You must,' he insisted gently before she could argue. 'Sit with Sabra. She will make sure you are comfortable. May I pass on your good wishes to the Sheikh?'

'Yes, please do. I realise it must have been a shock for her, but–' she stopped, tried to shrug it off.

'As soon as Sheikh Imad and his bride-to-be's father announced the contract, I guessed what would happen. She behaves like a spoiled child. I wish I could have reached you before she–'

Caseley turned her face into his shoulder. 'You came.'

'I wish I could stay.'

Taking a deep breath she straightened. 'I'm all right now.'

'I had hoped ... but Pawlyn and I must honour our obligations as guests.'

'Of course you must. You cannot risk the good-will you have built up over the past few days.'

'Besides, tonight we distribute the gold.' A muscle jumped in his jaw.

'What is it, Jago?'

His tension dissolved in a wry smile. 'I have talked myself hoarse. No one could ever accuse me of patience but I have surprised myself. Pawlyn has been invaluable. He and the Sheikh negotiated with immense skill on my behalf.' He rubbed his forehead.

'But?' she asked softly.

'We have not achieved a commitment. Yet without the gold, we wouldn't even have got this far. But our time is up.'

'When do we leave?'

'In the morning.'

'Perhaps there is still time. Whatever the out-come, you could not have done more. Now you must go.'

He raised her hand, his gaze holding hers. His lips brushed her knuckles and she felt a tug deep inside. 'I miss you.' Releasing her hand he strode away, his sleeveless robe billowing.

'That was unkind and uncalled for, Antonia,' Robert Pawlyn scolded, torn between wanting to offer comfort and shake her until her teeth rattled. She was disappointed, hurting. He knew how that felt.

She sobbed in a storm of fresh tears. 'Have you turned against me as well?'

'No. Nor will I. Though you do make it a tempting notion. I understand you being drawn to the Sheikh. He is a charismatic man. His urbane manner and fluency in French make it easy to forget he is Bedouin. But he is proud of his culture and would never betray it. The men of his tribe say they would prefer their daughters be eaten by crocodiles than marry "outside".'

'Yes, but–'

'No, no *buts*. As a prince who may one day be elected leader of his tribe, Sheikh Imad values honour above all things.'

'Then why didn't he warn me?'

'Why should he? Antonia, his engagement is none of your business. You asked to join the wedding party, remember? He kindly consented. As it happened, travelling in a mixed group provided excellent cover for Captain Barata's mission. Although the engagement announcement was made today, discussions between the families will have been under way for months.'

'Oh,' Antonia said in a small voice. She wiped her eyes and nose with the end of her scarf. 'I feel very stupid.'

He hardened his heart. Sympathy would give her an excuse to wallow. 'You'll get over it.' He was brisk. 'Now while I walk you back to the tent, we will talk of other things. What are you most looking forward to on your return to Cairo? For myself, it is a proper bath. Though I shall miss wearing Bedouin clothes. They are cooler and far more comfortable for the climate than European dress. Don't you agree?'

'Why can't I ever stay angry with you?'

'Why would you want to?'

'I should apologise to Caseley.'

'Yes, you should.'

'She'll gloat.'

'You know better than that.'

Antonia blew out a breath. 'She's nicer than me.'

'So make an effort.'

'I hate her and I hate you.'

'No you don't.'

'What would you know?'

I know you. 'Be sure to eat well this evening. We have a long journey tomorrow.'

'Don't *fuss*, Robert.'

Fighting a grin, he watched her march away, stiff-backed, her head high.

Chapter Seventeen

Caseley woke early. Quickly covering her hair, she put on her thick cloak and left the tent, picking up an empty water pot as she passed. Outside, the air was cool and fresh. In the east, the rising sun tinted a pearl sky with gold.

She went first to the latrine, then to the well. Boys moved along the camel rows, putting down fodder for them, as several men milked the females. Caseley paused for a moment to watch a baby camel try to butt a man out of the way. He glanced round, smiling, and murmured to it without breaking rhythm.

At the well Caseley waited among women and girls. To ward off the morning chill some wore a wide-sleeved jacket over their *thobe*, others a long black cotton coat edged with red or blue braid. She murmured a greeting; relieved and delighted when it was returned.

When her turn came she filled the pots with care and moved out of the way before tipping a little water from one into her hands. She washed them, then with a little more in her cupped palm, rubbed her face and dried it with the end of her scarf.

As she walked back, the air was growing warmer as the sun climbed. Soon the rocks would shimmer with reflected heat. The scent of a dozen fires, roasting coffee and fresh bread made her hungry.

Back at the *bayt*, Fayruz had rekindled the embers. Behind her in the shadows, Caseley was aware of other women moving about. Greeting Fayruz she set down the full water pots within reach and was rewarded with a smile.

Taking off her cloak she rolled it up and pushed it into the fabric bag, then returned to the entrance and sat down. Flouring her hands she dug into the bowl of dough and set to work. Fayruz brushed off the metal plate and laid it on stones surrounding the glowing embers.

Women came and went from the tents, shaking rugs and blankets then rolling up the tent wall to air the interior. Young girls carried toddlers. Boys ran to and fro, shouting to each other while they did their morning chores.

The pile of flatbreads in front of Caseley grew larger. She and Fayruz alternated dropping them onto the hotplate, flipping them over as they cooked, before lifting them onto a large platter. The smell made Caseley's mouth water. It felt good to be hungry. It felt good to be alive.

Even as the thought formed, guilt welled up. She fought it, crushed it. Grief would not bring them back. She had so many treasured memories. They, and her sons, would live forever in her heart. She swallowed the lump in her throat, took a deep breath, then another, and knew the raw wound had begun to heal.

The babble of conversation increased. Rashida placed a dish of yoghurt and another of dates on the rug, then settled herself down next to Caseley. Greeting the older woman in Bedouin dialect, Caseley was rewarded with a pat on the arm and some delighted babble. Not understanding a word, she smiled back.

Fayruz handed her a warm piece of bread then showed her how to fold it and scoop up yoghurt. Moving to one side to allow another woman to take her place, Caseley ate her breakfast. She would not want to live like this all the time. But she would not have missed a single moment.

Zainab raised the coffee pot, but before Caseley could respond, Rashida shook her head and passed her a mug of camel milk. '*Shukran*,' she smiled, touched that they remembered.

After breakfast, repacking the fabric bag took just a few minutes. There wasn't a container large enough to hold all the memories she was taking home.

She carried the bag outside. She wasn't the same person who had left Falmouth. She and Jago would hold on to the best of the past and build a new future.

'Are you all right?'

She looked up into his concerned face and

nodded. 'Yes. I was just– I know it's unlikely we would ever have– I wish the boys might have experienced this.'

She saw his jaw clench as he gripped her shoulder for a moment. 'You took the thought from my head.'

The camels were brought over and it was time to leave the camp. Fayruz, Zainab and Rashida kissed Caseley. Others had crowded into the tent and added their voices, gripping her hands, their smiles and touch telling her she had been forgiven for her hair.

'*Shukran. Ma salaama,*' she said over and over again.

Antonia was not kissed. On both sides, leave-taking was polite but cool.

As they left the tent and walked to the camels, Caseley saw Sheikh Imad and his bodyguards with Jago and Pawlyn. The two servants waited with the baggage camels.

'It has been very interesting,' Antonia said to Sabra. 'But I'm not sorry to be returning to civilisation.'

Though Caseley winced inwardly at the implied insult, Sabra merely nodded. 'This life is hard for those born to it. Outsiders would find it impossible.'

Antonia moistened her lips. 'Before we leave, perhaps I should offer my good wishes to Sheikh Imad.' Her voice wasn't quite steady and Caseley felt both sympathy and admiration.

Sabra nodded. 'I am sure he will appreciate them.'

Pawlyn and Jago joined Caseley and stood on

each side of her, watching as Antonia approached the Sheikh. He tucked his hands into his sleeves as he listened. She spoke in Arabic. He replied in the same language, dignified as always.

'He's telling her she is rare among the Europeans he has met,' Pawlyn said. 'And she is to be commended for learning the languages spoken in Egypt. Her photographs show her love for the country and its people. He wishes her happiness in her future.' He sighed. 'Heaven knows Antonia has her faults. But she doesn't lack courage.'

'You're very generous,' Caseley said.

His gaze stayed on Antonia as he murmured, 'I have plans.'

'Come.' Jago's hand was warm under her elbow. His touch sent a thrill through her and she leaned into him for a moment, reassured by his strength.

She glanced at him, felt his fingers tighten briefly. She saw the hunger in his eyes and a blush heated her skin. Releasing her with obvious reluctance, he bent and linked his fingers. She placed her sandaled foot in them and he boosted her onto her camel.

As she hooked her leg around the post and arranged her robe, one of the servants handed him two switches made from date palm stems. He passed one to her. Their gazes locked again. There was so much to talk about. But now was not the time. Her camel lurched to its feet and he went to mount his own.

Others were packing as they left the camp and headed up the track in single file. A while later it broadened out. No sooner had Jago moved his camel up to hers than Antonia appeared at her other side. 'May I speak to you?'

'You have said enough,' Jago's tone was cold.

'Please?' Antonia kept her eyes on Caseley. 'I owe you an apology.'

'At last,' Jago muttered. Not bothering to hide his disdain, he dropped back to ride with Pawlyn. In front, with two of the guards riding ahead, Sheikh Imad and Sabra were deep in conversation.

'I spoke in haste,' Antonia said. 'Hearing the news – I was hurt. I know that is no excuse. But ... the trouble is I don't fit in. My mother died when I was a baby. My nurse, Hamida, raised me. She taught me Arabic. My father indulged my interests but had no time for me. I hoped to win his approval by doing well in my studies. He was more concerned with my skill as a hostess. Because I wanted more than to be simply a decorative dutiful wife, I was – am – disapproved of.'

Antonia's defensive self-absorption would not have helped, Caseley thought. But nothing would be gained by saying so. 'You and I share similar backgrounds,' she said. 'My mother was my father's second wife. His first wife and son died in an epidemic. My mother was killed in an accident when I was twelve. After that, my father devoted all his energy to the business. I think it was the only way he could cope.' Had it not been for Rosina she would have been desperately lonely.

Antonia nodded, but Caseley sensed it was simply a reflex. She hadn't been listening. Her next words proved it.

'When I met Sabra and Sheikh Imad I was

fascinated. They seemed so sophisticated and European, and yet so exotic. I thought maybe – then the chance to attend the wedding – but the camp–' she shuddered. 'The way they live is not at all like I imagined.'

'Sheikh Imad can move between European and Bedouin life because he is a man. Sabra's wealth and position allows her far more freedom than most women. But it is still much less than his. While we were at the Bedouin camp she visited many of the women in their *bayts,* but not once did she approach the men.'

'I had such dreams–' Antonia shook her head. 'I feel very stupid.' She looked up suddenly. 'Do you think I'm a coward?'

'Accepting the reality of a situation is common sense, not cowardice. And you know you aren't. If you were you'd have given up photography long ago. But you didn't. Despite the difficulties and criticism, you worked to develop your talent. That demonstrates courage and commitment.'

'Thank you.' Antonia smiled. But it quickly faded and she raised troubled eyes. 'What will I do now? Marry Spencer Blaine? Join the ranks of women I have no respect for?' She shuddered. 'I can't. I'd die of boredom. He is so *hollow*. But my father is determined. Yet if I don't, what's left?'

'Only you can decide that,' Caseley said. As Jago returned, Antonia turned her camel away.

'Did you receive the promised apology?'

'Not exactly.'

Jago snorted. 'Why am I not surprised? I have not forgotten her attempts to undermine you. As I told you before, she's jealous.'

241

Caseley's laugh broke. 'Why would she envy me?'

'You have a husband who would give his life for you; and will do *anything* to win back your esteem and affection.'

As day faded into evening, they continued the pattern established on their journey to the camp and during their stay. The three women laid their camel saddles, blankets and cloaks on one side of the fire, the men on the other.

In the look Jago sent her, Caseley read frustration and impatience. But respect for Sheikh Imad and Sabra kept him silent as they settled down for the night. Caseley was torn. She yearned for the comfort of his arms and the warm strength of his body. But though his declaration of love and commitment made her quake with relief, each time she relived them, a new uncertainty gnawed at her.

As a girl, managing the house and daily walks between house, yard and town had kept her slender. Happiness in her marriage and the birth of two children had rounded her figure and the contours of her face. Jago had adored her transition from girl to woman. But grief had pared her to the bone.

When they first met, he had taken her breath away. Handsome, broad-shouldered and hard-muscled from the physical demands of shipboard life, his half-Spanish heritage gave him a patrician air while from his Cornish ancestry he had inherited immense stamina and a tender heart none but those closest to him even suspected.

Now, still lean, he had the solid strength of oak,

yet moved like a cat. The silver that threaded his black hair added distinction. The creases at the outer corners of his eyes were deeper, scored by hours spent scanning the horizon on long voyages.

She did not doubt that he loved her. But would he still find her desirable? She felt herself blush beneath her long robe, and dreaded that he might not.

The following morning Caseley noticed the camels constantly turning their heads and sniffing the air. She knelt to roll up her cloak and push it into the striped bag. 'Sheikha? Why are the camels doing that?'

Sabra glanced up from her own packing. 'They are probably anxious to get home.' She smiled. 'As I'm sure you must be.'

They made an early start, and instead of stopping at midday, Sheikh Imad insisted they keep going.

During the afternoon, Caseley's camel became restless. She tapped its shoulders with her stick to keep it moving. Jago came alongside.

'Something feels wrong. If we were at sea, I'd say I could smell a storm.' He shaded his eyes with one hand. 'But here, if there are signs I can't read them.'

Caseley looked up. The cloudless sky resembled polished pewter. Heat pressed down like a weight on her head and shoulders. When, at last, the narrow wadi widened into a stony plain bounded by low hills, the intensity of her relief surprised her.

She became aware of a sound. Barely audible, it was low and continuous, different from the wind.

243

She looked round.

'What is it?' Jago asked.

'I don't know. Can't you hear it?'

Before he could answer, the bodyguard at the rear shouted a warning. Sheikh Imad glanced back and abruptly changed direction towards the low hills edging the valley's sides, slapping his camel's rump with a stick.

Sabra had seized Antonia's rein. Robert Pawlyn's camel broke into a run to remain with them. The servants towing the baggage camels were urging them on with shouts.

Responding to Sheikh Imad's bellowed order, the bodyguard at the rear started towards Caseley and Jago.

Unsettled by all the shouting, Caseley's camel jerked its head violently and swerved sideways. Thrown off-balance, the rein torn from her hand, she tumbled from the saddle. Her camel bolted after the others racing towards rising ground.

The breath knocked out of her by the fall, she looked along the wadi. A low rumble vibrated through the ground. The valley floor seemed to be moving. She blinked to clear her vision, then realised she was seeing tongues of foaming debris-laden water hurtling towards her.

Fighting the scream that rose in her throat she scrambled to her feet, and saw Jago jump from his camel. It galloped after the others. Staggering as he landed, he managed to avoid falling and ran towards her.

Seizing her hand he looped her arm around his neck and wrapped his other arm around her waist. 'Are you hurt?'

Her heart was hammering wildly. She felt light-headed from the shock of her fall.

'Caseley?' As he hauled her to her feet, she winced. Her hip and shoulder ached where she had landed on them and her grazed hand stung.

'N – nothing broken.'

He took most of her weight to spare her crippled foot as they ran towards higher ground. But the flood was quicker. A few yards from safety the brown-grey water poured over their sandals, splashing up their legs, soaking the bottom of their robes.

The force was terrifying. Their wet robes dragged. Caseley bit her tongue to stifle a scream as she fought to keep her balance. Stones and debris slammed against her ankles. The pain made her eyes sting. She clung to Jago. If he let go, the water would sweep her away.

He waded the final few steps, grunting with effort as they stumbled up the rising slope. When they were well clear of the water he stopped, panting, as they both looked back.

Gasping for breath, held hard against him, she could feel the rapid thunder of his heartbeat. Her own was even faster. The flood swept by with a hissing roar, carrying broken tree trunks, date palm fronds and scrubby thorn bushes ripped up by the roots.

Caseley was mesmerised by the power of the silt-laden torrent that stretched the width of the valley floor. Above the tumbling racing water a fine mist cooled the air.

'Are you sure you're all right?' His voice was hoarse.

Her heart still hammered wildly. She felt queasy from shock and reaction to their narrow escape. She nodded, forcing a smile. 'J – just b-bruised.' Her teeth chattered. 'I'll b-be all c-colours of the rainbow tomorrow.' His strength gave her comfort. His body against hers kindled a kaleidoscope of vivid memories; powerful, passionate, tender. Despite the heat, her skin tightened in a shiver. 'Thank you. If the water had reached me before you did–'

'Don't.' His voice was raw, his compressed lips bloodless.

Seeing the others watching, Caseley raised a hand.

'You should not have let go of the rein,' Antonia called.

'The camel was far stronger than you and she knows it,' Jago said. He caught her hand and she winced.

'What?' He turned it palm up and his indrawn breath hissed.

Caseley looked, then wished she hadn't. When the camel's violent movement tore the rein free it had scored her skin. Then her hand had scraped across the gritty ground.

'It's not too bad.' She was trying to convince herself as much as him.

'It must sting like the devil. You need to get the grit out.'

'For that I need clean water. Perhaps when we stop for the night. I wish we had some honey.'

'Honey?'

'Rosina swears by it as a healer. She used to smear it on the boys' knees whenever they took a

246

tumble.' Her breath hitched and her eyes filled. She started to turn her head but he caught her chin, his callused fingers gentle.

'Please, Caseley,' his voice was unsteady. 'Don't shut me out. They were mine, too.'

Scalding tears spilled down her cheeks as she met his gaze, saw his agony, and realised how alone he must have felt. Night after night, Rosina had held her while she rocked with grief too deep for tears. Jago had faced the loss of his sons alone.

Sheikh Imad's bodyguards approached with the two recaptured camels. Jago wiped away her tears with his thumbs. She whispered thanks, her smile tremulous.

Remounted once more, they followed the Sheikh higher up the hill then through a fissure in the rocks. Filled with shadow it was cool and soothing to the eyes after the sun's glare. They emerged onto a small plateau with a view over the valley. Stopping, Imad quietly ordered his camel to kneel.

Looking down, Caseley saw the flood had slowed and the tumbling surface was smoother.

While the camels were being fed, cooking fires lit and the meal prepared, Jago led Caseley back to the rocky fissure. 'I thought I saw – yes, here it is.' He stopped beside a small drip-fed pool of water. The size of two cupped hands, it was crystal clear.

'Will you shield me?' Caseley placed herself so he was between her and the others.

'Of course, but why?'

'I need a bandage for my hand.' Lifting the bottom of her robe she tried to rip the bottom of her shift.

'Here, let me.' Kneeling, Jago caught the material between his teeth at the side seam. It gave way, and a moment later he had torn a four-inch wide strip from around the hem. He handed it to Caseley. 'Your servant, ma'am.'

Blushing and laughing, she dipped one end of her scarf into the water. 'It's really cold. I didn't expect that.' She wiped the blood, mud and grit from her palms.

'Why don't you put your hands in?'

'Sabra said these pools are rare and highly valued. We take water for granted. But this little rockpool might mean the difference between life and death for someone. I don't want to be the person who taints it.'

The following morning the only signs of the torrent were large puddles and broad snaking channels that had been carved out of the ground.

'Within a few days,' Sabra said, 'grass will grow and flowers will bloom. Insects and birds will come.'

'Then the sun will dry everything out and it will die,' Antonia sighed. 'It's so – brutal.'

Sabra shrugged. 'It is the desert.'

Chapter Eighteen

They reached the outskirts of Cairo at mid-morning the following day. Underlying the oppressive heat and smells of the city was a tension that hadn't been present when they left.

Four uniformed Egyptian police were trying to disperse a group of shouting men. Sheikh Imad spoke tersely to Pawlyn.

Sabra turned after nodding to let Pawlyn know she had heard. 'Cover your faces.'

Caseley obeyed at once, tucking the now very grubby end into her headband.

'Why?' Antonia asked.

'There has been some trouble in Alexandria,' Pawlyn explained.

'What kind of trouble?' Antonia demanded as she drew her scarf over her nose and mouth.

'The kind that might have been expected, given the continued presence of the English fleet. Some see it as unwanted interference, others as a safeguard. Tempers on both sides are short. Scuffles broke out and people were injured.'

'Where in the city? Was it near the Consulate? How many people? Were they badly hurt?'

'I don't know yet,' he replied patiently.

He knows more than he's told us. Even as Caseley caught Jago's eye and knew they shared the same thought, she understood why Pawlyn was saying little. They were at least four hours by train from

Alexandria. News of events there must have reached Cairo by telegraph. But the information was only as accurate as the person sending it. Until he'd had a chance to check the facts he wouldn't want to cause Antonia unnecessary anxiety.

'I'll be able to give you more information after I've been to Reuter's office,' he said, confirming Caseley's guess. 'Try not to worry.'

'I'm not *worried*,' Antonia retorted, contradicted by the tremor in her fingers. 'I simply want to know what's happening.'

Though the city was crowded, there were few European faces. Black-shrouded women shopping in pairs at stalls piled high with fruit and vegetables did not linger to bargain. Men had gathered on street corners or were sitting outside coffee houses holding earnest discussions.

When they reached the square from where they had set out on their journey, Caseley noticed that the bodyguards and servants remained mounted, forming a protective ring around the rest of the party as their camels knelt and they slid down from the saddles.

As Caseley stretched her back Jago and Pawlyn approached Imad, who offered his hand. Jago shook it, glancing quickly at the journalist.

'Please tell the Sheikh, in French if you please, how very much I appreciate his generosity and his efforts on my behalf.'

Caseley's heart swelled. He had done that for her, knowing the Sheikh would respond in the same language.

Imad released Jago's hand. 'I regret you were not

250

able to win a firm commitment. Yet there is reason to hope. Your conduct and manners found favour with those who have little regard for the English.'

As Pawlyn added his own thanks, Jago turned and beckoned Caseley.

Shielded from public view by the guards' camels she uncovered her face, folded her hands and bowed her head politely. 'Thank you, sir, from the bottom of my heart, for a life-changing experience.'

'You will not be forgotten, Madame Barata.'

Touched and delighted, Caseley moved back so Antonia could take her place. But she didn't move.

Covering her face again, Caseley didn't try to hide her anger, though she kept her voice low. 'For shame, Antonia. You demanded to go on this journey. The very least you owe him is the courtesy of a polite farewell.'

Blushing scarlet, Antonia stepped forward and thanked him for the opportunity of experiencing Bedouin life.

'I wish you well, Mademoiselle Collingwood.'

Remounting his camel, he rode away surrounded by his bodyguards. Having unloaded the bags containing cloaks and other belongings, the servants followed.

'Come,' Sabra spoke quietly in French as Jago picked up the bags. 'You will want a bath and a meal before you leave for the train station.'

Caseley quickly translated for Jago, glad of the dusty robes and head coverings that ensured no one looked at them twice.

'Sheikha, with your permission I'll go to Reuter's office first,' Pawlyn said. 'I'll be back as

251

soon as I can.'

As she walked into Sabra's house and the door-man closed the wrought-iron gate, Caseley felt safe for the first time since they had entered the city.

'Considering the situation in Alexandria,' Jago murmured, 'it might be safer for us to remain in Bedouin clothing.'

'I was about to suggest it,' Sabra responded when Caseley translated.

As they entered their bedroom Caseley thought how much had changed in the nine days they had been away. Jago dropped the fabric bag on the floor, caught her arm and drew her to him.

'I have missed you so much. You have no idea–' He leaned back, frowning. 'You're trembling.'

'I know. Silly, isn't it?'

He laid one hand along her face, his callused palm gentle. 'Not at all. I'm awed at how well you have coped with everything.'

He thought it was a reaction to events. Part of it was. But the rest– The rest was about him, about them. Realisation of how much she loved him, fear of his disappointment.

At the sound of water being poured in the bath-rooms on either side, both stiffened. He muttered a curse. She raised a warning finger to her lips.

Catching her hand, he kissed her knuckles. As his gaze met hers she glimpsed diffidence. It helped to know he, too, was nervous.

'Go and enjoy your bath,' he released her. 'I certainly need one. You will enjoy my company more when I no longer smell like a camel.' He pulled off his head cloth, shrugging out of his *aba* as he headed for his bathroom.

Caseley knelt to take her towel and facecloth from the striped bag, grimacing at their state. Leaving them on the chest lid, she picked up her soap and toothbrush and crossed to her bathroom.

'*As-salaamu-aleikum*,' she greeted the servant, pulling off her scarf and headband, wincing as she unrolled the bandage around her hand.

The woman blinked then responded politely, '*Wa-aleikum-as-salaam, hanem.*'

Crossing to the small jug of water standing in a china basin, Caseley poured some into the glass, opened her small tin of tooth powder and cleaned her teeth, rinsing and spitting into the basin. Already she felt better. The servant waited patiently for her to finish, then indicated Caseley's robes.

Taking off everything but her shift, she handed the garments over. The woman didn't move. Instead she held out her hand and waited, curling her fingers repeatedly against her palm.

Powerfully reminded of Rosina, Caseley abandoned modesty and pulled the shift over her head.

The woman gasped, her expression concerned and sympathetic. Gabbling in Arabic, she pointed at the dark red and purple bruise that had spread over Caseley's hip. Another mottled bruise extended from her foot almost to her knee, the skin scratched and scraped.

Still talking and shaking her head, the woman picked up an empty pitcher and hurried out.

Caseley climbed into the bath, releasing a sigh of pleasure as she slid down into the water, wincing as her hand stung. For a few moments, she simply enjoyed the sensation of warm water against her sticky, dusty skin.

She wished she didn't have to move. But they could not afford to miss the afternoon train. Reluctantly, she stood up, soaped herself all over then sat down again to rinse off the lather.

The servant reappeared with two more pitchers of water, set them down by the bath and started removing the pins from Caseley's hair. As it cascaded over her shoulders and down her back, the woman lifted one of the pitchers, emptied warm water over Caseley's head, and began to massage her scalp.

'Oh, that's wonderful,' Caseley said in French, adding, '*Shukran*,' in case the woman didn't understand. After thoroughly massaging from forehead to nape, the woman emptied the second pitcher over her.

Wringing water out of the long ropes of hair, she motioned Caseley to stand up, handed her a towel to wrap around her head, another to wrap around her body, then offered a steadying hand as she stepped out.

While Caseley dried herself, the woman disappeared, returning a few minutes later with a clean shift and *thobe*, sandals and a small pot of salve. She pointed to Caseley's hip.

'*Shukran*.' Caseley removed the lid. It smelled pleasantly of herbs with a hint of wintergreen. She dipped her fingers in and rubbed the salve gently into her hip. Quickly absorbed, it soothed and eased the ache. She smiled at the woman, put on her shift and *thobe*, and freed her damp tresses.

Returning to the bedroom, Caseley saw on the

bedcover a folded scarf and headband for her, and a clean *thobe*, head cloth and *aba* for Jago.

Hearing a cascade of water, she realised he was receiving similar attention. Setting the little pot on the table, she towelled her hair some more, then sat on the edge of the bed and began to comb out the tangles.

Warm air from outside flowing in through the louvers would soon dry it enough to put up.

A few minutes later Jago padded in on bare feet, a towel round his hips. 'It was a relief to wash off the desert. How are you feeling now?'

'Clean. It's wonderful. Sabra sent up fresh clothes. She has been so kind.'

He dressed quickly then searched the bag.

'What are you looking for?'

'My comb.'

'Here, use mine.' As he took it she reached for the pot of salve.

'What's that?' With a few swift sweeps his tousled hair was neat, his beard smooth.

'A salve for my bruises.'

Handing back the comb he took the little pot and sniffed the contents. 'It smells pleasant enough.' He dropped to his knees. 'Show me.'

'It's all right, Jago, I can–'

'Finish your hair?'

She extended her leg and winced. Her foot looked worse now than when it was caked with mud, blood and dust.

'Dammit, Caseley.'

'It's really not that bad.' As he eyed her she admitted, 'It's uncomfortable but not painful.'

Kneeling in front of her he cupped her heel in

his hand then bent to kiss the livid bruise. His lips were warm and soft. Caseley's heart fluttered.

Dipping his fingertips into the salve he began to massage it gently into the discoloured, abraded skin. She looked at his bent head, his hair curling on his strong, tanned neck. He was a proud man, aware of his achievements and his position in society. Now he knelt at her feet.

As if sensing her gaze he raised his head. Their eyes met. On his feet in an instant he drew her up, held her close, his head resting against hers. He waited, allowing her to choose what happened next. She felt the tension in him, recognised the cost of his control.

It was too soon. No, the past was past. He had given her his word. She breathed in the familiar scent of his skin, welcomed the comfort of his strong arms. Too long away, she had come home.

Her hands crept up to rest briefly on his shoulders, then slid around his neck. She pressed her lips to his throat, his jaw, and felt a tremor run through him. 'Oh, Jago, I've been so lonely without you.'

He turned his head so his mouth brushed hers then covered it. For a long moment the kiss cherished. Far better than words it conveyed his gratitude, her forgiveness, his grief, her solace. It broke down walls and bridged chasms.

Then his tongue moved lightly across her lower lip and lingered on the scar where she had bitten it. Passion arced like lightning. As the kiss deepened she met his hunger with her own. As she gloried in his strength and need for her, her fears dissolved. His hand swept down her spine, moulding her against him. They fitted together so well, but not close enough. She wanted – ached – burned.

A knock on the door made them both start. Tearing his mouth from hers he raised his head. Breathless, bereft, trembling, Caseley rested her hands on his shoulders to steady herself.

He eased away, raked a hand through his hair. 'I–' he cleared his throat.

Stepping away from him, heart racing, she took a deep breath and pulled the layers of cotton away from her heated skin.

There was another knock. They glanced at each other, then Caseley went to the door with Jago close behind. A manservant bowed and repeated the message he'd been given. Caseley thanked him and, with another bow, he retreated silently along the passage.

'Our meal is ready and Mr Pawlyn is back,' she said as Jago closed the door. 'He will join us downstairs as soon as he has changed.' She picked up her comb.

'Caseley, I–' Jago began.

'Don't,' she pleaded. 'Don't say you're sorry. Unless you really do regret–'

'No! God, no. How could I? I have craved – but I didn't intend–' He stroked his fingertips down her face. 'You are so beautiful.' His fingers rested lightly on her lips as she drew a soft breath, her heart too full. 'Don't argue.' He dropped his hand, stepped back. 'Please.'

Instinct told her to lighten the moment. His love gave her strength. 'Did I seem reluctant?' Still watching him, she tipped her head sideways and

257

drew the comb from root to tip in swift strokes.

One corner of his mouth tilted up. 'Not that I recall.'

Straightening up, she swung the wavy bronze curtain back over her shoulder. Handing him the comb she gathered her damp hair into a twist, coiled it on top of her head, and quickly pinned it in place.

By the time she had put on her scarf and headband, he had finished dressing.

'I'm ready,' she said.

'Just one thing.'

'What?' She glanced round to see what she'd forgotten, and caught her breath as he gently grasped her shoulders.

'This.' Bending his head he kissed her. It was a slow, deep kiss that made her heart turn over and her eyes sting. When his mouth left hers she opened her eyes slowly.

He was watching her, his face troubled. 'I loved you when I married you. I loved you even more when our sons were born. That love is nothing to what I feel for you now. When you collapsed during our voyage here – I have known fear, but never like that. I had already failed you. But the possibility I might lose you forever–' the bleakness in his eyes pierced her soul. 'Don't leave me, Caseley.' His voice was rough, the words both plea and command.

'Never.' She caught his hand, pressed her lips to his palm. 'You are – everything.'

His arm around her shoulders held comfort and promise as they crossed to the door.

Moments after they joined Sabra and Antonia

in the salon, Robert Pawlyn hurried in, dressed in clean robes, sandals, and head cloth, his face scrubbed shiny above the stubble he had not taken time to shave.

'Madame Caseley,' Sabra said, combining the courtesy she observed in mixed company with the friendship that had evolved between them. 'Please sit beside your husband. It will be easier for both of you.'

Thanking her, Caseley quickly explained to Jago as they settled on the floor. Less than two weeks ago this had felt totally alien. Now it was so familiar they thought nothing of it. A steaming platter of spiced rice, vegetables and chunks of meat in a yoghurt sauce was placed on the cloth next to a plate of thin, soft flatbreads. They helped themselves, scooping up sauce-soaked rice with the bread.

'What–' Antonia began in English. Seeing Pawlyn's frowning glance she blushed and switched to French. 'I beg your pardon. What have you found out?'

'Colonel Arabi has continued reinforcement work on the forts,' Pawlyn replied. 'As minister of war he could not have stopped without orders from the Khedive. Obviously none were received. Now the commander of the English fleet, Admiral Sir Beauchamp Seymour, is threatening to bombard Alexandria.'

'On what grounds?' Jago demanded, as soon as Caseley had translated.

'The danger posed by the forts to the English fleet. Colonel Arabi has repeated his promise not to interfere with the Suez Canal. It's an honourable move that will cost him dearly. It has cut no ice with Admiral Seymour. Meanwhile, the British press has branded Arabi a villain, claiming he is hostile to both Britain and France. They demand action in the name of national pride.'

'What is the British government's position?' Jago demanded after Caseley translated.

'Both houses are deeply divided. But invasion looks certain. Marines on Malta and Cyprus are waiting for transport, and the War Office is planning to send troops from Britain, Bombay, Aden and Gibraltar.'

Caseley's throat was dry and her hand shook as she reached for her glass. She swallowed quickly then continued translating as Pawlyn went on.

'All foreign ships are leaving Alexandria. Admiral Conrad has taken the French fleet to Port Said. He refuses to be party to an act of aggression against a country that has every right to defend itself. The French Consulate has closed and its staff sailed with him. Trains from Alexandria are packed. Some people are coming to Cairo. But others are leaving at Banha for Zagazig and Ismailia.'

'Ask him where they will go from there,' Jago said.

'North by ship down the Sweet Water canal to Port Said,' Pawlyn replied. 'Or south on the single track line. They might also take ship through the Suez Canal, to the Red Sea.'

'You will want to leave as soon as possible,' Sabra said, signalling the servants who brought water and towels for them to rinse their hands.

Turning to Caseley, Jago spoke quietly. 'I will

260

take you to Ismailia and put you on a ship for–'

'No.'

The skin around his nostrils whitened. 'It was not a request and this isn't a debate.'

She saw through his anger to the fear that inspired it. 'Jago, you cannot come with me and it will not be safe for me to travel alone. We came here together on *Cygnet*. We will leave together the same way.' She met his glare, spoke for his ears alone and challenged him to remember. 'You asked me not to leave you.'

'That's different.'

'No. It isn't.'

'I will send for calèches to take you to the station,' Sabra said as they left the salon. 'The servants have packed for you and will bring your bags down as soon as you are ready.'

Jago had the bag open on the bed as Caseley emerged from the little cubicle next to the bathroom.

'These robes have no pockets, and we will need money to pay the calèche driver and for our rail tickets.'

Caseley delved into the bag and gave him a soft kid-leather drawstring purse. 'Use this.' She looked at the rolled felt cloaks lying on the bed. *So many memories.* 'I want to keep mine.'

He looked at her, gave a quick smile. 'They were a gift. It would be discourteous not to.'

Her clean gowns and underwear, Jago's jacket and trousers and their shoes filled the bag. Fastening it, Caseley rolled the cloaks and put them in the striped fabric bag. With notes and coins in the leather purse, Jago pulled the cords tight then

261

looped them twice around his wrist.

A servant arrived for the bags. After a last look round Caseley went with Jago to the door.

In the lobby at the bottom of the stairs she gripped the Sheikha's proffered hands. 'I will never forget your kindness.'

Sabra kissed her on both cheeks. 'Nor I yours. Be happy.' She offered her hand to Jago, who bowed over it. 'I wish you a safe and speedy journey back to Cornwall.'

'*Shukran*, Sheikha,' Jago said after Caseley had translated. He bowed again.

Sabra turned to bid farewell to Antonia and Robert Pawlyn.

'You need not look so surprised,' Jago whispered as Caseley smiled. 'I have a clever wife and learned from her.'

When Jago insisted Caseley ride with him, Pawlyn was visibly delighted to escort Antonia. As they neared the railway station they found themselves fighting a human tide of different nationalities. Men, women and children, all laden with belongings, streamed out of the station.

As Jago paid off the driver, scuffles broke out among people wanting to claim the calèche. He roared at them in Spanish, waving them away as he reached in for the bags and helped Caseley down.

'Let me carry the fabric one,' she insisted and looped it across her body.

'Link your arm through mine and don't let go. I know we should not touch while dressed like this. But I will not risk your safety.'

'Why Spanish?' she asked as Jago shouldered

262

his way through.

'We are in Bedouin robes but I don't speak Arabic, there wasn't time to ask you correct French phrases, and I didn't think it wise to use English.'

Ahead of them Pawlyn had commandeered two porters, one to carry Antonia's camera boxes and tripod, the other their bags. Caseley stayed close.

Despite all the people leaving the station, the concourse was still crowded. Pawlyn bought their tickets, waving Jago away. 'We'll settle up later. The train is waiting. You find our seats while I see the luggage safely loaded.'

A few minutes later, as they settled into their carriage, there was a shrill blast from the whistle. Amid clouds of steam as the engine roared and puffed, the carriages jerked and the train slowly picked up speed as it left the station.

Chapter Nineteen

Caseley gazed out of the window for a while, but the heat and jolting were unpleasant. She rested her head against the high, padded back of the seat and closed her eyes, comforted by the pressure of Jago's arm against hers.

'Do you feel unwell?' he asked quietly.

Opening her eyes, she saw the concern in his and gave a rueful smile. 'No. But I was much more comfortable on my camel.' Her smile widened. 'It feels very strange to hear myself say those words.' She pulled the loose cotton away from her damp

263

skin, relieved that she wasn't confined in a corset and multiple petticoats.

He pressed his arm against hers. 'Try to sleep. You will feel better for rest, and it will help the journey pass more quickly.'

She closed her eyes and let her thoughts drift. They had been in the desert for just a few days, but so much had changed. She became aware of Robert Pawlyn talking quietly to Antonia.

'No, you do yourself an injustice. Your photographs show artistry in the way you have framed the image. But the balance of light and dark, sharpness and diffusion demonstrates technical skill. That has to be learned, and it takes dedication.'

'It doesn't feel like hard work if you enjoy it.' Antonia sighed. 'I wasn't very successful at the Bedouin camp.'

'Getting permission was always doubtful. But you took your equipment anyway. I'm looking forward to seeing those you took of the camp, and of us.' He coughed. 'What would you say to working with me?'

'Doing what?'

'Providing photographic images to illustrate my articles. These are momentous times for Egypt. Someone should be documenting the changes and their effects on people at all levels of society.'

'That someone being you?'

'Yes. You cannot tell me the idea doesn't appeal.'

The silence stretched. Waiting for Antonia's reply, Caseley hardly dared breathe.

'You know it does. How could it not? But my father would never allow it. Me go travelling with an unmarried man? Heavens above,' she mocked bitterly, 'what would people say?'

'Yes, about that, the thing is, I was thinking – please don't answer now. You may want time to–'

'Robert,' Caseley heard Antonia's all-too-familiar impatience and exasperation. 'How can I answer when I have no idea what the question is?'

'Of course you – though this wasn't – but–'

'For goodness' sake, Robert!'

'All right, here it is then.' He took a breath then blurted, 'Will you marry me? Wait, let me finish. When we get back, your father will want to ship you off out of harm's way. I understand his concerns. But I can't leave. There has been too much distortion and too many lies printed already. No doubt it is selfish of me, but I should very much like you to stay as my wife. Will you at least consider it? We get along well. I admire your talent too much to ever try and stop you pursuing it. Indeed, I should like to see you achieve the recognition you deserve. Working with me will afford you opportunities to reach a much wider audience. I was thinking, in time, maybe a book? A collaboration?'

Caseley opened her eyelids a fraction and saw Antonia gazing at him, her features slack with astonishment. Then she looked down at her clasped hands.

'I know I'm no one's idea of a romantic figure,' he pressed on. 'But I have dreams and ambitions. I care about this country. I care about you. Probably more than is wise, but there it is...'

Touched by his honesty, Caseley closed her eyes again before unexpected tears betrayed her.

'I know you are unhappy and want more from life,' he continued with quiet urgency. Having plucked up the courage to start, clearly he intended to say everything that had been building up inside him. If he failed it would not be for want of trying.

'I would support you in that. I think – no, I truly believe we would make a good team. I don't have your artistic temperament. But I consider that an advantage. Emotion and creativity need the balance of pragmatism. Were we alike we would probably kill each other.'

Caseley heard the smile in his voice. Robert Pawlyn's insight surprised her. Yet it shouldn't. He had shown deeper understanding and compassion for the problems of this country than anyone else she had met. He also saw something in Antonia beyond her talent with a camera.

'I – I'm not an easy person, Robert.'

'I know that. But you've not had an easy life. I hope you will forgive my suggesting that you yearn to belong. In such circumstances it is very easy to mistake a mirage for reality. The thing is, true happiness is only found with someone who understands you, who loves you enough to let you be yourself.'

Caseley had never questioned the truth of that. She'd never had reason to. But everything was different now. For so many months she had been unable to imagine ever being happy again. Yet the desert had given her what she least expected – peace.

It was a land of sand, bare rock, heat and thirst, where a camel and water jar were all that stood between – between life and death. Yet amid the harshness she had found friendship, acceptance and shared experience.

Two nights ago, sitting on a rock with Jago, she had looked up into a vast black sky sprinkled with stars as numberless as the sand grains at her feet and felt a loosening of the constriction around her heart.

She had been ravaged by grief, guilt and rage. Time and this journey had blunted the raw edges. Now there were moments in each day when she actually forgot those terrible weeks. Then a sight, smell or sound would bring it all flooding back, sometimes so sharp, so brutally vivid it stopped her breath. The bad memories would always be there. But she could bear them. And now she could focus on good ones, too: golden treasures that would never fade or tarnish.

'You make me sound selfish,' Antonia said.

Caseley wondered if Jago was listening. She kept her eyes closed, her breathing steady, anxious not to embarrass Antonia or Robert Pawlyn by revealing she could hear their conversation.

'If you are, I think it's because you're unhappy. A happy person finds it easy to be generous. Their happiness warms everyone they have contact with. Being happy makes it easier to shrug off irritations, ignore discomfort and deal with difficulties.'

Caseley knew that for a fact.

'I have never felt like that.'

'Then surely it's time that you did?'

'You make it sound easy.' She sounded wistful.

'Being happy is a choice, Antonia. Of course there will be problems. And pain. Life is full of challenges. How dull and boring it would be without them. The happiness I'm talking about is the kind that grows between two people whose differences complement one another, who are stronger together than they are apart.'

Jago hadn't moved but Caseley sensed he was awake. Robert Pawlyn's words pierced deep into her soul. They perfectly described how she had felt about Jago, about her marriage. But that had been *before*. She was no longer the woman he married. There was no going back. They could only move forward, trusting in their love for each other. Antonia's voice broke into her thoughts.

'It never occurred to me– Do you really think – you and I–?'

'If I did not think so, we wouldn't be having this conversation. I don't expect you to share all my opinions. I want a wife, not an echo. Fortunately I know you well enough to have no fears on that score. I should enjoy talking to you about my work, and I hope very much you will want to share yours with me. Together we could create something special.'

'You aren't just being kind? About my photographs?'

'No, I'm not. Were I to be so foolish I would forfeit your trust.'

'You really would take me with you on assignments?'

'Haven't I just said so?'

'Yes. But that's now. How can I be sure that once we are married you won't suddenly decide it's too dangerous, or you prefer to go alone and I should remain at home and cook or sew–'

He laughed. 'Have you ever cooked anything?'

'You know what I mean.'

'You have my word, Antonia.' The silence stretched and Caseley had to fight the urge to open her eyes.

'It is very tempting.'

'Then say–'

'No, wait. You took me by surprise. I want to be fair, Robert. I don't love you.'

'Not right at this moment. But I believe you will, in time. We're friends and that's a start. I'm good for you, Antonia, and I'll be good to you.'

'My father – my father dislikes very much that people talk about me. He says it reflects badly on him. Before we left he announced that marriage to his aide, Spencer Blaine, would put an end to the gossip and settle me down.'

'Is that what you want?'

'Of course it isn't. How can you even ask? Spencer cares nothing for me. I embarrass him. But he's ambitious, so he would even put up with me if it gained him my father's good opinion. He need not worry. I wouldn't marry him if he were the last man in Egypt.'

'Bravo. You deserve better.'

Silence fell. To Pawlyn it must have seemed endless.

'Thank you, Robert, I accept.'

'You do?' Relief, surprise and delight combined to lift his voice an octave. He cleared his throat. 'Right. Jolly good. As soon as I've been to the telegraph office I'll come to the Consulate and speak to your father.'

It was early evening when the train arrived at

269

Alexandria station. They parted company outside. Handing Caseley into the first calèche, Jago listened as Antonia gave the driver the address of the Consulate, then followed in the second with the luggage. Pawlyn took a third.

'While you were asleep,' Antonia turned to Caseley as the horse clopped briskly along the street, 'Robert asked me to marry him.'

Caseley felt guilty about pretending ignorance, but Antonia would be unlikely to forgive her for having overheard. 'Have you accepted?'

'Yes.'

'I hope – no, I am sure – you will be very happy. Though I haven't known Mr Pawlyn very long, he impressed me as kind and sincere.'

'I shall certainly enjoy working with him. He wants me to take photographs to illustrate his articles, and later for us to work together on a book.'

Impulsively, Caseley pressed her hand. 'How exciting.'

'Actually, it is.' Antonia blew out a breath. 'Although – I daresay you will think me foolish and ungrateful – but it is not the love match I dreamed of.'

'*His* feelings must be deeply engaged or he would not have proposed. For him it is definitely a love match.'

Antonia shrugged. 'He is my consolation prize.'

'Forgive me, Antonia, but he deserves better from you. Surely having stayed with the Bedouin and seen the importance to them of their way of life, you must see that your dream of a future with Sheikh Imad was simply a mirage? It had no connection to reality. You have received an offer of marriage from a kind, intelligent man who recognises your talent. Compare him to Mr Blaine, who would never take your side against your father and to whom your photography is an embarrassment, he would expect you to give up the day you married.'

Antonia shuddered. 'Hell will freeze first!'

'Then be grateful for Robert Pawlyn. Not only does he support your passion, he wants to use it to complement his own work. Can you not see what a compliment that is?' As the words left her lips, she recalled sitting at the table in Jago's day cabin aboard *Cygnet,* writing letters in Spanish on his behalf, talking about cargoes at breakfast and discussing repairs to company ships and potential expansion at the yard over dinner at home on Greenbank.

'Don't you get bored with always being right?' The ironic tone of her retort showed Antonia had accepted her point.

'He's a good man, who cares deeply for you.'

'But do I deserve it?'

Hearing genuine fear beneath Antonia's flippancy, Caseley squeezed her hand briefly. 'He obviously thinks so. Trust him, and trust yourself.'

Antonia blew a slow breath. 'I'm scared,' she admitted. 'But I won't let it stop me.'

Caseley smiled at her. 'I should hope not.'

They arrived at the Consulate. While Jago paid both drivers, two servants came out to pick up the luggage and camera equipment. Antonia followed them inside. Caseley and Jago entered the building together. Spencer Blaine came out of the general office and stopped, visibly shocked.

'You have been out in public like that? Your father will be appalled.'

'Oh, for heaven's sake, Spencer. Dressing in English fashion would have put us at risk of being attacked. Would you have us sacrifice our safety to appearances?'

His face flushed crimson. 'There is no need to be offensive. I am only too aware that you have little patience with protocol. However, we have a reputation to maintain, and–'

'What is all the noise?' Sir Douglas stopped halfway down the staircase. 'Good Lord!'

'I was just telling Miss Collingwood my concern–'

'Yes, I heard. Normally I would agree with you. However, on this rare occasion my daughter has shown uncommon good sense.'

Antonia lifted her chin and Caseley felt a pang of sympathy. Sir Douglas's remark revealed his attitude towards his daughter. At best impatient, at worst contemptuous, it certainly helped to explain her prickly attitude.

While respecting Antonia's fierce devotion to her photography, Caseley hadn't realised what it must have cost her to continue when faced with constant belittling. Robert Pawlyn had seen through her defensiveness to her courage, and loved her for it.

Sir Douglas came down the stairs, his gaze passing briefly over each of them. He gave a brief nod. 'Though I dislike the necessity of such disguise, current circumstances make it a sensible decision. Well, Captain Barata? Were you successful?'

'We did our best, sir.'

The diplomat's expectant smile faded. 'Considering the value of the gold involved, I expected a more definite result.'

'As I say, sir, we did our best. Sheikh Imad graciously acted as intermediary, and Mr Pawlyn's knowledge of the language and customs proved invaluable.'

'Dealing with such people is impossible—' Spencer Blaine began.

'The Bedouin could not have been more generous or hospitable.' Jago ignored the interruption, his gaze on the Assistant Consul. 'We were welcomed into their tents and treated as honoured guests. The elders discussed our proposal at great length. By the time we left, opinion seemed to be turning in our favour.'

'Why did you not stay longer? Another day or two might have secured the agreement.'

Caseley remembered what Pawlyn had told her. Unexpected guests – even enemies – were welcomed for three days with no questions asked or payment requested.

'Sheikh Imad had business back in Cairo. Besides, pressing for a commitment might have had the opposite effect.'

'Then all we can do is hope.' He beckoned to his daughter. 'Antonia, here in the Consulate you are on English sovereign territory. I suggest you go up and change.' He turned back to Jago. 'Captain Barata, you are to carry Mrs Williamson and two Maltese gentlemen to Port Said. Admiral Seymour has threatened to bombard the city—'

'I am aware of the threat, sir. We learned of it on our return to Cairo.'

'Yes, but what you don't know is that Sir Charles is out of hospital and has been called to meet with our Consul-General in Cairo, leaving me in charge. By the time you have changed your clothes, a calèche will be outside to convey you and my aide–'

'With respect, Sir Douglas, I am not going to Port Said. I'm taking my wife home to Cornwall.'

'It was not a request, Captain Barata. As the accredited representative of Her Majesty's government whose business brought you here, I am giving you a direct order.'

'My wife–'

'Will await your swift return. The distance is not great, 121 nautical miles, according to Blaine's calculations. You will be back in less than a week.'

Caseley laid her hand on Jago's arm, feeling rigid muscles vibrating with barely suppressed fury. 'The sooner you go then the sooner you will return. I will wait for you at the hotel–'

'No.' Jago and Sir Douglas spoke together.

'You cannot stay there alone,' Jago said.

'I would not hear of it,' Sir Douglas added. 'You will remain here with us. Antonia will be glad of your company. As for the threatened bombardment, I believe it may yet be called off. Messages have been exchanged between Colonel Arabi, the Khedive and Admiral Seymour.'

'It is most unfortunate,' Spencer Blaine broke in, 'that the Admiral's personal servant was killed while they were both ashore during the trouble a few weeks ago. By all accounts the Admiral took it very badly.'

'Yes, thank you, Blaine,' Sir Douglas said.

'Whatever the Admiral's personal feelings, he is an Englishman and will not allow them to influence a matter of such international importance.' He bared his teeth in a brief smile. 'There is no cause whatsoever for alarm. The forts are all along the shoreline. We are in the centre of the city. We will be perfectly safe.' He turned to Jago. 'Your trunk is upstairs. You will oblige me by leaving as soon as possible.'

Caseley opened the trunk. 'Will you change?' Her headband and scarf hung over the bed's brass foot rail.

Jago shook his head. 'No, I'm safer like this. I'll change on board. Is there a clean work shirt and trousers in there?'

She took them out, rolling them together, her movements deft despite the tremor in her hands. Sir Douglas might say there was no cause for concern. But his smile had betrayed fear. Had Jago seen it? If she asked, he would worry.

'I suppose I should be grateful,' Jago growled bitterly. 'At least he didn't commandeer *Cygnet*.'

Take me with you. She clenched her teeth to stop the words escaping. There wouldn't be room. *Cygnet* was not built to carry passengers. If Nathan gave up the mate's cabin to Mrs Williamson and took the sea berth in Jago's day room, the other two gentlemen would have to sleep on the benches in the saloon. *Don't go.* He had no choice. Refusal could cost him his ship. Her throat was dry, swallowing painful. She moistened her lips.

'Comandeer *Cygnet*? First he would have had to get past Nathan, Jimbo and Hammer.'

'And Martin. Remember Santander? Fire in the fo'c'sle yet he held off that mob, and him only a boy.'

'I'll never forget it.' Picking up the striped bag containing the two felt cloaks, she added his rolled shirt, trousers and clean underwear. 'May I ask you something?'

'Anything.' He opened the leather drawstring purse, pressed a gold coin into her hand.

'I have no need of it, Jago. I am Sir Douglas's guest.'

'Take it anyway. There may be something you want.'

You. Come back safely. 'Jago, the berth in your sleeping cabin – why did you have it made narrow, again?'

'When Philip was born I knew you wouldn't be able to sail with me any more. What I hadn't realised was how much I would miss you. In my sleep I would reach for you and find only space. So I told Hammer to alter it. Why?'

'When I drew back the curtain and saw–' she shook her head.

'Tell me.'

'I felt– I thought you wanted to wipe away any sign that I had ever been with you.'

'I did.' He cupped her face between his hands, his mouth gentle on hers. 'I could not bear the constant reminder of all the times you had shared it with me. I wanted you there even though I knew you couldn't be. What kind of man is jealous of his own children? But I was.' He held her away from him and the crease between his brows deepened. 'I thought you would understand.'

'I do – now.' She should have realised. Had it not been the same for her? Every time he went away on a voyage their bed felt vast, cold and empty. But that was *before*.

Once more he drew her close, rested his cheek against her temple. 'I'm so sorry,' he whispered and she felt a muscle jump in his jaw.

'What for?'

'Everything.' He tilted her chin. His lips brushed hers then lingered.

Hunger, rigidly controlled, prowled behind the tenderness and drew its echo from her. She buried her hands in his hair and poured her whole heart into the kiss.

With time so short, holding him, needing him, knowing he felt the same, was both comfort and torture.

Reluctantly he drew away, and tucked a fallen curl behind her ear. 'Stay safe, *querida*. I'll be back as fast as *Cygnet* can bring me.' His voice grew rough. 'Don't come down until I've gone. I can't– I hate leaving you.'

Somehow she held her voice steady. 'Fair winds, Jago.'

Seizing the bag, he walked out.

She heard his footsteps on the stairs growing fainter. A cold breath whispered across the back of her neck and her skin tightened in a shiver.

Wiping her eyes, she pulled herself together. He'd be back in just a few days. Then they could go home. *To what?* The house with all its memories would be waiting for her. It had not changed. *But she had.*

The horror and sadness of those final weeks

had obscured everything that was happy. Crushed by grief, all she had been able to think of was her loss. But even the most violent storm eventually passes. Black clouds part and the first golden shaft is a promise of the sun's return.

She tucked the coin deep into the folds of her headband, bathed her face and tidied her hair, then crossed the upstairs hall to a drawing room where a tray of tea and a plate of dainty pastries sat on a low table. Even on the brink of potential invasion routine had to be maintained and appearances observed.

'There you are,' Antonia said. 'Come and have some tea.' Obeying her father she had exchanged her *thobe* and headscarf for a stylish gown of pale blue silk with lace-frilled three-quarter length sleeves. Her hair was gathered into a simple chignon on her nape, a style that would be easy to manage. Perhaps Robert Pawlyn's proposal had already begun to have an effect.

'I was just telling my father about your famous flatbreads.' She handed Caseley a cup and saucer. 'You must be quite expert after all that practice.'

'I enjoyed learning something new.' Raising the cup, Caseley sipped. She missed Jago already. Though they had seen little of each other at the camp, she had known he was there. Now he wasn't. She was alone again.

Sir Douglas bit into another pastry, dropping crumbs down his waistcoat. 'I wish my daughter might take more interest in the domestic arts. A sensible young woman knows that this is the route to contentment. But I fear she is a lost cause.'

Antonia glanced away but Caseley saw her embarrassment and anger. Though his complaint was clearly not new, that he would voice it to a relative stranger revealed the depth of his frustration.

'With respect, Sir Douglas, if I had Miss Collingwood's talent, I should want to spend every spare moment trying to develop and perfect it.'

'Would you, indeed? I wonder what your husband would think about that?'

'As he has found my fluency in French of great help to him over the past week, I believe he would encourage me.'

'Hmph,' he snorted and turned again to his daughter. 'I trust that having insisted on taking all that expensive equipment you brought back some interesting photographs?'

'Fewer than I would have liked. Bedouin women are very modest and shy. As their guest I could not insist. But I did take one that shows the way they dress.' As Antonia's gaze met hers, Caseley read a plea that she would keep their secret. 'I also took some wonderful images of the camels we rode. They belong to a very valuable herd, so we were privileged to have use of them.'

'Perhaps while Mrs Barata waits for her husband's return, she could help you in your dark room.'

'I think not.' As her father's brows shot up, Antonia looked at Caseley. 'Father has never been in there so he has probably forgotten it is little bigger than a closet. There is barely enough room for me. And to anyone not used to them the smell of chemicals can be very upsetting.'

'I much prefer fresh air and would be more hindrance than help.' Caseley understood why, fighting a constant battle to be taken seriously, Antonia didn't want to share. 'I shall look forward to seeing the finished prints.'

After a brisk knock, Spencer Blaine put his head round the door.

'Come in,' Sir Douglas said irritably.

'I took Captain Barata to Mrs Williamson's house. Mr Theotakis and Mr Roussos were already with her. They left immediately for the harbour and should arrive there at any time.'

'Good. That is one less concern.'

'Mr Theotakis said there are only a handful of doctors at the European hospital. He insisted we should consider leaving. Naturally. I told him it was out of the question. But he continued to press, reminding me that the French have closed their Consulate. No doubt this is purely a temporary measure

'Why are there so few doctors, Mr Blaine?' Caseley interrupted. It was clear the aide wanted to follow the French example. But he wouldn't risk his position by suggesting it.

'Most of them left after the riots in June. They took their families and possessions so it is unlikely they will return.'

Realising she had been handed a lifeline, Caseley swallowed the last of her tea and lowered the cup to its saucer.

Blaine turned to Sir Douglas. 'I came back via the telegraph office. There are no new messages from Cairo. Mr Pawlyn was there and asked me to tell you he would be coming to see you shortly.'

Sir Douglas chewed and swallowed the last of his pastry. 'I wonder what he wants.'

Antonia blushed pink. Caseley placed her cup and saucer carefully on the tray and rose to her feet.

'If you'll excuse me, I shall go to the hospital.'

Reaching for another pastry, Sir Douglas froze. 'Why? Are you ill?'

'No. I am perfectly well, thank you. I intend to offer my help.'

His shocked expression mirrored that of his aide. 'A hospital is no place for a lady.'

'Indeed it is not,' Spencer Blaine echoed.

'I appreciate your concern. But surely we should be thinking of patients who have no one to tend them?'

'Mrs Barata, I must protest. You are not a doctor. Nor are you a nurse.'

She thought of her father, of her sons. 'You are mistaken, sir. I have considerable nursing experience.'

'Be that as it may, until your husband returns I am responsible for your safety.'

'What safer place can there be than a hospital?' Caseley maintained her smile with an effort.

'You are a stranger here, Mrs Barata,' Blaine's condescending smile made her hand itch with the desire to slap him. 'Given the current level of tension, for an Englishwoman to venture onto the streets is the height of folly. Nor can we spare anyone to accompany you–'

'I would not expect it, Mr Blaine. I am fluent in French and dressed like this with my head covered no one will know my nationality. Now, you must excuse me.'

As Caseley went to the door, Antonia jumped

281

up and followed.

'Try and talk some sense into her.' Sir Douglas did not try to hide his impatience. 'It is too bad. I have enough to do without—'

'You aren't going because I didn't want you to help me, are you?' Antonia's question drowned her father's complaint.

'No, I'm going because I can be useful. And because if I don't keep busy while Jago is away I shall go mad.'

'I have no experience of illness.'

And I have too much. 'Truly, I didn't expect you to come with me.'

'I have to be here when Robert arrives.'

'Of course you do.' Looking into Antonia's troubled face, Caseley touched her arm in reassurance. 'This is the most important day of both your lives.'

'One of the servants will show you the way. It's not far.'

Chapter Twenty

The hospital was a long two-storey building with a cornice edging the flat roof and a tall, arched entrance. As they reached the grounds, Caseley turned to the woman servant Sir Douglas had insisted went with her and thanked her in French and Arabic. The woman nodded and hurried back the way they had come.

A large, airy foyer with deep windows and

282

square columns supporting the ceiling was thronged with people. She caught snatches of French, German and other languages she couldn't identify. The men wore suits. The women's dress varied. Some wore European fashion; others wore long, dark skirts and high-neck long-sleeved bodices, their hair covered by printed headscarves.

Catching sight of a tall, thin woman in a long grey habit and white apron, her hair covered by a white cloth fastened at the back, Caseley crossed to intercept her.

'Excuse me,' she said in English. 'Are you a nurse?'

The woman nodded. 'I am Soeur Jeanne.'

'I understand you are short of staff? I should like to offer my help.'

Drawing her back against a wall so they did not impede people hurrying to and fro, the woman's gaze flickered from Caseley's scarf and *thobe* to her sandals.

'Why you are dressed this way?' Soeur Jeanne asked in heavily accented English.

Caseley switched to French and saw the nurse's relief. 'My husband and I attended a Bedouin wedding in the desert. When we returned to Cairo we learned there had been unrest here, directed at English people. Our hostess advised us to remain in Bedouin dress.'

'A wise suggestion,' Soeur Jeanne nodded. 'The unrest was violent. At least fifty Europeans were killed. The injured were brought here. But with so few doctors... Where is your husband?'

'The assistant British consul ordered him to carry some people to Port Said. He is a ship-

283

owner and master. I cannot simply sit and wait for his return. So I came here.'

'Do you have experience of caring for the sick?'

Caseley swallowed. 'I nursed my father and my two sons through their final illnesses.'

Jeanne's nod held sympathy. 'You are a gift from God. Come with me.' She led Caseley along a wide corridor, through doors that swung shut behind them then down a short passage. Ahead, another set of doors was propped open. 'This is one of the men's wards. Usually, there are six but because we have only two physicians and two surgeons we have had to close two.'

The ward was large with tall windows that opened at the top along one wall, a row of beds beneath, and another row on the inside wall. Every bed was occupied. Some men were propped up on pillows, with limbs or heads swathed in bandages. Others lay on their backs, eyes closed, faces as white as the sheets.

'Wait here.' Jeanne went into the ward. She returned a few moments later with a short, plump woman also wearing the grey habit and white apron. 'This is Soeur Marie. She will show you where everything is. You are to assist her. You realise many of the tasks will be unpleasant?'

'Even more so for the patients,' Marie said, her sharp gaze assessing.

'I understand.' Beneath Caseley's calm façade, trepidation writhed and churned. She pushed doubts aside. The swift acceptance of her offer showed how desperately help was needed. She could not back out now. Nor could she bear to spend the coming days waiting in the Consulate with nothing to do while Antonia was occupied in her darkroom.

'I'll leave you in Marie's capable hands.'

'Thank you.'

As the tall nun hurried away, Marie clicked her tongue. 'Soeur Jeanne has a heart of gold and a head like a colander. What's your name?'

'Mrs Barata, Caseley Barata.'

With a brisk nod she led the way to a supply closet and gave Caseley a white apron to cover her thobe and a white cloth to replace her black scarf. 'Fold it into a triangle and tie it at the back over the pointed end. The other staff will recognise you as an aide.'

From that moment on, Caseley didn't stop. She helped Marie change beds and carried the dirty linen to the large hamper by the door to be collected by a laundrymaid. She emptied various receptacles and washed them in a special room, where piped water fed through a boiler came out steaming from one tap and cold from another over a vast metal sink.

After a few hours another sister shepherded her away to a small rest room equipped with a couch, a table and some chairs. Telling her to sit down she left, returning a few minutes later with a bowl of rice and chicken and a cup of mint tea. Instantly Caseley thought back to the journey into the desert and the Bedouin wedding.

The sister left and Caseley sat at the table to eat. Was Jago making good time? Were sea conditions good? She pictured him in shirtsleeves in the day cabin, wearing his salt-stained and sun-bleached jacket, taking his turn at the wheel.

After her meal she returned to the ward to assist Marie as she changed dressings. She carried basins of disinfectant and took covered buckets of bloodstained cotton to the boiler room to be burned. Darkness fell. Lamps were lit. Another sister arrived to take over for the night. Dark circles under her eyes and pale skin spoke of exhaustion.

'Come,' Marie said as they left the ward. 'You have done enough. Go home.'

Caseley smiled wearily. 'I wish I could. But Cornwall is a long way. I can't leave without my husband, and he won't be back from Port Said for several days.'

'I meant home to where you are living in the city.'

'I'm a guest at the British Consulate. Please, I would prefer to stay here. After a few hours' sleep I will be fine again. You need me, and I want to be useful.' *Keeping busy allowed her no time to worry.*

'I'm glad to have you. You aren't afraid of hard work. I will go and ask Soeur Jeanne.' Taking Caseley to the sisters' quiet room she gave her a gentle push. 'Sit down before you fall down.' The door closed behind her and Caseley was alone.

She sank onto the couch. Images of Jago floated through her mind: standing at *Cygnet's* helm; seated at the table in his day cabin, his dark head propped on one hand as he completed the log; leaning against a camel saddle beside the campfire, at ease in his Bedouin robes. She had not prayed since the night the boys died. But as she closed her eyes her last conscious thought was a plea: *please let me see him again.*

An explosion jolted her upright, her heart hammering. Where was she? As salvo after salvo created a deafening thunder, she remembered: the hospital. The bombardment had started.

The door opened and Marie came in. She set the cup of tea and plate of fresh flatbread on the table and laid the clean apron hanging over her arm on the couch. 'I looked in on you during the night.'

'You should have woken me,' Caseley rubbed her face to banish the fog of sleep, then untied the stained and creased apron she had slept in.

Marie shook her head, wincing at the roar and *crump* as a shell landed. 'You are awake now.'

'Soeur Jeanne–?'

'Is grateful for your offer. Come to the ward when you are ready.' She pointed to the plate. 'Eat. You will need all your strength.'

After visiting the bathroom, washing her face and hands, and swallowing her breakfast, Caseley put on her clean apron, refolded and tied her white headscarf and hurried to the ward.

Two hours later she no longer flinched at the gunfire. But her jaw ached from clenching her teeth. Quickly she stripped damp and blood-stained sheets from a bed. The previous occupant had died twenty minutes ago. A new patient slumped semi-conscious in a chair, waiting. Marie hurried over, concern furrowing her forehead.

'There's a Mr Blaine in the foyer asking to speak to you. He says the gunfire is hitting buildings in the city.'

Horror was a dark void inside her. *Antonia, Sir Douglas.* 'I won't be long.'

'Don't run,' Marie whispered. 'The patients

have been frightened enough.'

As Caseley entered the crowded foyer, the smell of blood, sweat and fear triggered a surge of panic that squeezed her heart and tightened her throat.

She dug her fingernails hard into her thumbs and made herself take a slow, deep breath. The noise was deafening. Terrified people shouted for help, the wounded groaned or screamed in pain and the thunder of heavy guns was relentless.

She saw a man in shirtsleeves flanked by two nursing sisters moving slowly among the injured slumped on benches against the wall or laying on the tiled floor. The apron that covered him from chest to shin was as bloody as a butcher's.

Caseley realised he must be one of the doctors. She had not seen him on the ward. But by the time the sick or injured reached a bed, their care was in the hands of the nursing sisters. He crouched, rose, bent and straightened with the ease of a young man. But, as he glanced round, she saw his face was lined and haggard with exhaustion.

Pausing at each person, he gave quick instructions regarding those who needed immediate treatment and who could wait. People beyond help were identified by a reassuring touch, a glance at the nurse and an infinitesimal head-shake.

She spotted Spencer Blaine. His cream linen suit was streaked with dust, dirt and blood. One hand shook as he mopped his face with a crumpled handkerchief. In the other he held a small suitcase.

'Mr Blaine?' Caseley had to raise her voice above the thundering guns. 'Are you hurt?'

'Me? No. The Consulate– I was at the telegraph

office. When I got back– It's gone–'

'What do you mean, gone?'

'It's not there any more. The building is just a pile of rubble. I can't believe–'

'Antonia? Sir Douglas?'

He shook his head. 'They must be – no one could have survived. I saw one of the clerks – his legs – crushed.' Nausea tightened his face and he recoiled as weeping dust-shrouded relatives carried in more wounded. 'I have to go.'

'Go? Where?'

'Cairo. I can't stay here. Our wonderful British navy is destroying the city.' He turned away.

Caseley caught his arm. 'Please stay. We need help. And you're as safe here as anywhere.'

He backed away, shaking his head. 'I can't– I don't know what to–'

'You could show people where to wait, reassurance or a drink of water.'

'No – I–'

Caseley's patience snapped. 'How would you feel if you were injured and no one would help?'

'How dare–' he spluttered. 'You have no right–'

Caseley saw two men stagger in. Their suits, dust-caked and torn, marked them as businessmen or bankers. The younger man half-carried the elder who swayed, one arm hanging useless in a saturated sleeve, blood dripping from his fingers.

'Please, tell them to wait over there,' she pointed. 'I'll fetch some water.' She hurried to the kitchen, filled a jug, grabbed a cup from the cupboard and returned to the foyer. Spencer Blaine had gone. She crossed to the waiting people. One woman had looked up as she approached.

'Are you hurt?' Caseley asked in French, then English. From the woman's modest garments and covered head Caseley guessed she was Jewish. Her eyes were huge and dazed but she shook her head. 'My m-mother. She– I was told to wait.'

Caseley held out the jug and cup. 'Please will you help? A sister will find you when – when you can see your mother.'

After a moment's hesitation the woman nodded.

'They will be so grateful. When you need more water the kitchen is through there.' Caseley pointed.

She raced back to the ward. Marie and Jeanne had laid mattresses down the centre of the floor. Unconscious men occupied three of them. Two had truncated limbs swathed in fresh bandages. Caseley's gorge rose and she swallowed hard.

The doors swung open as two orderlies carried in a stretcher.

'Come,' Marie touched her arm. 'We must open another ward.'

As Marie opened the windows, revealing bare mattresses on basic bedframes Caseley gritted her teeth. Over the guns' roar she heard the scream of shells passing overhead, the *crump* as they landed. The floor vibrated with the crash of falling masonry.

Caseley jumped. 'How can you be so calm? Aren't you scared?'

The nun raised her eyebrows. 'Would it help? I hope I am spared to tend those poor souls out-side. But if I should die–' she crossed herself and her smile was luminous. 'I will be safe in the arms of my Lord. So what have I to fear?'

For weeks after the boys died Caseley had wanted oblivion. Each time she woke she dreaded the pain of facing another day. Now as shells supposedly directed at the forts were overshooting and destroying the homes and lives of ordinary people, she knew she wasn't ready to give up. She wanted to live. She wanted to see Jago again.

While she mopped the dusty floor with a solution of chloride of lime to disinfect it, Marie threw blankets onto the beds. Before they had finished, patients were being carried in. Relatives came too, some willing to help, others too afraid to leave.

Back on the main ward time flew as Caseley fetched and carried whatever was needed. She jumped as Jeanne tapped her shoulder. 'You need food and a rest.'

'What about you?'

'We are used to this. You are not. Go to the women's ward across the foyer, down the corridor and turn right. Ask Soeur Marie-Claude if she can spare me one of her nurses.' She made shooing motions with her hands.

'I can stay–'

'You will do as I ask,' Jeanne said gently, 'or you must leave.'

'I beg your pardon. I only–'

'I know. And I appreciate it. Now go.'

Torn between reluctance and relief, Caseley left the ward. She was tired out, yet every nerve vibrated like an overstretched wire.

Where was Jago? How close to Port Said? How long would it take him to get back?

Short, choppy waves and a strong current had

made *Cygnet's* departure from Alexandria uncomfortable. But after Jago had manoeuvred the schooner between the British ironclads and out into deep water, the voyage to Port Said was swift and uneventful.

When he heard the first salvo of gunfire he had nearly turned the ship around. But with British guns hurling barrage after barrage of shells at the forts, and the Egyptians firing back, it would have been impossible to get near the harbour. He must keep going. He had no choice. The Consulate was in the centre of the city, nowhere near the forts that spread along the shoreline like beads on a necklace. Caseley would be safe.

Maud Williamson quickly revealed her true character through her selfish disregard for those left behind in Alexandria. She also tested the crew's courtesy to the limit.

'Asking for table linen she was,' Nathan told Jago in a private moment below. 'All clicking tongue and frowns when Mart told her we didn't have no call for nothing like that.'

'Surely a little sociability at the table isn't too much to ask?' she demanded of Jago as he bolted his dinner, anxious to get back on deck and wring every last knot of speed from the schooner. He glanced up.

'This is not a pleasure cruise, Mrs Williamson.'

'Indeed it is not.' She wrinkled her nose. 'I have to say I would have expected a little more–'

'Madam, your expectations are not my concern. As for conversation, let the gentlemen oblige you. I have more pressing concerns,' Jago snapped and abruptly left the saloon. It was their fault he was not with his beloved wife. Returning to the deck, he looked into the galley shack.

'Until we reach Port Said I want my meals in my day cabin.'

'Aye, sir. Cap'n?'

'Yes?'

Martin's throat worked. 'Missus all right, is she?'

Jago rubbed the back of his neck. Tension had pulled the muscles tight and a dull ache throbbed at the base of his skull. Hammer and Jimbo would have told him to ask. Nathan would have backed them. They all thought the world of Caseley.

'She was when I left. But I'll be glad to get back.'

A strong north-west wind filled every sail. He drove *Cygnet* hard. The crew, knew without a word spoken, that this was to be the fastest turn-around possible.

They moved crab-like around the canting deck, ignoring foam-streaked water that kissed the lee rail, going about their tasks with a determination that matched his. The passengers were allowed on deck but politely asked to stay out of the way. Remarks or questions regarding the captain were ignored.

After delivering the message and receiving a promise that a nurse would be sent directly, Caseley reentered the foyer.

'Mrs Barata!'

Robert Pawlyn had one arm around Antonia who leaned against him, barely conscious. In his other hand he carried her camera case. Blood from a head wound covered half her face and neck and had soaked into the shoulder of her *thobe*.

Hurrying to them, Caseley put an arm around Antonia's waist to help support her. 'Thank God you're safe. I was afraid– What happened?'

'We were on the roof of the Reuters building. Antonia was taking photographs when the bombardment started.' His face was tight with anger and anxiety. 'From the moment the guns opened fire, shells were landing in the city.'

'Do you think it's deliberate?'

He moved a shoulder. 'The British guns are supposed to be shelling the forts along the shoreline. Are we really supposed to believe they are simply guilty of poor marksmanship? But only Admiral Seymour knows whether he is acting on his own initiative or following orders from back home. Will you take care of her?'

'Of course. What of her camera? She's sure to ask.'

He held up the case. 'Probably smashed to bits, but knowing how much it means to her I couldn't leave it.'

'Spencer Blaine came in earlier. The Consulate's been hit. He said it's just a pile of rubble.'

'Oh, God.' Pawlyn passed his hand over his face. 'Sir Douglas?'

Caseley shook her head.

'Where is Blaine now?'

'If the trains are running he will be on his way to Cairo. I pleaded with him to stay and help but he refused.'

'He'd be as useful as a headache. Maybe I should stay.'

'No. When this is over and each side is blaming the other, your account of today's events will be vitally important. Who else cares enough to describe the devastating effects of all the political manipulation and deceit on ordinary people?'

'Thank you.' It was heartfelt. 'I'll come back later.'

Taking Antonia's weight, Caseley half-dragged, half-carried her to a corner space at the end of a bench and propped her up. Her closed eyes were screwed tightly against pain and the blood-free side of her face was ash-pale.

Caseley pushed the camera box underneath the bench and left to fetch a basin of warm water. She saw Soeur Jeanne, who frowned. 'Why are you not–?'

'Miss Collingwood is the daughter of the assistant British Consul. The Consulate was hit this morning. She was injured and a friend brought her here.'

Jeanne looked at Antonia's forehead. 'It needs stitches. Clean it with warm water and a pinch of chloride of lime. Then take her to the benches down there.' She pointed down the corridor. 'They are close to the operating theatre so the doctor will see her waiting.' She glided away, moving quickly without seeming to hurry.

Fetching water, cotton wool and a bandage Caseley began to clean the wound. It wouldn't stop bleeding. Panic stirred like mud in a pond.

Wincing, Antonia tried to push Caseley's hand away. 'Don't – hurts.'

'Antonia? It's Caseley. You're at the hospital.' Setting the basin and bloody cotton wool under the bench so they wouldn't get kicked over before she had time to take them back to the sluice room,

Caseley hauled Antonia up and supported her along the corridor. Her heart sank. The benches here were almost as crowded as the foyer. Lowered to the bench, Antonia folded her arms across her middle and curled forward over them, head bowed. Knowing there was nothing more she could do, Caseley returned to the foyer as a young woman holding a baby ran in, sobbing.

Caseley went to her. 'Are you hurt?' As the young woman swung round, wide-eyed, she asked again in French, 'Are you hurt?'

'No. No. My husband is a doctor at the Greek-Egyptian hospital. He was supposed to come home at eight. When the house next to ours was hit I was afraid to stay. I ran all the way here.'

Caseley looked at the silent baby's closed eyes and waxen skin. *Oh no. Please, no.*

'He's sleeping,' the young woman said with a glassy smile. 'That's best, isn't it? Then he won't be frightened.'

Caseley felt her heart break. She knew she should rest and eat. But how could she when so many people needed help?

Chapter Twenty-one

After thirty-six hours the blue Mediterranean turned brown with muddy outflow from the Nile. *Cygnet* was approaching her destination.

Protected by two breakwaters, one supporting a tall lighthouse, several basins along the main waterway were lined with jetties. Warehouses and buildings stood behind them. The water was crowded with lighters ferrying cargo and dhows laden with handicrafts to offer to ships waiting to enter or leave the Suez Canal.

Night was falling and Jago's eyes were gritty with tiredness. The sun's fierce glare and the fast passage had taken their toll. As soon as the passengers were ashore, he went down to his day room. Martin had already lit the overhead lamp. He knocked on the open door while Jago was writing the log.

'Cocoa, Cap'n,' he set the mug down carefully, keeping it away from the chart. 'One of the boatmen was selling fresh milk.'

'Thanks, Mart.' Dropping his pen, Jago rubbed his face.

'Leaving tonight, are we?'

He was tempted. But common sense prevailed. 'No, we'll go at first light. Get some sleep. Ask Nathan to come down.'

They divided the watches while Jago swallowed his cocoa. Nathan moved his gear back into his own cabin. Falling onto his bunk Jago was asleep in seconds.

Woken by Martin bringing in a pitcher of water, Jago glanced up through the skylight and saw the pearl grey of dawn. He washed, buttoned up a clean shirt, pulled up his braces, dragged a comb through his hair and walked through to the saloon.

Breakfast was porridge with treacle, bread, cheese and dates.

'Dear life, Mart. Fattening us up for Christmas are 'e?' Hammer demanded.

'Leave 'n be,' Nathan grunted. 'Boy got his head

screwed on. Need a good start, we do. Bleddy wind can't make up its mind. If he stay in the nor'west we'll be tacking back and forth all the bleddy way.'

Jago felt his heart drop like a weight in his chest. The wind had to change. It *had* to.

Against the roar of guns, and the crump and rumble of explosions, Caseley fetched water for parched throats and helped the walking wounded to dressing stations or the lavatory.

A dark-haired man burst through the doors, frantic with worry and shouting his wife's name. Looking round, Caseley heard the young woman cry out to him, watched as he fought his way through to her. He looked down at their child and she saw him flinch as realisation struck like a blow. He gathered his wife close. Tears slid down his face, cutting tracks through the dust.

That was what Jago must have felt: helplessness, guilt, rage. Many hundreds, perhaps thousands, of people would have been killed today. All over the city parents would be weeping for dead children.

She returned to the corridor, retrieved the basin and bloody cotton wool from under the bench and took them to the sluice room. When she got back Antonia hadn't moved, but Caseley's stomach twisted on seeing that rivulets of blood had flowed over her arms to soak her skirt. Fewer people were waiting and the theatre doors stood open.

Caseley hauled Antonia to her feet. One nurse was wiping blood off the floor while another laid instruments on a clean towel. She looked up as Caseley staggered in.

'Soeur Jeanne says it needs stitches.'

'Put her on the table.' She peered at Caseley. 'Who are you?'

'A volunteer. I've been helping Soeurs Jeanne and Marie.' Suddenly dizzy, Caseley crumpled and slid down to sit on the floor. 'I'm sorry.'

'How long is it since you ate anything?'

Caseley tried to remember. 'I'm not sure.'

'Too long.' The nurse gently pushed wet blood-thickened hair back from Antonia's forehead. She went to the instrument table. The doctor strode in and, as Caseley struggled to her feet, he beckoned her forward.

'Hold her head still.'

Caseley went to the head of the table, placed her hands on each side of Antonia's face, and looked away from the gaping cut and all the blood.

'Camera?' Antonia slurred.

'It's safe,' Caseley reassured. 'Mr Pawlyn had gone to find more plates. He promised he would be back very soon.'

The nurse caught hold of Antonia's hands as the doctor came to the table.

'Keep her still,' he repeated.

Antonia's screams pierced Caseley like knife thrusts. She wanted to press her hands over her ears and run away. Instead she held Antonia's face, told her how brave she was and it was nearly over.

The doctor stepped back. Caseley received another weary nod. Then he left.

'Sit her up.' As soon as Antonia was upright, the nurse placed a pad over the neatly stitched wound and bandaged it in place.

'Dreadful headache,' Antonia whispered.

Pouring a little water into a small glass, the nurse took a dark brown bottle from a cupboard and added a few drops to the glass then held it to Antonia's lips. 'Find her somewhere to sit,' she told Caseley. 'Then get yourself something to eat. You did well.'

Back in the foyer, now less crowded, Caseley settled Antonia in the corner so she leaned against the wall. Her eyes were closed and all the tension had drained from her face.

'Antonia? Your camera box is under the bench. Rest here. I'll be back soon.' Caseley turned away and saw a familiar figure walk in from outside. She picked her way through to meet her.

'Sheikha! Are you injured?'

'No, I am unharmed. But Sheikh Imad was shot by an Egyptian soldier.' She turned as four servants carried in a litter bearing the inert figure of the Sheikh. 'This hospital has the finest surgeons. If he is not operated on immediately–'

'I'll fetch a sister.' Running to the ward, Caseley found Soeur Jeanne accompanying the doctor on his rounds. Within minutes, Sheikh Imad was taken into the operating theatre.

Caseley watched them go, queasy with hunger and exhaustion. There was something she should do, but she couldn't remember what it was.

'Go and eat!' Soeur Marie insisted.

In the quiet room a covered plate had been placed on the table. It held bread, cheese and dates, and there was also a covered jug of juice. She sat down, swallowed some juice. It slid down her parched throat, cool, soothing and so welcome. Tiredness dropped over her like a heavy blanket. She felt herself falling and everything went dark.

She woke with a jolt. Something was different. Then she realised: the gunfire had stopped.

What was she doing on the couch? She didn't remember lying down. She sat up and, in the light from a lamp on the table, saw Sabra sitting nearby gazing out into the darkness.

'How long–?' She croaked and cleared her throat.

Sabra looked round. 'So you are back with us. Not as long as you needed. What are you doing here?'

'Sir Douglas ordered my husband to take passengers to Port Said. I was to remain at the Consulate until he returned. But I couldn't – with nothing to do I would have – so I came here and offered to help.'

'It's as well you did.'

'Mr Pawlyn brought Antonia in. She had a gash on her head that needed stitches.' Caseley's skin tightened as she recalled the screams.

Sabra nodded. 'Does she know about her father?'

'I'm not sure. I haven't told her. How is Sheikh Imad?'

'Recovering. The bullet had lodged in a muscle so he did not lose too much blood. As soon as the doctor will allow, I shall take him to my villa. When he is fit to travel we will return to Cairo.'

Caseley nodded, biting back the question that hovered on her tongue. But Sabra had noticed.

'You are wondering why we did not tell you we were coming to Alexandria.'

Caseley felt her cheeks warm, and nodded.

'We went to speak to the Khedive who was then at Ras-el-Tin palace.'

'Why?'

'Colonel Arabi's offers of negotiation had been rejected by Admiral Seymour so we knew the British were determined to go ahead with the bombardment. They claimed it was necessary to restore the Khedive's authority. But their true intent has always been to destroy any chance of Egyptians ruling their own country. We don't want Egypt's ruler to be a puppet of the English. We tried to persuade the Khedive that achieving a compromise with Colonel Arabi would be a demonstration of statesmanship and understanding of what his people want.' Her voice faltered but pride lifted her chin. 'We talked until our voices failed. Tewfiq was offered safety aboard one of the English ships but he declined.'

'Surely that shows his loyalty to—'

Sabra's smile was bitter. 'He declined because he couldn't make up his mind which side was most likely to win and didn't want to be on the losing one.' She folded her hands in her lap. 'During the night he fled to Cairo. Soon after the bombardment started the palace was hit and caught fire. We got out just in time.'

'What do you think will happen?'

'To Egypt?' She inhaled deeply. 'While you were sleeping I was brought information that Tewfiq sent Colonel Arabi a letter claiming the bombardment was his fault, because he had refused to disarm the forts. Yet how could he disarm them when, as Minister for War appointed by the

Khedive, it was his responsibility to ensure the city was protected against attack by a foreign power? A truce has been declared and seems to be holding. Now the Admiral has sent a letter to Colonel Arabi claiming that he has no desire to make war on Egypt and is ready to hand over the city – what is left of it – to a disciplined and obedient Egyptian army. To that end, Colonel Arabi is invited to return to Ras-el-Tin to agree arrangements.' Irony and disgust shaded Sabra's tone. 'I suspect Tewfiq's sole contribution to that letter was his signature. The rest will have been dictated by his English advisors, who know perfectly well that Arabi cannot obey.'

'Why can't he?' Caseley asked. Even as she wondered how Sabra knew about the letter, she remembered Jago telling her what Sheikh Imad had said about having many sources of information. 'Surely if it means peace–'

'It doesn't,' Sabra said flatly. 'It's a trap. If he goes to the Palace he will be arrested. If he refuses to obey the summons he'll be labelled an outlaw.'

Caseley stared at her, appalled.

'So in answer to your question, I fear Colonel Arabi's forces will be crushed and this country will be occupied by the English on the pretext of protecting the Suez Canal which was never in danger. But an occupying power needs the goodwill of the governed. We will play the English at their own game.' Caseley had no idea what Sabra intended but she felt her skin prickle. 'However, Sheikh Imad needs time for his wound to heal first.'

Reluctantly, Caseley stood up. 'Will you excuse me?'

'Where are you going?'

'Back to the ward. With so many new patients the nurses will have had no rest.'

After a night doing whatever the nurses asked of her, Caseley was walking wearily across the foyer when Robert Pawlyn entered. He was carrying another box. His suit looked as if he had slept in it.

'How is Antonia?'

'Her head is sore but otherwise she is well.'

'Does she know about her father?'

Caseley nodded. 'She asked if I had heard anything so I told her what Mr Blaine had told me. She could not face the wards. So she has been helping in the supply room, rolling bandages and making pads from old sheets.' As his brows rose, Caseley smiled. 'The sisters are very persuasive. What were those explosions?'

'Admiral Seymour sent a shore party to the forts to destroy the remaining guns. The Egyptians have suffered heavy losses. Most of the European quarter of the city has been reduced to rubble. There are bodies everywhere and fires are spreading. Colonel Arabi and his army have withdrawn under a flag of truce. As they were leaving he ordered the jails to be opened and the prisoners set free. Now people are blaming him for the looting. What should he have done? Left them to burn?' He passed a hand over his face. 'I'm sorry.'

Caseley waved away his apology 'Sheikh Imad was shot. The Sheikha brought him here. He's had the bullet removed and is recovering. As soon as it is safe, the Sheikha will move him to her villa. Then they'll return to Cairo. I saw no

304

benefit in telling Antonia any of this.'

He nodded gratefully. 'I appreciate it. Marines have arrived from Cyprus and are starting to restore order. I'd better go. Please tell her I came, and that I'll be back later.' His cheeks reddened. 'Give her my love.'

'I will.' Caseley walked to the ward, tired to her bones and desperate to keep busy.

Jago climbed the companionway. Golden in the east and turquoise overhead, the sky softened to clear, pale blue.

'Go down and get your breakfast, Jimbo.'

'Aye, Cap'n.'

As Martin clattered dishes in the galley shack, Nathan relinquished the wheel to Jago who watched the smoke from the stove chimney. It blew one way then the other. Then it steadied. He glanced at the compass. North-east. He offered up silent thanks.

Glancing back at him with a grin, Nathan turned to Hammer as they prepared to tack. 'Come on. Put your back into it. Missus will be wondering where we're to.'

Jago stepped out on deck soon after sun-up on the 13th July. It had been two days of hard sailing. But the wind had held steady, blowing fresh to strong as it drove *Cygnet* along parallel to a coast of low sandhills fringing a vast lake.

Looking shoreward his mouth dried as he saw a pall of smoke darkening the sky. As *Cygnet* passed the ruins of two forts, then the burning palace, the crew on deck was silent. The lighthouse still stood but huge chunks had been blown out of it. The

305

surrounding area was a scene of carnage and devastation.

The entire city seemed to be on fire. Hungry flames flared within the thick choking smoke, adding weight to the humid summer heat.

Caseley.

The rising wind had created a heavy swell that made manouevering in the harbour difficult. But the crew knew what to do and shortened sail without a word from Jago while he steered them past the naval ships. Many had buckled plates, jagged holes in the superstructure, and broken spars, damage inflicted by the fort batteries.

Two boats packed with armed marines rowed shoreward. As *Cygnet* headed for one of the jetties, Jago heard a volley of small arms fire.

As soon as *Cygnet* pulled alongside, Jago jumped down. He stumbled but caught himself and ran towards the Custom House. The stout wooden doors were closed, the stonework pocked with huge holes. He saw mangled bodies, grotesquely swollen in the heat, lying where they had fallen.

Caseley.

Trying to remember the route the calèche had taken he headed east. But with many of the buildings in ruins and streets blocked by rubble, bodies and raging fires, he was forced to detour. He crossed a wide avenue, saw a square with a Napoleonic fort in it, and released a gasp of relief as he realised where he was.

He continued east then north, barely seeing the sprawled eviscerated bodies, deaf to the screams of the injured and the wailing grief of dazed survivors.

He reached Midan Muhammad Ali but the devastation had left it barely recognisable. The Consulate was just a pile of broken walls, rubble and twisted iron.

Caseley

Looking towards the hotel he saw more ruins. He wanted to roar his fury at the English guns. She couldn't be dead. He would know.

He'd had no suspicion when the boys died.

That was different. Caseley was – everything. Without her...

He shut the thought off. He could not return to the ship without her. The crew would never forgive him.

He swiped at wet eyes, dragged a breath into lungs that ached, and forced himself to think. She might have been hurt. If so, she'd have gone to a hospital. He had to find someone who spoke English.

Hearing another volley of shots he ran towards the sound and emerged into an open space in front of a church. A line of British sailors wearing white caps and dark blue coats and trousers had just lowered their rifles. A dead Arab lay slumped at the base of a tree.

'Bloody fire-raiser,' one of the sailors spat.

Jago grabbed him. 'Where's the nearest hospital?'

'Right there, mate.' The soldier pointed to the rear of a long building.

Jago raced round to the front and ran through the main door, skidding to a halt in the foyer. He saw an elderly nun wearing a white apron over her grey habit. She had a mop and bucket and was washing the blood and dirt-smeared floor.

'Excuse me.' Fear roughened his voice. 'My wife... Is she here?'

The nun straightened. Leaning on the mop for support she shrugged apologetically and replied in French.

Jago looked wildly round. There had to be someone who spoke English. He strode towards the back of the foyer where a wide corridor led off in each direction and almost fell over another nun who was on her knees scrubbing a large splatter of crimson whose edges had dried rusty-brown.

'I beg your pardon. Do you speak English?'

She sat back on her heels. 'A little.' Her accent was strong. 'How may I help you?'

'I'm looking for my wife.'

'Her name?'

He had to moisten his lips before he could speak. 'Barata, Caseley Barata.'

She smiled. 'Yes, she's here.'

His eyes closed for an instant. 'Is she–?' He couldn't finish.

'She wasn't hurt.'

'May I see her?'

'Of course.' She dropped the scrubbing brush into the bucket and struggled to her feet, ignoring the hand he offered. 'Thank you, but I can manage.' As she stood, lean and tall, he saw her face was pale and etched with exhaustion.

Moving the bucket back against the wall out of the way, she led him down the wide corridor. 'Her arrival was a gift from God. We are so grateful for her help.' She opened a door and stood back to let him pass.

Caseley lay where she had fallen on the couch. She still wore her stained and dusty *thobe* with a bibbed apron over it. A white scarf was crumpled under her head. Curls had escaped from the untidy coil and clung to her temple and cheek.

He knelt beside her, his hungry gaze taking in the plum-coloured shadows beneath her eyes, skin grey-white with fatigue stretched tight over her cheekbones. He had never seen her in such a dirty dishevelled state, nor had she ever looked more beautiful to him. She was alive and safe. He stroked her face with gentle fingertips, fighting the sobs that wrenched his chest, and heard the door close quietly.

Caseley opened her eyes. They were blank, un-seeing. She gazed at him and he watched aware-ness return. Relief and love lit her slow smile even as tears spilled down her cheeks. 'You're back.'

'I promised.'

She sat up, wrapped her arms around his neck and pressed her face to his. 'Oh, Jago.'

He held her, breathed her in. He could feel her bones. She looked so fragile. God alone knew what she had seen and dealt with these past days. The need to protect her sent a violent tremor through him.

He moved to sit beside her, one arm around her shoulders, his free hand holding hers against his heart.

'You appear to have been busy.'

Glancing down at her dirty clothes she made a wry face. 'After you went I would have gone mad just waiting. Mr Blaine said most of the doctors had left so I came here and offered my help. When the bombardment started – the noise–' she shook her head. 'I have never heard – it was terrifying. But soon injured people were pouring through the doors and we were so busy there wasn't time to think about what was happening outside. Mr Pawlyn brought Antonia in. She had left the Consulate early to go with him to take photographs so she wasn't there when it was hit. She had a deep gash on her head that needed stitches. Sabra brought Sheikh Imad who had been shot. The doctor removed the bullet and he will recover.' She ran out of breath, turned to him. 'I kept telling myself you would come. You had to. I closed my eyes and pictured your face and that gave me the strength to do what the sisters asked–'

He stopped her desperate words with his mouth, kissing her until both were breathless.

She eased back, looked into his beloved face, and saw strain and exhaustion that reflected her own. 'Please can we go home now?'

They stopped at the supply room. Caseley opened the door just as Antonia and Robert Pawlyn were coming out. Antonia had a bandage around her head. She caught Caseley's hand. 'Thank you. Soeur Jeanne told me what you did for me.'

'I was glad to.'

'Captain, I am happy to see you safely back.'

Jago inclined his head. 'Thank you, Miss Collingwood. My wife and I wish you both every happiness.' He shook hands with Pawlyn.

'Where will you–?' Caseley began then stopped.

'Antonia's coming home with me,' Pawlyn said, picking up her camera box. Caseley saw pride and love in his gaze. 'The building I'm in escaped the worst of the shelling and the landlord has spare rooms. We'll marry as soon as it can be arranged.'

'But today,' Antonia said, 'I am determined to take photographs. Alexandria was a beautiful city. Now I hear it is destroyed.'

'You will need to take care,' Jago said. 'Fires are raging all along the waterfront and in the European Quarter.'

Antonia shook her head, compressing her lips to stop them trembling then dragged in a breath. 'How could the ships not have realised? Surely they must have seen that the shells were overshooting and landing in the city?'

About to say that Sabra was of the opinion that the damage had been deliberate, Caseley stopped herself in time. Antonia would want to know how she knew. It would not serve anyone for her to discover Sheikh Imad was in the hospital.

'There must be a record for the future, images that show what happened here,' Antonia declared. 'Forgive me, you will be anxious to leave. I– We–' glancing at Pawlyn she corrected herself, winning a quick smile from him, 'wish you both a safe journey home.'

Impulsively, Caseley gave her a quick hug. 'Be happy,' she whispered.

'I think – I hope – I will be. Robert believes in me. You cannot know how much that means.' Antonia murmured.

Caseley knew, far better than Antonia realised. Smiling she stepped back, and Antonia reached for the case of photographic plates.

After looking into the wards and saying

311

goodbye to Soeur Marie and Soeur Jeanne, who thanked her again, Caseley covered her head with her scarf and with her arm through Jago's, walked out into the mid-July heat.

It took them nearly an hour to reach *Cygnet*. They saw parties of sailors and marines fighting the fires. In areas that had escaped the worst, shops were open.

Jago helped her along the gangplank. 'Good to see you, missus,' Nathan said.

Martin poked his head out of the galley shack. 'Missed you awful we have.' He glanced warily at Jago. 'Beg pardon, Cap'n.'

'Hot water,' Jago growled as the corners of his mouth twitched.

'Aye, sir.'

Hammer and Jimbo both raised a forefinger to their foreheads in salute. 'Can we leave now, Cap'n? Fresh water tank is full. While you was gone Hammer rowed over to one of the ironclads and begged a sack of flour, some salt pork and fresh veg.'

'Get the sails up.' Jago led the way down the companionway. Inside his day cabin he kicked the door closed and pulled her close. 'When we came near on our way back from Port Said and I saw the smoke–' His arms tightened. 'Never in my life have I known such fear.'

Arms around him she nestled her head against his warm neck and breathed in his unique scent. 'Even if the sisters hadn't needed me I would have had to keep working.'

'Did it help the time pass more quickly?'

'Yes, but that wasn't the reason. I was bargaining

312

with God to bring you back safe. If I had lost you too–'

'You will never lose me. I am yours, body and soul. Never again, Caseley. I will not be parted from you again. Either you must sail with me or I shall leave the sea and spend more time on the yard.'

Before she could respond there was a knock on the door. 'Hot water, Cap'n.'

Reluctantly, he released her. 'As soon as we're out of the harbour we'll have a meal. Then you should rest.'

He brought in the water pitcher and set it down beside the washstand. Pausing briefly to touch her face, he went out, closing the door behind him.

Stripping off her grubby garments, Caseley rolled them up and put them in the trunk, taking out a clean shift and her sprigged cotton dress, relieved she had something clean to put on. Everything she had taken ashore lay beneath the ruins of the Consulate.

The cabin floor tilted beneath her feet and she was careful not to overfill the basin.

Washed, dressed and her teeth cleaned, she was still tired but felt much restored. Finding a spare comb amid the sea junk on the shelf she redid her hair and had just replaced the last pin when Jago opened the door.

'How are you now?'

'Better.' Dropping the comb on the table she went to him. As his strong arms closed around her she knew this was where she belonged. 'I missed you so much.'

'When I saw the smoke and the flames–'

Feeling the shudder ripple through him, she held him tighter. 'All I could think of was finding you.'

She put a finger against his lips. 'I am with you so I am safe.' She reached up and laid her mouth on his, felt his arms tighten around her.

'Dinner, Cap'n, Missus,' Martin yelled through the door.

'Dammit,' Jago murmured against her lips. He drew back. 'Wait until I get you home.'

Caseley gazed at his beloved face, saw new lines scored by anxiety. When they left Cornwall she had been unable to picture being happy ever again. But she was, beyond anything she could have imagined. She smoothed a lock of hair back from his forehead. 'Must I?'

'Must you what?'

'Wait?' Feeling a blush burn her cheeks she turned away to open the door, catching her breath and feeling herself quake as he gently bit her neck.

His hand rested, warm and possessive, on her waist as they entered the saloon where Martin had just removed the lid from a steaming pot of stew.

Caseley's mouth watered at the savoury aroma. 'Martin, that smells delicious.'

Footsteps clanged on the brass stairs. Nathan came in followed by Hammer.

'Jimbo got the helm, Cap'n,' the mate said.

Jago nodded. 'Hammer, are we carrying any spare timber? The berth in my sleeping cabin–'

'Be done by sundown, Cap'n.'

While they ate and Caseley answered their questions she was acutely aware of the man at her side, his knee touching hers. Her husband. Her beloved. *Jago.*

Author's Note

Claims in the British Press that rising unrest in Egypt might endanger the Suez Canal brought the British and French fleets to Alexandria in May 1882. In June there was a riot in the city during which the trusted body-servant of British Admiral Sir Beauchamp Seymour was killed.

Admiral Seymour issued an ultimatum ordering reinforcement work on the forts to cease immediately. Responsible for ensuring the city was adequately defended, Colonel Arabi, the nationalist leader who was also minister for war, could not stop work on the forts without orders from the khedive. These were not forthcoming. Refusing to take part in an unprovoked act of aggression, the French admiral removed his fleet.

British naval guns opened fire at 7 a.m. on 11th July, their supposed aim to destroy the forts sited along the coastline of the city. But when the bombardment ceased at 5.30 p.m., the wealthy cosmopolitan heart of Alexandria had been totally destroyed.

The publishers hope that this book has given you enjoyable reading. Large Print Books are especially designed to be as easy to see and hold as possible. If you wish a complete list of our books please ask at your local library or write directly to:

Magna Large Print Books
Magna House, Long Preston,
Skipton, North Yorkshire.
BD23 4ND

This Large Print Book for the partially sighted, who cannot read normal print, is published under the auspices of

THE ULVERSCROFT FOUNDATION

THE ULVERSCROFT FOUNDATION

... we hope that you have enjoyed this Large Print Book. Please think for a moment about those people who have worse eyesight problems than you ... and are unable to even read or enjoy Large Print, without great difficulty.

You can help them by sending a donation, large or small to:

**The Ulverscroft Foundation,
1, The Green, Bradgate Road,
Anstey, Leicestershire, LE7 7FU,
England.**
or request a copy of our brochure for more details.

The Foundation will use all your help to assist those people who are handicapped by various sight problems and need special attention.

Thank you very much for your help.